DEEP DESERT DECEPTION

A Smoke Tree Series Novel

Gary J. George

Cover photograph by Paul Moore

For Ginny. For making my life so good.

Prologue

Sergeant Burke Henry was not a happy soldier. *Escorting an agent from this newly created bunch they were calling the CIA down the Cagayan River in the Philippines was not his idea of a warrior's work. He had been in the Cagayan Valley before, during World War II, helping the Huks drive the Japanese Army off of Luzon Island. At the same time, he had been involved in that bitter fight, losing men he revered as friends and compatriots from his platoon, the man he was escorting had been stationed in London, a place he had never left during the war, pushing a pencil in some vague military-intelligence unit. Sergeant Henry wished his boss had at least assigned him someone from the old OSS: an experienced hand who had actually run missions during the war. Unlike this new outfit, the OSS had not treated ground-level military personnel with condescension and even contempt*

And now this man, whose lack of combat experience was matched only by his lack of understanding of Filipino politics and the Filipino character, was lecturing Sergeant Henry about the need to put down the Huk insurgency.

"It's simple, Sergeant. These people are Communists."

"So?"

"So? They're Communists, damn it! They're the enemy."

"I fought alongside these people. They're tough, brave, dedicated. Superb fighters. They don't give a damn about any politics except local politics. They couldn't tell a Communist from a cockroach. You're completely off base."

Agent Fletcher sighed.

"Sergeant Henry, I don't like working with you. But my boss says the agency has to interface with USAFFE. Says there has to be military oversight of this kind of transaction, though heaven knows why. So here we're stuck with each other."

"You've never explained this 'transaction,' as you call it."

"We're delivering money. A whole lot of money. We need the cooperation of this local official and others in his group to help in the fight against the Huks."

"The exact same people who helped USAFFE drive the Japanese off Luzon Island?"

"That was a marriage of convenience. Just like having Stalin for an ally in Europe. You don't see us being buddy-buddy with Stalin anymore! And like Stalin, these Huks are Communists. These are new times. This is a new war. Get your head out of the old one! Our job is to put down the Huk Rebellion, and to do that, we need the cooperation of this man."

"This government official."

"Right."

"If he's a government official, why don't we just go to his office in Tuguegaro City and knock on his door?"

"I hope you're being intentionally naïve. You're not really that stupid. It's a bribe. Money to guarantee that he, and the others he will pass some of it on to, will stay on our side. The Huks would kill him if they knew he was taking this money. And if we did it in Tuguegaro City, the Huks would know it before we got out of the building. They already think the man we're meeting today collaborated with the Japanese during the war."

"And did he?"

"Probably."

"Then we should kill him ourselves. Do you know what the Japanese Army this man collaborated with did to American soldiers? Has anyone told you about the Bataan death march?"

"This man is our guy now, and we want him to stay our guy. I'm done arguing with you. You do the soldier stuff. I'll do the political stuff. That includes the thinking."

An hour later, the river emerged from a long, twisting stretch through a steep canyon with rocky ledges, a stretch that made Sergeant Henry very nervous and kept him scanning the hillsides above them. Relived to be in a broader valley, he steered their boat toward a small opening in the trees where a well-worn path led away from a sandy beach. He climbed out of the boat and tied it off to a stump.

Agent Fletcher shouldered a rucksack and jumped to shore, careful not to get his feet wet.

"You stay with the boat. I don't want somebody stealing it and leaving us stranded in the middle of this jungle."

"You don't want me to scope out the meeting spot and make sure it's safe? You know, do my 'soldier

stuff'?"

"I was a soldier too, Sergeant."

"Yeah, but I was a real one."

The agent's face got even redder than his sunburn.

"I've had extensive training in counterinsurgency work. You haven't. I'll know if the place is okay."

"Right. I'll wait for you here. As ordered."

When agent Fletcher had disappeared down the trail, Sergeant Henry left the small beach and faded into the tree line. No sense in being a sitting duck if someone happened by.

A half hour later as he crouched sweating in the shrubbery, fighting mosquitos and watching the river, a firefight erupted in the distance. He got to his feet and headed toward the sound, M-1 carbine in hand, staying parallel to but clear of the trail Agent Fletcher had taken through the fecund, teeming, rank-smelling and humid jungle.

The closer he came to the source of the small arms fire, the more sporadic the shooting became. Soon, there was an ominous silence. The sergeant stopped. He remained perfectly still until the normal sounds of the jungle returned. Moving with a stealth born of *experience, it took him another fifteen minutes to reach the edge of a small clearing.*

Agent Fletcher lay face down in the middle of the clearing. Next to him was a Filipino man in khakis and a colorful shirt. Both men were motionless. It was obvious they were both dead. There were other bodies nearer the perimeter of the clearing. None of them showed any signs of life. He stood and silently surveyed the scene for a long time. Then he began to move slowly through the fetid vegetation surrounding the clearing, looking for other personnel.

It took him an hour to complete the small circle, and in that time, he found seven dead men wearing the uniform of the Philippine Constabulary. He also came across three men in peasant clothing who must have been part of the Huk movement. Two were dead. One was badly wounded but still alive. Blood ran from his mouth as he struggled to speak. Sergeant Henry turned the man's head sideways so he wouldn't drown in his own blood. He was speaking Tagalog, and Sergeant Henry's knowledge of that language was rudimentary. He did, however, understand the phrase, "all dead." Soon after the man gasped out those final words, he too breathed his last.

By the time Sergeant Henry returned to his starting point on the east side of the clearing, the sun was filtering through the trees at an oblique angle as sundown approached. After another long pause, and feeling very exposed, he entered the clearing. Next to Fletcher and the Filipino government official, the canvas rucksack lay on the ground. He opened the flap and removed parcels wrapped in heavy paper that was damp with humidity and bound with string. He cut one open. It contained bundles of one hundred-dollar bills. He assumed the other parcels contained the same, but he had no intention of staying in the clearing long enough to find out.

He closed the flap on the rucksack and slung it over his shoulder. He faded deeper into the tree line. When he was a good distance from the clearing, he stood for a long time and thought about the money. It was a lot of money, and it belonged to the CIA. Apparently, they were tossing it around like candy. Must be nice to be an agency that didn't have to account for cash. What would they do with the money if he returned it? Probably use it to bribe some more corrupt Filipino legislators, many of them former collaborators with the Japanese. Sergeant Henry didn't much care for that idea.

He thought about the money some more.

He was a career soldier, but someday he would retire. Then what? NCOs didn't get much in the way of a pension. His skill set centered around killing people, and while he was very good at his job, it didn't translate well into a paying job in the civilian world. He remembered the draftees in Korea saying NCO stood for "No Chance Outside."

Burke Henry decided to keep the cash. He didn't try to delude himself into thinking the act was justified. He didn't rationalize the decision. He was keeping the money, and that was that.

As he reached his decision, he heard the sound of an outboard motor starting up on the river. So much for an easy boat ride home.

He retrieved a machete from one of the dead men. He was in for at least two days of chopping his way through the jungle. Those two days would give him plenty of time to find a suitable place to bury the rucksack so he could come back and retrieve it someday

As he set out in the near darkness, he was already writing the after-action report in his mind. About the dead CIA agent. About the dead government official.

About the Huk ambush. About the stolen money.

Table of Contents

CHAPTER 1 17

CHAPTER 2 21

CHAPTER 3 41

CHAPTER 4 59

CHAPTER 5 75

CHAPTER 6 81

CHAPTER 7 105

CHAPTER 8 117

CHAPTER 9 141

CHAPTER 10 165

CHAPTER 11 171

CHAPTER 12 183

CHAPTER 13 191

CHAPTER 14 197

CHAPTER 15 209

CHAPTER 16 213

CHAPTER 17 215

CHAPTER 18 223

CHAPTER 19 253

CHAPTER 20 257

CHAPTER 21 263

CHAPTER 22 273

CHAPTER 23 285

CHAPTER 24 287

CHAPTER 25 299

CHAPTER 26 353

CHAPTER 27 365

CHAPTER 28 375

CHAPTER 29 385

CHAPTER 30 405

CHAPTER 31 415

CHAPTER 32 441

CHAPTER 33 453

Epilogue 467

Deep Desert Deception

CHAPTER 1

May 18, 1964

Captain Carlos Caballo, known as 'Horse' throughout the Lower Colorado River Basin, was in his office early on a hot Monday morning working with Sergeant Kensington on the patrol schedule for Smoke Tree. The sergeant was one of the few lateral transfers from the now-defunct Smoke Tree Police Department. Horse had hired him two years before to help smooth the transfer of the policing of the town from the STPD to the San Bernardino County Sheriff's Department's Smoke Tree Substation, a substation that was already responsible for policing the entire east end of San Bernardino County, the largest county in the United States.

The hiring had paid dividends many times over. Sergeant Kensington had proved to be dedicated, trustworthy and competent.

The intercom buzzed.

"Yes, Fred?"

"Call for you, line one."

"What's this about?"

"It's Burke Henry. Says he has to talk to you."

"Okay."

Horse walked back to his desk and punched up line one.

"Hello, Burke. Haven't heard from you for a while."

"Been busy.

I have to be gone for a while. When I get back, there's something important I want to show you. Any chance you can come out to my place in about three weeks?"

"Of course. Is this official business?"

Burke was silent for a moment before replying.

"Yeah, Horse, I guess it is."

"Sure, I can come out. Let me check my calendar"

Burke could hear papers rustling.

"Okay. How about June Eighth, three weeks from today? All that Memorial Day Weekend craziness on the river will be over by then."

"Fine. See you when you get here.

One more thing, Horse. Just in case I'm not at the house when you get there, the key is under that big rock by the northwest corner of the corral. Go ahead and let yourself in. There's grape soda in the refrigerator."

"Okay. See you in June."

After Horse hung up, he wished he had asked Burke two questions. First, since when did he lock his house? That was something new. And where was he calling from?

Well, since he didn't know where Burke was, there was no way he could call him back. He'd have to settle for asking his questions in a few weeks.

He and Sergeant Kensington went back to work on the schedule. Things were a lot more complicated now that ninety thousand servicemen were spread out all over the Eastern Mojave for Joint Force Desert Strike. Every one of them in Horse's area of responsibility. Many of them looking for any excuse to come into Smoke Tree and check out the local girls.

And the locals none too happy about it.

Plus, the carnival was coming to Smoke Tree the first week of June. That usually created a problem or two all by itself. Mix the Army with the carnival with the unhappy locals and the Smoke Tree High School Graduation, and there was potential for some real

CHAPTER 2

January 1956

The motorcyclist was westbound on 66 at two in the afternoon on a cold January day. A vicious wind was quartering out of the northeast as he rode into Holbrook, Arizona, a hard-looking town on the Santa Fe Railway line.

He passed the Wigwam Motel. The places looked no more like real wigwams than Brahman bulls looked like burros. He stayed on the highway until he was nearly to the west city limit before he decided to look the town over before travelling on. Even though he was pretty sure of his ultimate destination, he was always on the lookout for a place that might better suit his purposes.

He turned north on Thirteenth Avenue and then west on West Buffalo to Erie. That brought him to Holbrook High School. He pulled to the curb and took in the condition of the buildings. They were not in good shape. Class was in session, but the two furtive-looking young men in Levi's and flannel shirts moving quickly down Erie must have decided to take an early quit.

A sign on the corner pointed the way to Hunt Park and the Navajo County Fairgrounds. He made his way to the park. A town often reveals much about itself by the condition of its parks and schools. In the parking lot, he shut down his motorcycle and put it on the kick stand. He removed the panniers from the rear fender. He draped them over his left shoulder and walked into the park. The smell of dust was mixed with a faint undertone of farm animal odor blowing toward him from the county fairgrounds.

A meandering stroll convinced him Holbrook thought no more highly of its park than its high school.

He returned to the parking lot and re-attached the panniers. He kicked the motorcycle to life and drove through the residential areas of town. The homes he saw reinforced his initial assessment. They looked as badly used as the buildings housing the town's businesses.

He made his way to Navajo Boulevard and headed south. Before he reached the Santa Fe tracks, Navajo

Boulevard became Apache Boulevard.

They love Indians here, he thought. Indian street names and fake wigwams.

As he approached the railroad crossing, lights flashed and the gates came down. A freight train was rumbling into town from the east, engines thrumming and horn blaring for the crossing. He slipped the bike into neutral and spread his feet wide on the pavement as he watched the train pass. He didn't mind the delay. He liked trains.

A police car pulled up beside him. In his peripheral vision, he could see the driver giving him a studied appraisal. The officer shifted into reverse and backed up enough to see his plate. Subtle. In his rearview mirror, he could see the officer calling in the number to dispatch.

The train cleared the crossing. The clanging of the signal ceased and the flashers shut down. The gates lifted. He shifted into gear and eased the bike into motion. The black and white pulled in behind him and followed. When the two-vehicle parade reached the oddly-named Bucket of Blood Street, the officer turned left. The rider continued on to the south, now completely convinced that Holbrook would not do at all.

Outside the city limits, he turned east-southeast on Highway 180 and rode across the bridge spanning the Little Colorado River. He cranked the throttle open and the bike leapt forward. He sped down the deserted highway into a vast, sere and mysterious vista of great depth and complexity.

He crossed a low bridge over Five Mile Wash and then re-crossed the Little Colorado. He saw a sign advertising curios for sale at the Petrified Forest. The sun was angling to the west in his rearview mirror, revealing a panorama behind him that, but for the receding sun itself, differed little from the one opening before him.

The temperature, which had been just barely above forty at high noon, was dropping rapidly. As the sun neared the horizon behind him, it tinged the tableau ahead ever deeper hues of red and orange. The changing light was turning the browns and grays of distant mountain ranges to lavenders and darker purples.

He backed off the throttle to take it all in. He was driving very slowly when he noticed a road that cut away at an angle from the long, straight stretch ahead.

When he reached the intersection, there was a sign for the Painted Desert Inn. He took the turnoff.

The Inn sat very near an intersection on the edge of a plateau that sloped away to the southeast. It was a large, adobe building with many windows. Sunlight was caught and held in those facing west. Others gleamed soft and yellow. Lights already burning against the fall of night. Lights beckoning travelers to a refuge against the coming darkness. He slowed even further and drove into the parking lot.

There were a number of cars and one other motorcycle. He brought his bike to a stop and hit the kill switch. The engine died. He leaned it onto the kickstand and climbed off. The engine was already pinging and popping in the cold air. He took his goggles off and turned the Army field cap they had held in place so the bill faced front. He hooked the goggles over the handlebars and unfastened the leather panniers from the rear fender. He was adjusting them on his shoulder as he neared the inn when a large, burly, bearded man wearing a leather jacket much like his own came out of the building and stepped into the lot. The man nodded. He nodded back.

He stopped at the door to remove his hat before entering.

Inside, his boots rang on the hardwood floor as he walked into a large dining room where young women in crisp, Harvey House uniforms circulated among the seated customers. The spicy, warm aroma of Mexican food filled the room. When a waitress came out of the kitchen balancing a tray of food, the smell of frying meat followed her out the door.

I'm afraid this is too fancy for me, he thought. He was turning to leave when he realized the walls were covered with murals. He was drawn to one in particular. Crossing the room, he stood in front of it. It depicted a journey undertaken by two Indian boys. They were walking from their village to a distant lake to gather salt.

As he studied the story the mural told, some of the nearby patrons became aware of a slender man of above-average height with an olive drab cap in his right hand and saddlebags slung over his left shoulder. There was an air of intense concentration about the dark man with short, blonde hair.

One of the Harvey Girls approached him.

"Beautiful, isn't it. I never get tired of looking at

it."

The man continued to study the mural as he spoke in a surprisingly deep voice.

"Who painted this?"

"A man named Fred Kabotie. A Hopi Indian. He painted all the murals in here."

"Man can tell a story. Pulls you in."

"Yes, it does.

Will you be joining us for dinner, sir?"

He turned to face her. She was struck by the blue eyes in the dark face.

"No, thank you ma'am. Just passing through."

"Well, most people are."

The hint of a smile tugged at the corner of his mouth.

"I expect that's so.

Do you have time to answer a question?"

"Yes."

"I just came off 180. If I stay on this road, where does it go?"

"Into the Petrified Forest and then on to Adamana

on Highway 66."

"And if I go back to 180 and take it southeast?"

"You'll see lots of empty desert. A couple wide spots in the road, but no towns of any size until you get to St. Johns, and there's not much there either.

"And it's a long way to this St. Johns?"

"Oh, yes."

"Thank you, kindly."

He left the dining room and passed out of the building into the parking lot beyond.

The other motorcycle was gone.

He lashed the panniers to his back fender and retrieved his goggles from the handlebars. He turned his cap around and snugged it tightly to his head with the goggles. He climbed on and started the bike and drove back to the intersection of the two roads. At the stop sign, he turned southeast.

He was soon in Apache County, the sixth largest county in the United States, home to less than 70,000 people within its eleven thousand square miles. The majority of those people were Indians of various tribes. By an immense margin, there were more cattle and sheep in the county than people: Indian, Mexican, white or otherwise.

As he drove past Hunt, Arizona, more a ghost town than a living community, the sun touched the western horizon. The sky cascaded with reds and oranges and golds, recoloring the Twin Peaks to the east. He slowed and eased his bike to the side of the road and shut down the engine.

The world grew quiet, but not silent. He could hear the sigh of the wind and bursts of muffled sound as flocks of small birds moved from shrub to shrub. Absorbed by the play of the rapidly changing light on the immensity spreading out to all sides of him, he turned in a circle to take it all in. It was like standing on the edge of an unknown and empty planet. His motorcycle and the blacktop road beside it seemed artifacts of some civilization long since extinct from the face of that barren world.

The temperature continued to drop. He would have stayed until all the light left the sky, but he realized a new sound was coming from the north. A vehicle of some kind. He strained to define it as it faded and then returned as the originator of the sound moved through the hilly country. Then he heard it clearly. It was a Harley.

He smiled.

He climbed back on the bike and stomped hard on the kickstarter. The motorcycle responded with its own distinctive sound. He got back on the road.

He maintained the same speed he had held before stopping. The light from his headlamp became visible against the blacktop as twilight dropped over the land. Purple began to replace the brilliant colors of the sunset. As he approached Volcanic Mountain, he slowed again and turned onto a dirt road running to the north atop Black Ridge. He drove slowly until he was over a mile from the highway. He shut down his engine and leaned his bike onto the kickstand.

Without the noise of his own machine, he could hear the Harley on the highway. The sound level dropped as the rider slowed. The bike idled for a while. Then, there was silence.

He's listening for me, the man thought. Listening and not hearing anything.

He started the engine again and revved it a few times before turning it off.

Now he knows I'm up here. He'll either drive up or come on foot, and he doesn't look like a man who takes much to walking, so I'm betting he'll drive. But first, he'll wait a while to see if I come back down the road.

The gibbous, waxing moon that had risen pale and almost unnoticed in the bright glare of day was now well above the eastern horizon in a cloudless sky. It provided all the light he needed. He left the panniers attached to the fender, but removed five canvas bags. He hid them in a snakeweed bush a good distance away.

It was getting very cold. Every breath expelled vapor. Mid-thirties would be his guess, dropping into the twenties by morning. Absent the sound from the other motorcycle, the immense stillness engulfed him. The wind had stopped. The birds gone silent. The only sound was the crunch of his boots against the hard ground and the sound of his own breathing.

He gathered rocks and made a crude fire ring. He side-stepped down the steep ridge into the broad wash below, grateful for the moonlight. Once down, he gathered cheat grass, rip-gut brome and some small, dead sticks for kindling. When he had all he could carry, he took everything up to the fire ring and then climbed down the hill to find more substantial fuel. There was lots of desert willow in the sandy wash, the orange and gold leaves visible in the pale, ghostly light. Beneath the willows, he found enough dead limbs to make a bundle. He went back up the hill.

Setting the wood aside, he arranged the grass in a substantial pile inside the ring. He pulled a Zippo lighter with the raised emblem of the 11th Airborne Division from the pocket of his Levi's. He sparked it to life and moved the flame under the dry grasses. White smoke blossomed immediately, followed by small flames. He began to add twigs and small sticks. Once they ignited, he added the desert willow.

When he had a substantial blaze, he walked to a nearby stand of sage brush and kicked two of the bushes into pieces with his Corcoran jump boots. He carried the pieces to the fire ring and added them to the mix. The resinous sage flared, giving off the pungent odor that is the mark of high desert country.

A wind sprang up, gusting in from the north. The fire intensified, and sparks blew off into the night, leaping high into the air before they winked out.

There, he thought, if he can't see this fire, he should be able to smell it.

The intermittent wind made his fire cast flickering shadows on the rocks and sparse plants. After he warmed his hands, the man rose and untied his sleeping bag from the handlebars of the motorcycle. He spread it on the ground north of the fire ring.

When he was finished, he faded into the shadows, leaving his motorcycle and bedroll sole and silent witnesses to the little campfire. It was the only manmade light visible in that vast emptiness. Small beacon indeed in that immensity, but beacon enough for his purposes.

It was not long before he heard the Harley rumble to life. It moved slowly toward him along the route he had recently traveled.

Didn't think he'd come afoot, he thought.

The beam from the Harley's headlight soon appeared on the ridgeline, wobbling as the rider struggled to keep the heavy machine upright on terrain that was, by increments, rocky and then cloaked in sand to a depth of over two feet. Once it wavered as it veered sideways. He could hear the heavy machine slipping on the unevenly angled and sand-covered hard pan as the rider adjusted the clutch and throttle to keep it moving forward.

As it completed the final section of road to the campsite, the headlight did not touch the man's hiding place. Even so, he kept his eyes averted to preserve his night vision.

The rider killed the engine at the edge of the glow from the fire. The headlight blinked out. The bulky rider dismounted, leaned the Harley onto its kickstand, and stood looking toward the fire. He looked for a long time before moving to the man's motorcycle. Unbuckling the flaps on the panniers, he pulled out the contents and dumped them at his feet. As he lowered himself ponderously to one knee to better paw through the items, the man left his hiding place and silently closed the distance between himself and the kneeling man.

"Find anything interesting?"

The hulking man lurched to his feet and turned. He did not speak, just stood assessing the figure that had materialized behind him.

He came to some conclusion.

"Thought you had something valuable in them saddlebags, way you carried them with you when you went inside back there."

"I did."

The big man shuffled toward him, feet splayed,

unzipping his leather jacket as he came. His big, hard gut projecting in front of him.

"Where is it?"

The would-be thief continued forward. As he drew closer, the man could smell sweat, gasoline, motor oil and cigarette smoke.

"Somewhere your fat fingers can't get hold of it."

It took a moment for the insult to register.

One big hand reached inside his jacket.

The man closed the remaining distance between the two with startling speed. He grasped the bulky rider's arm with both hands, one on the elbow and one on the forearm, simultaneously turning into the man and twisting until the elbow dislocated.

The rider swore and released his hold on the gun he had been pulling from an inside pocket. The chrome-plated .45 winked in the moonlight as it clattered to the rocks. But he was game for all that he was injured. He roared in rage as well as pain as he swung his good hand at the man who had just done him grievous harm.

He should not have done that. The man released the injured arm and grasped the ponderous, oncoming fist with both hands. He twisted the fist to one side and seized the thumb in a fierce grip that brooked no retrieval. The fat biker did not know it, but the fight was over now but for the epilogue.

Maneuvering the biker's bulk by leveraging the thumb joint that all humans instinctively protect, the slender man went into what would have looked like a delicate dance to an untrained observer of the strange and intricate maneuver. His steps turned the rider in a wide and accelerating circle before he suddenly forced the larger man's hand toward the ground and released his grip. The man's momentum carried him sprawling head first into the fire.

He screamed as the fire burned his face and set his greasy hair asmolder. Like a walrus struggling onto shoreline boulders, he levered himself by means of his good arm over the rocks and out of the fire ring. He ended up on his back, staring into the night sky.

The slender man turned away and collected the .45 from where it had fallen. He carried it to where the man lay on his back, t-shirt twisted up to expose an enormous pale gut that quivered like a monstrous, obscene maggot with each shuddering breath.

"Nice gun."

The man released the clip. He pulled back the slide and ejected the round that had been in the chamber. He bent over and picked up the round and tossed it into the wash below. Then he field-stripped the weapon in a few practiced and efficient motions. He threw the pieces off into the darkness. He thumbed the rounds out of the clip and dispersed them to all points of the compass, followed by the clip itself.

He walked away.

The downed rider pushed himself up on his good elbow and strained to see over his own stomach. The other man was at his Harley doing something to the gas tank. As the prone biker stared in horror, he saw the man toss the gas cap aside and begin filling the tank with handfuls of dirt. He struggled to get to his feet without further injuring his dislocated elbow, no easy trick for a man who weighed nearly three hundred pounds.

The slender rider turned and came back to him, clapping the dust from his hands. As he drew closer, he realized the smell of burnt hair had been added to the stink of the downed man's body.

"Stay down. If you don't, I'll kick you in the face."

The man ceased his efforts. He wasn't sure he

wanted to get up anyway.

"I'm going to pack up and go now, but I want you to know something. I don't like people on my back trail. I see you again, I'll kill you."

The big man slumped back to the ground and stared into the void above. He turned his head to watch as the man moved away and retrieved something and brought it back to the emptied panniers before repacking them and tying them to his back fender. He could see the man's feet as he rolled up his sleeping bag and carried it to his bike, tying it on before he threw a leg over the machine.

The bulky rider rose onto his elbow again.

"Hey you. You can't leave me here like this."

The man hesitated for a moment and then dismounted.

"You're right. No reason for you to have this warm fire."

He threw dirt on the flames. The fire smoldered and died.

He returned to his bike without speaking again. He remounted and kicked it to life and rode off into the night, leaving the vanquished rider next to a dead fire beneath the cold light of a winter moon.

Deep Desert Deception

CHAPTER 3

February 1956

The man rode into Smoke Tree on a Royal Enfield Interceptor on a cold day in February. It was very windy. There was so much grit in the air, his face was stinging with countless tiny abrasions as he entered the town.

He turned off Highway 66 onto Front Street at the point where the highway curved away from the railroad tracks. He continued down the street until he came to a tired, used-up-looking building called the California Gateway Hotel. He turned left and drove up onto the sidewalk and stopped next to one of the green metal posts holding up the colonnade. Hitting the kill switch, he climbed off and leaned the bike onto its kickstand. Because the cycle had a magneto ignition and required no key, he chained it to the post. The fact that it could be driven away by anyone with enough leg strength to punch down the kickstarter made securing it necessary.

After he snapped the lock, he stood for a moment and watched a westbound freight rumble into the rail yard on the other side of the deserted street as it slowed for the depot. He had once, many years before, ridden a flatwheel boxcar all the way from Oklahoma to Los Angeles to join the Army. A boxcar that had rolled into Smoke Tree at dawn carrying an already-homesick, hungry and cold seventeen-year old who was away from home for the first time in his life.

At the time, *he hadn't even known the name of the town. As the train slowed that morning, he had been huddled in the corner of the car. He untangled himself from the discarded shipping waste he had been using for both bed and blanket and moved to the door. He could see the south side of the tracks through a gap in the partially open door. In the far distance were the Black Mountains in Arizona.*

The freight came to a stop for a crew change. There was a lot of concern on the west coast about railroad sabotage in the days following Pearl Harbor, so he pulled his eye away from the door, afraid someone might see him. He moved to the back corner of the car and stayed there until the train was underway again.

When it lurched to a start, he returned to the door. He caught the odor of creosote and ballast from the railbed beneath the slowly-turning wheels. As the long freight crawled out of the station, he saw a few rows of old, wood-frame houses. Some were white and some were pastel shades. There were a few red-tile-roofed adobes mixed in. Brown Bermuda grass surrounded some of the houses, and some had only dirt yards. There were chinaberry trees, leafless and bleak in the early morning winter light, desiccated clumps of last year's fruit clustered thickly on their limbs. The people he saw outside were all brown.

A lean and hungry-looking dog trotted up the street. It stopped to sniff something discarded at the curb and then moved on. A filigree of delicately twisting smoke from a trash fire wisped in the door. The scene reminded him of the reservation where he had grown up.

When he thought about the reservation, he realized again that he could never go back there. Nor to anywhere in Oklahoma. Not after what he had done. On the heels of that conviction came another thought. He was going off to fight a war. He needed a place to hold in his mind as somewhere to return to. Not the home he couldn't go to, but a place to serve as a marker for home. A mental talisman of sorts. As the train picked up speed and the neighborhood receded from view, he decided to make this little town, with its brown yards, brown trees and brown people, that place. He promised himself that if he survived the war he would learn the name of the town and return someday.

He no longer had anywhere else to go.

When the freight across the street stopped with a clanking of couplings and a final hiss of airbrakes on that February morning, his thoughts returned to the present. He removed the panniers from the back fender of his motorcycle. He untied his bedroll from the handlebars and went up the worn cement steps into the seedy, deserted lobby of the sad building.

He crossed to the counter. There was no one there. He banged on a tarnished bell a few times. A disheveled clerk wandered out of the back room and told him about the rates. He paid for two weeks in advance. He signed the register as Burke Henry, the name he had used since the day he enlisted in the Army shortly after Pearl Harbor. A name he had been using for so long it now seemed more real than his given name.

"Is there a bank in town?"

"Yes."

The clerk stood staring at him.

"Think you might tell me where it is?"

The clerk waved vaguely to the north.

"On Broadway."

"And the post office?"

"Block above the bank."

The clerk handed over an old-fashioned key hooked by a few links of flimsy chain to a block of wood.

"Room 213. Upstairs. Bathroom's down the hall. Keep the noise down after eleven. No women in your room."

Burke took the key and climbed the bare-wood stairs, the panniers slung over his shoulder and the sleeping bag under his arm. The clerk watched him until he was out of sight and then turned and went back into the room he had come out of.

Burke found 213 and unlocked the door to the musty odor of a sparsely-furnished room with cheap, worn linoleum on the floor. A faded pattern of some sort, barely discernible. His boots crunched grit as he walked across the threshold. It was as cold in the room as it had been on the street. Single bed. Mattress with no box springs suspended from the frame by metal straps. Reminded him of the Army. An ancient, worn dresser with several knobs missing from the drawers. One wooden chair. A stained sink with a badly-silvered mirror on the wall above. No cabinet behind the mirror. No soap on the sink. A grayish-white, threadbare towel hanging from a wooden bar with the varnish long since rubbed away. Remembering the clerk's words about the bathroom being down the hall, he wondered how many men had pissed in that sink in the middle of the night. He made a mental note to buy a quart of bleach.

He pulled open the closet door. Inside, a metal pipe was screwed into flanges that had been nailed to the wall. No hangers on the pipe.

He left his bedroll in the room and went out without locking the door. He went down the stairs and through the lobby. The clerk was back at the counter. He stared at Burke with eyes as unblinking and expressionless as a carp but did not acknowledge him. Outside, he unslung the panniers and attached them to the rear fender. He unchained the motorcycle and started it up and drove off on a slow tour of the streets of the town he had barely glimpsed all those many years before.

There was a small park in front of the Santa Fe depot. The depot spoke of faded glory, but the park, with its towering palm trees and World War One field gun, was well-maintained. The houses he drove past on the residential streets were almost all in good condition, with the usual exceptions that can be found in any town. He liked the neighborhoods. Nothing fancy, nothing pretentious, except for the one spread up the side of a hill on the south end of town.

He drove by the high school, a majestic old, vaguely gothic, well-cared-for building that looked like it belonged in New England. He rode past two community ball fields. Even though baseball season was long over and the close-cut Bermuda grass had gone dormant, the facilities were in good repair: no holes in the backstops and no vandalism to the dugouts.

Satisfied, he drove to the post office he had passed earlier. With the panniers over his shoulder, he went inside and rented the smallest size box before driving back down the street to the Bank of America. He did not re-attach the panniers to the fender for the short ride.

He carried them over his shoulder when he went inside.

He opened a checking account with a hundred dollars, using the post office box as his address. When he was finished, he inquired about a safe deposit box.

"How big, Mr. Henry," asked the teller, an older, very thin, irritated-looking woman with downturned frown lines at the corners of her mouth whose starched, white blouse gave off the improbable odor of witch hazel.

"Biggest one you have."

"Fifteen by twenty-two is our biggest box. It's quite expensive. Fifty dollars a year. You can rent a small one for five dollars."

"I'll take the large size."

"You'll have to pay in advance."

He produced his wallet and extracted two twenties and a ten.

The woman wrote him a receipt for his payment and completed the paperwork for box number one hundred and twenty-one. She produced a card for him to sign so his signature could be verified when he wanted access. After he signed, she took the card and handed him a key and led him to the safe deposit vault.

She asked him to turn his back as she entered the combination and opened the door. They went inside.

"Takes two keys to open it: your key and the one we keep here."

They both inserted and turned their keys to open the door. He pulled out the box.

She led him out of the vault to a small room.

"This is the private room. The door locks from the inside. When you're ready to put the box back, just come out and push the button outside the door."

In the locked room, he opened the panniers and took out five canvas bags. All but one bag contained one hundred thousand dollars in banded, hundred-dollar bills. He put four hundred and ninety-six thousand in the box, keeping out five hundred dollars from the one broken stack for immediate expenses. He had spent over two thousand of the original five hundred thousand during his travels around the southwest. Mostly for gas and food. He had kept his expenses low by sleeping outside most nights, only occasionally checking into a cheap motel to shower. Sometimes, he even slept in the bed, but usually he unrolled his sleeping bag on the floor.

He was glad to finally have the money in a safe place again. Not that he had ever thought anyone was good enough to take it away from him, but there was always the unforeseen. Accidents. Unfortunate traffic stops. Things that could not be predicted.

He had performed similar post-office-and-bank-box operations in other towns that had interested him during his winter journey. El Paso in Texas. Silver City and Lordsburg in New Mexico. Prescott and Flagstaff in Arizona. Tonopah and Carson City in Nevada. None of those towns were quite what he wanted, but he had wanted to look at other places before he returned to the town he had seen so briefly in 1942. He was pretty sure it was the town he wanted, but it never hurt to have options.

In each of those other places, after spending a few days, he had retrieved his money and set out again. He never cancelled either the safe deposit or post office boxes before he left. He had no curiosity about what the bank or the post office would do when the rental terms on the boxes ended.

Outside, he climbed back on the midnight-blue motorcycle and drove to the smaller of the two markets in town. Might as well help the little guy, he thought. Inside, he bought a bag of apples that would have been culls in the supermarket in any big city. He also bought a quart of orange juice, cans of sardines and Spam, a box of saltines, cans of condensed milk, two bars of soap and a quart of bleach.

In the parking lot, he balanced the groceries on the seat between his legs and drove onto the street.

At the hotel, he put the food on top of the ancient dresser and poured the quart of bleach into the sink, turning his face away from the powerful smell. He unpacked the saddlebags. He put his spare Levi's, olive drab t-shirts, and socks and underwear in the drawer that had both knobs. He put his shaving kit and toothbrush in another.

He tossed his leather jacket on the bed. He arranged the empty saddlebags in what seemed like a random position beside the jacket before taking the soap and the threadbare towel with him and leaving the room. He locked the door behind him.

He went down the hall to a bathroom with "mens"

crudely hand lettered on the door with a marker of some kind. Inside, he saw chipped, black and white tile and water puddled on the floor. Attached to the wall was a solitary, cheap, towel bar that may have once been chromed. When he hung his towel, the bar sagged from its moorings.

He filled the claw-footed bathtub with rusty-looking and not-quite-hot water that smelled strongly of alkali. The old pipes groaned and banged the whole time the ancient, greenish faucets were open. He undressed and got in the tub. He bathed and washed his short, blonde hair. A lot of very dirty water went down the drain when he pulled the stopper.

He dried himself as best he could with the inadequate towel, shivering slightly in the draughty, unheated room. There was no bathmat, so he left his own puddle by the tub. He put on his Levi's and t-shirt and carried his socks and boots out the door.

He unlocked the door to his room and went inside. The musty air now held a faint hint of aftershave. He walked to the bed and stood looking at the saddlebags. They were not quite in their original position, although whoever had moved them had made an effort to put them back as they had been.

He put on his leather jacket and went out the door and locked it again.

In the lobby, the clerk was once again nowhere to be seen. He banged hard on the bell he had rung earlier in the day.

The clerk took his time emerging from the door behind the desk. He didn't seem happy about being summoned.

"Help you with something?"

"Stay out of my room. I ever have reason to think you've been in there again, you'll regret it."

The clerk spread his hands, palm up.

"I have no idea what you're..."

"Shut up. I already know you're a sneak. Don't convince me you're a liar, too.

Do you understand?"

The clerk was suddenly not so bored. Something in the eyes of the man on the other side of the counter alarmed him

"Yessir."

The clerk turned quickly and went through the door, closing it behind him.

Burke walked out of the hotel and set off down Front Street. When he came to a nondescript Chinese restaurant grandly named The Peking Palace, he decided to treat himself to a hot meal. He went inside and sat at the counter. The restaurant smelled of burnt coffee, green tea and frying fish. The cheapest thing on the plastic menu tucked behind the sugar shaker was chop suey. He ordered it.

When it came, it was a uniformly gray color. Even though the menu had advertised beef, chicken or pork, and he had ordered beef, he had the feeling whatever he had ordered would have come out of the same pot: a pot containing anything returned uneaten from the dining room. A pot that was always simmering on the back burner.

The odor that rose from the steaming bowl was not particularly appealing.

Oh well, he thought, it's cheap, and there's lots of it. He dosed it with soy sauce. He pulled the basket of soda crackers toward the bowl. He opened every package and stirred them all into his meal before he started eating.

When he left the café, darkness had fallen. The cold wind still blowing out of the north pushed dust and paper debris down the deserted street. There were no streetlights. All the storefronts were dark. He walked past a bar called The Palms. He could hear country and western music playing inside. Bars did not interest him. Never had. He walked on.

The tiny sliver of moon had already set, leaving the black velvet sky to the stars glittering overhead.

When he reached the hotel and went inside, there was a different clerk behind the counter.

"Evening, Mr. Henry."

That acknowledgement, and the way it was delivered, told him the new man knew everything that had taken place between Burke and the day man, or at least the day man's version of those events.

"Evenin'," Burke responded as he crossed the lobby and went up the stairs.

There was no light in the hallway that led to his room. He pushed his key into the lock more by feel than by sight and opened the door. Running his hand over the wall inside, he punched the button on an ancient switch. The dim, bare bulb that hung from the ceiling by a frayed wire came to life. In the unheated room, he pulled the threadbare sheets and blanket off the bed and tossed them and the pillow on the floor.

He was rewarded with a cloud of dust.

He spread his bedroll over the thin mattress. After undressing, he crossed the room and turned out the light. There was no window in the room and consequently no light of any kind. He groped his way across the cold, gritty floor back to the bed and climbed into the sleeping bag.

As Burke lay in bed, he reviewed his impressions of Smoke Tree.

Isolated town on the southeast edge of California. Colorado River forming a border with Arizona to the east. Nevada border not far to the north. Working class town. White people on the west side of town. Brown ones on the east. Indians isolated and mostly forgotten in shabby, government housing down by the river to the north of everyone else.

Thinking about the Indians made him think of his older cousin, Burke Henry. Twenty years old when he died in a single car accident, driving drunk in his old pickup truck. Driving as fast as the truck would go before he hit a telephone pole on a straight stretch of an isolated road: a road where an accident probably wouldn't be discovered for hours. Leaving no skid marks. The man who now called himself Burke Henry still didn't believe it had been an accident.

Nor did his Aunt. So, when her seventeen-year-old nephew showed up on her doorstep and explained what had happened and what he had to do, she willingly handed over Burke's driver's license and metal social security card, sentiment pushed aside by necessity. More concerned for her living nephew than her dead son. She understood Kyle had to get out of town and head for a place where nobody knew him or his cousin. Or knew one of the three men who had raped his sister and was now lying dead in a bay at his repair garage. Somewhere far from the panhandle of Oklahoma. A big city where he could enlist in the Army.

In Smoke Tree earlier that day, the switch engine shuttling through the rail yard across the street had brought back memories of other trains in other places. Catching a Union Pacific eastbound freight on a cold, winter night, the sixteenth of January, 1942, as it pulled away from Anadarko, Oklahoma. Hoping he could reach Chickasha before anyone discovered Harold Nevins behind the closed door on West Central Boulevard.

When the train reached Chickasha, he jumped off

and started the thirty-three-mile overland walk to Purcell in the darkness of a moonless night. If the authorities put out the word to watch for him on the Union Pacific freights that rolled through Anadarko day and night, he wanted to be on a Santa Fe train heading south out of Purcell.

As he lay in bed, he could hear a radio with a bad speaker down the hall. Frank Sinatra was singing, "I'll Be Seeing You". The song recalled train stations during World War II. Servicemen kissing wives or girlfriends goodbye.

He was wondering what it felt like to have a girlfriend when he fell into a dreamless sleep.

CHAPTER 4

February 1956

The next day, Burke began riding out through the country around Smoke Tree. He loved the miles and miles of open space. He ventured as far downriver as Parker, but the way the town was situated did not appeal to him. Also, he knew about the Japanese relocation camp at nearby Poston that had held thousands of Japanese-American citizens captive. He could sense yet the ugly undercurrent of anguish and frustration generated by those desperate, demeaned and disrespected people. It emanated so strongly from the place that it reached all the way into town.

There was some interesting land near Topock, but it was too close to the backwater there, and he knew summer evenings would sing with the sickly whine of mosquitoes. He had unpleasant memories, from places far, far away, of mosquitoes and the diseases and fevers they carried.

Oatman was intriguing, but he was disconcerted by the furtive and fugitive look of so many of the people he saw during the day he spent walking the hills there. People who turned away if they thought a stranger was looking at them. The look of people who might bring unwelcome investigators to the collection of semi-inhabited shacks spread across the hillsides of volcanic rock like a tumbletown rash.

That concern was coupled with his dislike of the huge piles of tailings and barren stacks of hardened mud where whatever fragile desert soil that had managed to accumulate across millennia had been stripped away and rendered sterile in the fervent, feverish search for gold. There are those who think the desert has been dealt so severe and desiccated a hand by nature that it cannot be rendered more singular and sere by any act of man. But it can be. It had been. And would be yet again. Greed and avarice can always further denigrate even the bleakest of realms. He rode elsewhere.

One day, he took highway 95 north toward Las Vegas and pulled off in Searchlight, a former copper-mining town now reduced to less than three percent of the population that had filled the streets early in the century. There were many abandoned properties he could have purchased for next to nothing, but there was a casino there. Even though he would need to use casinos from time to time, he considered gambling a kind of sickness. He had no desire to be near it.

Also, there were sad-eyed prostitutes working out of two motels across the highway from the casino. They brought back memories of his unhappy and defeated mother in the days after his Ukrainian father deserted the family and moved elsewhere and to points beyond.

Over his next few days of scouting for the ideal location, he considered Baker and Nipton and Kelso and Goodsprings in Nevada. He dismissed each of them for various reasons.

In truth, there was nothing wrong with them. Just as there had been nothing wrong with Silver City or Santa Fe or Taos in New Mexico, or Prescott or Sedona or Tucson in Arizona. The real deciding factor was always that image of the town he had not yet even known was named Smoke Tree when he passed through in 1942. An image of a pseudo home he had held so closely in his mind he came to see it as his good luck charm. A charm he believed had protected him from death while others had fallen around him in the Pacific Theater and Korea and then back in the Philippines. Not only not dead but unwounded. Even if not unmarked in other ways.

While he explored other towns in the area, something about Smoke Tree kept calling him back. Whatever the attraction was, he inevitably found himself narrowing his search to places closer to the little community.

On one of his daily excursions, this one to look at a dot on the map called Goffs, he crossed the Santa Fe tracks on highway 95 and stopped at the old service station that stood isolated and lonely just north of Klinefelter. As he drove into the dirt parking lot, he saw a man sitting on a rocking chair in front of a faded wood building. Drawing closer, he realized the man was very old. The old man smiled and nodded in appreciation as Burke slowed his machine to a crawl so as not to raise a cloud of dust.

He hit the kill switch, and the engine died. The smells of spilled motor oil, split coolant hoses and leaking radiators rose from the dirt.

"Hep you, young man?"

"Two gallons of high test, please."

The old man smiled and got up. In spite of the

chill, he was wearing only a green t-shirt tucked into canvas pants and a pair of worn boots. There was a long-billed, green cap on his head. Burke noticed he didn't use the handles on the rocker to lever himself to his feet; he simply rose in one smooth motion. An impressive maneuver for a man his apparent age.

The pumps at the station were of the old, hand-cranked variety, each of them topped with a red Pegasus painted on a milky white oval. The man carefully rotated the pump handle until the fuel entering the glass measure above the pump and below the mythical horse reached the two-gallon mark. He pulled a shop rag from his back pocket and removed the gas nozzle from its hook.

"I know some of you motorcycle fellers is right particular about your tanks, but I guarantee you I can get your two gallons in there without spilling a drop on that beautiful paint job. But if you're concerned about these old hands, you're welcome to do it yourself."

Burke climbed off and angled the big bike onto its kickstand. He removed the gas cap and stepped back.

The man kept the nozzle pointed upward with one hand while he positioned the shop rag to protect the paint. He cupped the tip of the nozzle in the palm of his hand before carefully inserting it. Once he was satisfied with the arrangement, he tripped the gravity feed and drained the two gallons into the tank. When the glass measure was empty, the man withdrew the nozzle while covering it with the rag.

"Thank you for doing that so well, sir. How much do I owe you?"

"That's one dollar and a dime. And no need to thank me. Always been partial to them motors. Wanted a Indian real bad when I was a young man."

Burke got a dollar from his wallet and a dime from his pocket and handed over the money.

"Speaking of Indians, I'm guessing you've got some native blood in your background."

The old man smiled and removed his hat to reveal a full head of black hair.

"You'd be right. Daddy was one hundred percent Chickasaw. That's why there's not a gray hair on this head. You've got a good eye, young man, but then I suspect that's because you have some Indian blood yourself in spite of them blue eyes. It's the cheek bones tell the tale."

"Got me there. My mother was Kiowa Apache. Got the blue eyes from my father."

"If you don't mind my askin', what brings you out this way? Oklahoma is Kiowa country."

"I'm looking around for a house to buy or a place to build one."

"What kind of place you lookin' for?"

"I'm pretty particular. I don't want to be in town, but I want to be close enough to get there for supplies without driving too far. I'd like a place that's very private and well away from the highway."

"Do you need electricity?"

"Not as much as I need privacy. But I do need water, and it seems to be scarce hereabouts."

"Well sir, there's a place off to the west in the Piutes that might meet your needs. There was a army post up there in the eighteen hundreds. Fallen to ruins now. But they built the fort there because of Piute Creek."

"Doesn't the government own the land?"

"It does, it does indeed, but there's some private land near it that has access to water. Man named Thomas Van Slyke homesteaded a hundred and forty acres of it right next to the creek in 1930. Tried to make a go of it growing alfalfa and grapes and fruit. But them mule deer and rabbits and ground squirrels ate his crops almost as fast as he could plant them. Toward the end of World War Two, he give up and sold the property to as fine a family as you're ever likely to meet. People name of Irwin. The Irwins built a little house and put up fences and pens and tried to make a living raising turkeys, but they had the same problems with coyotes and bobcats Mr. Van Slyke had with them deer and rabbits.

Anyways, just before Van Slyke sold to the Irwins, he pieced off five acres and sold it to a friend of his named White, Robert White. Lived down to Smoke Tree. This Robert White built hisself a little shack there right next to the creek. Liked to go out there of a summer day when it was hotter than blazes down the valley. Elevation in Smoke Tree is five hundred feet, you see? Fort Piute is nearly three thousand. Twenty-five hundred feet makes a lot of difference out here on a August afternoon."

"If it's so nice, what makes you think he'd want to sell it?"

"Not him. His son. Robert up and died real sudden

two years back. He was a widower, so the property passed to his son, Billy. I hear tell Billy would like to sell, but it seems like no one wants to live way out in the middle of nowhere down a road that's so bad it's hardly any road atall."

"I'd like to take a look at it. Can you tell me how to get there?"

The old man pointed up the highway.

"Go north. After about nine miles, keep your eyes peeled for a pile of rocks on the west side of the highway. That dirt track is the Old Mojave Road. Fort Piute was built to protect the mail and freight haulers and other travelers on the road. Take the track west and just keep a goin' 'till you reach what's left of the fort. Mostly some old rock walls and such. Leave your machine there and walk toward the creek. Pretty soon, you'll see the fences and turkey pens the Irwins built and what's left of their house.

Down near their place, you'll find the shack Robert White built. Ain't much, but it looks over the creek and the cottonwoods and the willows. Right pretty little spot. One of the only places in the whole Mojave where water runs all year long, even if sometimes it don't run very far 'fore it goes underground.

"If it's privacy you're a lookin' for, that place'll suit you to a fare-thee-well. I doubt you'll ever see anyone out there, except maybe a quail hunter in two in October."

"Many thanks for the information. I'm Burke Henry, by the way."

Burke extended his hand.

The old man extended his and they shook.

"Hugh. Hugh Stanton. Mighty pleased to meet you, Burke."

"Likewise."

Burke remounted and started his engine and eased out of the parking lot.

Hugh Stanton's directions were good. Just after his odometer showed nine miles had passed, Burke saw the rock cairn and turned west onto a dirt road. The road was hardpan atop a rocky plain at first, the bluish-gray of burro bush competed with the stubborn green of hardy creosote for dominance. But then he came to a wide, sandy wash that was a challenge for his machine. Once he exited the desert willow and catclaw-filled wash, the primitive road ran across rough, rocky ground again for some distance. But soon, he realized what he had thought was level desert when he saw it from the highway was actually fractured with drainage after drainage trending mostly north to south. Some of them were shallow and not difficult to negotiate, but some were deeper. In some, the sand was so deep he had to stop and dismount and walk alongside as he carefully guided his motorcycle in first gear by careful use of the clutch and throttle. It was not long before he could smell the clutch beginning to overheat. He stopped to let it cool off.

The instant he hit the kill switch, a great stillness settled around him. Absent the noise of his engine, there was little sound else in the vast space. Waiting for his clutch to cool in a world silent but for the whisper of the wind, he felt like an insignificant speck on the face of the open terrain, alone among the rocky hillsides stretching away to all sides. If what Hugh Stanton had said was correct, Burke was the only human presence within miles in any direction.

He remounted and drove on. The ground he was traversing began to rise as he continued west. As it did, the vegetation began to change. What had been a monotony of creosote and white bursage became interspersed with Mojave yucca, bayonet yucca and Bigelow cholla. Clumps of stunted desert willow, chamisa, brittlebush and cheesebush began to appear in the bottoms of the washes. Small lizards skittered across the soft sand. Little gray birds flitted through the shrubs. A red tail hawk soared above.

In the distance were the Piute Mountains. At the south edge of the range, separated and almost distinct from it, a small butte jutted from the surrounding desert. It was early afternoon by the time he reached the ruins. They were surrounded on all sides by evidence of volcanic activity. The ruins themselves were exactly as Hugh Stanton had described them: a series of low, rock walls outlining old fortifications of which very little remained. The walls were of volcanic rock.

Burke studied the terrain with a tactician's eye. He saw why the fort had been built on this spot. Deny your enemy access to water in an otherwise waterless landscape, and you curtail his activities. It was also clear why the fort had been oriented as it had been. He realized the walls themselves had not been living quarters but defensible space built on terrain that offered excellent fields of fire and good lines of sight in all directions. The men stationed there must have lived outside in tents but retreated inside the walls if they came under attack.

He wondered what a soldier had to do wrong to get stationed at a post where he had to live outside in harsh conditions and only go inside if those conditions suddenly got even worse.

After he surveyed the remains of the fort, he continued onward. He walked past volcanic rocks covered with petroglyphs carved into the desert varnish. Some depicted game animals. Some depicted creatures not of this world. Creatures the stuff of nightmares. Soon, he came to the fences and structures of the abandoned turkey farm. They were still intact but beginning to deteriorate.

They spoke to Burke not only of neglect but of regret. He thought of the people who had tried to make a go of it here. Thought of them sitting at the kitchen table on a winter night studying the finances and prospects of their operation by the light of a flickering oil lamp. How desperate they must have been as the terrible truth relentlessly ground them down, year after year. Until the bank would not loan them enough money to get through one more season. People who had tried hard to derive a living here. Not because they hoped to get rich, but because they were reluctant to leave so beautiful a place.

Close by the evidence of their unfortunate failure, he came to a windmill turning in the breeze. It was pumping well water into a five-hundred-gallon stock tank. Two lines led away from the tank. One returned overflow from the tank back to the creek. One ran to a shack overlooking the creek. He followed the water line that led to the shack.

The door was partially open. Burke stepped inside.

On the west wall of the single room, a pipe with a faucet bib attached jutted out of the wall above a soapstone sink. He crossed the room to the sink and turned the faucet. It was mineral-encrusted and rough to the touch. Rusty water poured out. He let it run until it cleared. He cupped his hands under the flow and bent down and tasted the water. It was delicious: cold and sweet. He turned off the faucet and dried his hands on his Levi's.

The only other things in the room were a rusted bed frame, a crudely made table and a chair with one broken leg. There were no windows in the small building. No ornamentation on any of the walls. What daylight was in the room came from various bullet holes that had penetrated the structure. Dust motes danced and shimmered in the narrow shafts of light.

He went back outside and walked what he assumed were the outlines of the property. The exact perimeter was hard to determine because the only fence on the land marked the edge of the Irwin property. He stopped where the second water line was spilling water into the creek bed below. He stood looking at the line of cottonwoods and willows lining the creek. The cottonwoods were substantial and very old and barren of all but a few dead leaves. The willows were heavily burdened with mistletoe that was dotted with red berries. He heard the plaintive call of a phainopepla, sole lover of the bitter fruits of the destructive parasite and unintentional spreader of its seeds to other hapless hosts.

The sun had tilted to the west and was beginning to stain the sky red and orange shot through with rays of purple and gold. This place will do, he thought. It will do very well.

As the light softened in the sky and edged toward twilight, he suddenly realized he was no longer alone. He took a few deep breaths of the cold air and shouted,

"Spirits of those who carved on the rocks, I am a warrior of the *Na-ishañ-dina*. I ask your permission to live here in harmony with you and the world around us."

His deep voice boomed in the stillness.

He fell silent. He heard the wind blowing down the gorge from the north. The groan of the bushings in the windmill pump. The splash of the outflow from the drain line. The pulse of his own blood. There was no sound else. But he knew he had been heard.

He returned to the ruins and mounted his machine. He started back down the road, the pale, yellow light of his headlamp gradually growing visible against the burnt amber of the desert sands.

CHAPTER 5

February 1956

Burke found Billy White in the Smoke Tree phone book. It took him two days to make contact with the man. Billy was a brakeman working the Santa Fe extra board. He was single, so when he was on the line there was no one home to answer his phone. As soon as he got back to Smoke Tree, he marked up again so he could pick up another job after his mandatory twelve-hour rest period. When he got to his house, he unplugged his phone so he could sleep undisturbed. Once his rest period was complete, he was required to be close to the phone. That's how Burke finally reached him.

When Billy White answered the call, Burke asked him if he wanted to sell the property near Fort Piute.

"Yes, but I can't be away from the phone long enough to go out there and show you around."

"I've been there and looked it over. What's your price?"

The response was not immediate. It occurred to Burke that he might be the first potential buyer to inquire.

"I believe eight hundred dollars is fair."

Burke knew if he met the asking price, he would be viewed in town with suspicion or thought a fool. Or both.

"I'll go four hundred."

Billy maintained the property had great sentimental value because it had been left to him by his father.

Sure, it does, thought Burke. That's why you're willing to sell it.

The two men dickered for a while and then settled on six hundred, which was what Burke knew he was going to end up paying when Billy named his opening price.

"I don't believe I know you, Mr. Henry."

"New in town."

"I don't want the expense of an escrow, so I'm willing to sign a quit claim and turn the deed over to you, but I won't take a check from someone I don't know."

"Wasn't planning to tender one, Mr. White. This will be a cash deal."

"Okay. I don't keep the deed at the house. It's in a safe deposit box at the bank."

"All right. I'll meet you there in an hour."

"How will I know you?"

"I'll be in the parking lot on a midnight-blue motorcycle."

"Oh, you're *that* guy. Heard people have seen you riding that machine around town. Staying at the California Gateway, right?"

"That's right."

"I'll see you at the bank, then.

Burke arrived at the bank long before Billy White. He went to his safe deposit box and go out two thousand, six hundred dollars in one hundred-dollar bills. He put six of the bills in the pocket of his motorcycle jacket and divided the remaining bills between the two front pockets of his Levi's.

He was outside when Billy White parked next to his motorcycle.

The two men went into the bank together. Billy got the deed from his box and signed it over to Burke in the lobby in exchange for the six one-hundred-dollar bills.

The two men shook hands. Billy left. Burke was now the owner of five acres of land so far off the beaten path that very few people even knew where it was, let alone how to get there. He put the deed in his safe deposit box and left the bank. The entire process had taken less than fifteen minutes.

He drove to the Bluebird Café and parked on the street. He bought a copy of the Smoke Tree Weekly from a rack on the sidewalk and went inside and ordered blueberry pie and coffee.

The waitress brought his coffee. While he waited for his pie, he turned to the classified ads. He found a trailer for rent at the Sunset Beach Trailer Park. The rent was listed as forty-five dollars a month. Also, a 1949 Ford F-5 flatbed truck with dual wheels and a flathead V-8 engine was for sale for two hundred and fifty dollars.

The waitress came back with his pie. He ate quickly and paid and left. He walked down the street to the phone booth in front of the Greyhound bus station. Someone had been sick inside. Burke left the door open and was careful not to step in the puddle. He got out his change and called the numbers listed in the ads. The constant traffic passing on 66 made it difficult to hear, but he managed to make an appointment to look at the trailer the next day at ten in the morning. He arranged to meet with the owner of the truck at one thirty.

Back at the Bluebird, he got on his motorcycle and headed for Las Vegas.

He was on Fremont Street in that garish city by two o'clock. His circuit started at the Pioneer Club. He visited the Horseshoe Club, the Golden Nugget and the El Cortez before moving to the strip. Then he went to the Desert Inn, The Silver Slipper, The Showboat, The Sands, The Sahara and the Flamingo.

At each casino he visited, he bought two hundred dollars' worth of chips before playing a few hands of blackjack and then moving to the craps table to place bets on the pass line. He stuck some coins in the one-armed bandits. Sometimes he won a little, sometimes he lost a little. It didn't matter. He wasn't there to gamble.

Whenever he thought he had stayed long enough

to blend into the crowd, he cashed in his chips and left with the kind of small denomination bills he could use in Smoke Tree without calling attention to himself. No one seemed to take any particular notice of him.

He didn't worry about carrying so much cash as he moved from place to place. And although he chained the back wheel of his Royal Enfield to its frame each time he parked, he didn't bother to run the chain around a pole. The mob was in full control in Las Vegas, and criminals knew if they committed crimes that might upset gamblers, either inside the casinos, in the parking lots, or on the streets, their final resting place could well be a grave in the desert outside of town.

Heading back to Smoke Tree late that night, he hoped the time on the road would blow the stink of the casinos out of his clothing. He was carrying enough usable cash for the next phase of his project.

CHAPTER 6

February 1956

Just before ten the next morning, Burke drove to the Sunset Beach Mobile Home Park and stopped in front of the Sunset Beach Saloon and Grill. It was a simple, cement block building overlooking a boat dock floating on the river. The smell of cold water rose off the river as he tilted his motorcycle onto the kickstand and went inside.

The place smelled of cigarette smoke, grease from a grill, and an improbable mix of burnt coffee and spilled beer. There was a big woman in her mid-fifties dressed in a floral-print Mumu sitting on a stool behind a glass-topped counter. She looked like she was guarding the cash register next to her.

"I'm looking for Brenda?"

"I'm Brenda."

"I called yesterday about seeing the unit you have for rent."

The woman looked him over. Without speaking again, she got off the stool and walked to the big window next to the front door, no easy task for a woman about five feet tall who weighed at least two hundred pounds.

She peered outside before turning to Burke.

"Is that your motorcycle?"

"It is."

"I don't rent to rowdies."

"Good. I don't want to live around them."

She propped one hand on a massive hip.

"Where do you work?"

"Don't have a job, yet. Just got into town a few days ago."

"I'll have to have first and last and a security deposit. And I don't take checks from people I don't know."

"I think we're a little ahead of ourselves here. I'd like to look at the place."

The woman almost smiled.

"It's on the other side of the park. I'll give you the key and you can go see it."

"That's fine."

"I want a twenty-dollar deposit for the key."

"Okay."

The woman walked back behind the counter and sketched a crude map on a piece of scratch paper.

"Unit twenty-seven. Take your time looking it over, but don't be too long. Someone else is coming out to look at it. Be here any time."

I'll bet, thought Burke.

The woman hit the "no sale" button on the big silver cash register and removed a key from under the cash drawer. She held the key in one hand and turned the other hand palm up in front of him.

Burke got a twenty-dollar bill out of his wallet and handed it over. She gave him the key.

The Sunset Beach Trailer Park was a simple place, plain, sterile and graceless against the dirt of a desert hillside that sloped down toward the river. Two parallel rows of mobile homes and semi-permanent travel trailers fronted two narrow, crumbling, blacktop streets. The streets had no names. Nor did they have curbs, sidewalks or streetlights. There were no trees, no shrubs and no grass around any of the units. The streets were silent.

The masking tape stuck to the key in his hand read "27," but he counted only thirteen units on each side of the easternmost street. He looked at the crude map. Well beyond the end of the blacktop, he found an old Zimmer travel trailer set alone at an angle northeast of the other units. There were two grooves worn in the dirt where vehicles had come and gone. Cinder blocks beneath rusty, tireless axles held the unit above the ground. There was no skirting around the trailer. A white, corroded propane bottle sat just behind a trailer hitch supported by two more cinder blocks. Water, electrical and sewer lines snaked out from beneath the unit.

Two more cinder blocks placed side by side served as the first step to the door. A second rickety step had been fashioned from two wooden Pepsi Cola boxes piled one atop the other. Burke stood on the wobbly boxes and put the key in the door. It took some effort to get it to turn. When he stepped inside, he knew instantly the trailer had been empty for a long time. And hidden but not quite disguised beneath the odor of Pine-sol in the musty, long-enclosed space was the smell of isopropyl alcohol. Someone had suffered through a long illness inside these walls. Long enough that even a lot of disinfectant could not hide the smell.

There was another odor too, one not quite masked by disinfectant and alcohol: the fetid and sickly-sweet smell of death. Something with which Burke Henry was very familiar.

He surveyed the tiny living room. The décor was early desperation. A window covered by a dirty, nondescript curtain on the east wall. A smaller window on the north wall. Patternless linoleum above a sub floor that wobbled with each step he took. A dinette set formed by a tiny Formica table in front of a vinyl-covered bench beneath the north wall window. Cracks in the red vinyl had been covered with duct tape.

The kitchen held a propane stove that was little more than two Coleman burners. There was a small sink beside the stove, and next to the stove a small refrigerator. The refrigerator door was propped open to keep mold from growing inside. It was empty except for half a plastic ice cube tray.

Moving past the kitchen, he opened the door to the bathroom. Toilet and sink. No shower. No medicine cabinet. No towel racks.

Beyond the bathroom was a bedroom containing

an off-kilter dresser made of pressboard. A four by eight sheet of plywood was hinged to a two-by-four three feet above the floor on the back wall. The sheet was pinned at the top by two shorter pieces of two-by-four screwed into the wall. He crossed the tiny room and held the top of the plywood with one hand while rotating each of the blocks in turn to release the sheet. With both hands on the plywood, he lowered it slowly. Two chains connected to eye bolts stopped the descent when the makeshift bed was parallel to the floor.

He turned and left the trailer and re-locked the door. He walked to the front of the trailer and took in the view of the Black Mountains on the other side of the deep-blue Colorado River. Home sweet home, he thought, and walked back to the office to negotiate a price.

Brenda was on her stool smoking a cigarette in an ebony holder. An attempt at elegance that missed the mark by quite some margin.

"Who died in that trailer?"

"Pardon me?"

"Come on, Brenda."

The heavy woman took a deep drag on her cigarette and let the smoke trickle out of her nose. It climbed up her face and wreathed her graying and frazzled hair. She rested the holder in her upturned palm and squinted at him through the smoke for a long moment before replying.

"An old man passed away in there. Took him a while."

"And it was another while before anyone found him, right?"

"Yeah."

"So, who owns the trailer?"

"By rights, his son. But he doesn't want it. He bought it and set it up out here because his wife didn't want the old man dying in her house. Or anywhere near it, either."

"How sharper than a serpent's tooth it is to have a thankless child."

"Is that from the Bible?"

Burke shook his head.

"Shakespeare."

"You don't look like the Shakespeare-quoting type."

Burke shrugged.

"Books and covers and all that."

"I guess you're not interested in the place."

"I didn't say that. Now that I know what happened in there, we can talk price."

"Like the ad says, forty-five dollars a month."

Burke didn't say anything: just stood there and watched the woman smoke.

After a long silence, the ash fell off the end of her cigarette. She brushed it off the counter.

"All right, thirty-five."

Burke still said nothing.

Brenda sighed and took what was left of the cigarette out of the holder and stubbed in out in a black plastic ashtray with "Lucky Lager" printed on it.

"Thirty, then, but that's as low as I go."

Burke pulled out his wallet and removed seventy dollars and put it on the glass countertop next to the cash register.

"You've got the twenty I gave you earlier. This makes ninety. First, last and deposit."

"A lease would guarantee that price for a year."

"Month to month is fine."

"How long you think you'll be here?"

"Don't know yet.

I'd like a receipt for the ninety dollars."

Brenda reached under the counter and pulled out a receipt book.

"Full name?"

"Burke Henry."

She filled out the receipt and handed it to him.

He handed it back.

"Better write on there what the money's for."

"Don't you trust me?"

"Don't know you."

Two o'clock found him on Nineveh Street talking with Ellis McCready, the owner of the truck advertised for sale. The barking of the neighbor's dog, a high-strung collie, punctuated his statements.

"There's some things you should know about her if you decide to buy her," said Ellis, a congenial man in his sixties. "She has the four on the floor, but she has her quirks. The granny gear and the reverse are spur gears."

"What's that mean?"

Ellis smiled.

"It means a lot of clanging and banging and grinding and ruining the transmission if you try to shift into either one of those gears with the engine running. If you want to use either of them, turn her off, then put her in the gear you want, and then push in the clutch and start her up again.

A real good thing about her is the heavy-duty leaf springs in the back. Also, the bed is well above the wheels so you can carry quite a load without it scraping against the tires. She has the three hundred and thirty-seven cubic inch flathead. Real reliable engine. Had a ring and valve job two years ago, so she doesn't burn oil. Has the oversize radiator. Real important out here in the summer.

Brakes are mechanical. You have to stand on them pretty hard if you need to haul her down quick, but they're sound. Drums turned and new shoes a year ago. Battery's new. New brushes in the generator. Starter motor's good. Tends to go through starter solenoids though, like a lot of these older Fords, but if you get stuck you can by-pass the solenoid with that piece of copper wire in the glove box. Get you back to town so you can get a new one at the dealership. Cost you about two bucks, and real easy to replace.

Let's see, what else? Oh yeah, front end's sound. No play in the steering at all. That's real important when you're carrying a heavy load. And the tires are in good shape. Lots of meat left on them.

And see that thing on the back? That's a telescoping boom crane. You can lift over two thousand pounds off the ground with it and then swing it onto the bed."

"Sounds like a good truck. Can I ask why you're selling it?"

"Since I've been singing her praises, be surprised if you didn't. Don't need her any more. Retiring, you see. Been a stone mason all my life. Used her to haul cinder blocks and bricks and cement and sand and my mixer. In fact, for another twenty-five I'll throw in the mixer. We can load it up with the boom."

"No electricity where I'm going to be working."

"Then this is for certain the truck for you. Got a power take-off shaft that hooks to the mixer with a belt."

"Sounds good."

"Why don't you take her for a little spin?"

"Aren't you going to come along?"

"Nah. Key's in the ignition. Starter button on the floor next to the gas pedal. Pull the throttle a quarter of the way out and the choke halfway. Pump the gas pedal once, but only once. Be sure you have her in reverse before you start her up. When she warms up for a minute, push in the throttle and the choke and you're ready for the road."

Burke followed the instructions and was soon backing the truck out of a driveway lined with leafless elms. He drove south on Nineveh to where it dead ended into 66. There, he joined the flow of traffic heading south on eastbound 66. At the 66/95 split, he took 95 south. He had the road to himself. He took the truck up to sixty. The engine had a nice, throaty note and ran strong. There were no exhaust leaks he could smell in the cab. A series of small movements with the steering wheel confirmed that, as McCready had promised, there was no play in the front end. He pushed down hard on the brake pedal. The old truck didn't exactly stop on a dime, but it did come to a halt without pulling to either side, and he still had a lot of pedal left.

At five-mile road, he slowed and turned off the

highway onto the dirt. He shut down the engine and set the emergency brake. Climbing out of the cab, he wormed under the truck despite the rocks digging into his back. The bottom radiator hose was new and there were no radiator leaks. There were no obvious oil drips and no smell of burning oil leaking onto the engine.

He crawled back out from under the truck and lifted the hood and propped it open. The top radiator hose looked good. The heater hoses were sound. No corrosion around the battery. No chips or leaks in the glass fuel filter hooked to the firewall.

He removed the air cleaner and looked at the two-barrel carburetor. Clean as a whistle. The filter in the air cleaner was new.

He lowered the hood and got back in the cab.

He liked the fact that the truck had gauges for oil and water and battery instead of idiot lights. No rips in the bench seat. No liner on the roof, but that was to be expected.

Back on the highway, he reached over and turned on the radio. When it warmed up, Hank Williams was singing "Your Cheatin' Heart" on the local station. Even this close to town, the signal was weak, and Hank's voice had to compete with static from the sparkplug wires that increased with engine speed. When he got back to Nineveh Street, Ellis McCready was standing next to Burke's motorcycle. He pulled into the driveway and got out of the truck and walked over.

"This is a fancy piece of machinery, Mr. Henry. Is it English?"

"Yessir. Made by the same people who made the Lee-Enfield rifle for the British Army."

"When I walked over to look at it, I realized it runs on a magneto."

"That's right."

"That means anyone could just climb on and drive away. Thought I'd better watch over it until you got back."

"Thank you. I appreciate that."

"Well, what did you think of the truck?"

"It's just what I need. Normally, I'd dicker a bit, but you strike me as a straight shooter. It seems like a good truck for the asking price."

"Thank you, young man. That's good for a twenty-five-dollar discount! I'll just toss in the cement mixer at no extra charge."

Burke smiled.

"You've got a deal."

"I hope she's as good to you as she's been to me. Come inside and I'll trade you the money for the pink slip.

I'd introduce you to the missus, but she's off at the grocery store."

In the modest but immaculate kitchen, the two men sat at the table and completed the transaction. When they were done, they stood and shook hands.

"If you don't mind, I'll leave the truck here while I run an errand. Maybe we could load that cement mixer on when I get back?"

"Sure, that's fine. Doris should be home by then. I'd like you to meet her. A real fine person. Pretty as the day we got married."

"I'll look forward to it."

The two men walked outside, and Ellis watched while Burke got the motorcycle started. He smiled and gave Burke the thumbs up when the English twin came to life.

It was late afternoon when Burke pulled up in front

of Smoke Tree Hardware and Building supply. There were no other vehicles in the dirt parking lot.

When he walked inside, he saw a stocky man with sandy hair sorting nuts, bolts and screws in wooden compartments. The man peered at Burke over his bifocals.

"Seems I spend most of my time putting these things back into the right bins. People mix em up, and I sort em out. Dream about it at night sometimes. I'm just sorting away and can never get done. Wake up tired."

He smiled.

"That's enough about my problems. What can I do for you?"

"I need some help estimating and pricing building materials for a project."

"Well sir, you've come to the right place. I'm Keith Halverson. I'm the owner."

"Burke Henry."

"What are you building, Mr. Henry?"

"A house."

"How big?"

"A thousand square feet would be about right."

"What kind of construction?"

"Frame with wood siding will be fine. I want to insulate it real good."

"You looking at post and pier construction or flat foundation?"

"Which would you recommend?"

"Where are you going to build it?"

"Out by Fort Piute."

Halverson whistled.

"Well, you've got God's own number of rattlesnakes and other critters out that way. I don't think you'll be wanting them under your house. I was you, I'd want it sitting flat on the foundation.

Ever built a house before?"

"Sure haven't. I'm going to get a book about it."

"What have you got in the way of tools?"

"Don't have any. Have to buy those from you too."

"No electricity out that way. You're going to have to do all the cutting by hand."

"Yes."

"And you're going to have to mix the cement by hand too. That's a lot of mixing for a man with a wheelbarrow and a shovel."

"Got a mixer. Runs on a power-take-off from the flatbed Ford I just bought."

"Only guy I know with a truck and mixer like that is Ellis McCready. You buy it from him?"

"Just a while ago."

"I heard he was retiring, but I didn't really believe it. Well, you did good. There's a man who took good care of everything he owned. He might be willing to sell you some of the tools you'll need to work the cement. Save you a lot of money if he will."

"I'll ask."

"Since you've got that PTO, I've got an old timber saw that will run off a belt. Do your rough cuts and save you an awful lot of hand-sawing."

"What do you want for it?"

"Mr. Henry, if you buy your supplies from me, you can have it until the job is done."

"Sounds good."

"One more thing. If you buy everything from me, including the tools you're going to need, I'll give you a ten percent discount because of the size of the order."

"Mr. Halverson, I believe we can work together."

Halverson walked to the back of the store and opened a sliding glass door that led to the lumber yard. The smell of sawdust and sacked cement washed into the room.

"Steve," he yelled, "come and take over the store. I'm going to be in the office with a customer until after closing time. You lock up for me."

Burke and the store owner went into the back office. Keith sat down behind a cluttered desk and had Burke pull up a folding chair and sit beside him.

"Since there's no electricity, you won't be putting in conduit and wiring of any kind unless you intend to buy a generator."

"Not necessary."

"And I'm assuming no indoor plumbing, right?"

"An outhouse will be all I'll need, but I do want a water line for a kitchen sink."

"How about a sink in the bedroom for washing up and so forth?"

"That too."

"Okay, no electrical and very little plumbing. That'll keep the cost way down."

He pulled a red, spiral notebook out of a desk drawer and began to list items and calculate the costs. In less than an hour, the list was complete. He totaled the amounts on an ancient adding machine and ripped off the tape and stapled it to the list.

He turned to Burke.

"Having a contractor build a house like this in Smoke Tree would cost somewhere around twelve thousand dollars. Of course, that's with electrical and full plumbing. Yours will be a lot cheaper because of all the things it won't have. Also, doing all the work yourself is going to save you just a whole pile of money.

With your discount, the cost of the materials you'll need comes to a little more than forty-five-hundred dollars. That includes framing, plywood, wood siding, drywall, insulation, doors, windows, roofing materials and all the hand tools you'll need. I've got a book here about simple home construction. You can borrow that until you're done.

You're going to need a fireplace for heat and a wood-burning stove for cooking and more heat. You can buy a factory built fireplace and frame it right into the house. I'll give you the name of a place in Vegas that will sell you one for less than what my wholesale cost would be. Old wood burning stoves aren't hard to find if you can figure a way to get one onto that flat bed and then get if off and into the house. By the way, I'd recommend you do that before you do the framing. Just put your stove on the floor where the kitchen will be and build the house around it."

Burke took the list Keith handed him and reviewed the items. When he was done, he counted out four hundred and fifty dollars in cash as a down payment. Keith gave him a receipt and agreed to put together the materials to pour the foundation, build the sill and start the framing. Burke didn't have a phone, so he wrote down the phone number for the Sunset Beach Saloon and Grill and asked Keith to leave a message with Brenda when the order was ready.

When they came out of the office, the lights were out and the store was closed. Halverson flipped a switch and the fluorescents buzzed and flickered to life, casting soft shadows around the room. The two men walked to the front of the store together and Halverson unlocked the door to let Burke out. He handed him the book about building methods, and they shook hands. By the time Burke got the book tucked into the front of his Levi's and got the Enfield started, the store was dark again.

The sun had set. It was very cold.

It was after six when Burke pulled up in front of the McCready house and shut down his engine. Before he had the bike on the kickstand, the porch light came on. Ellis came out and walked down the sidewalk to the street.

"We've been waiting dinner for you. Doris wants to meet the man with the shiny motorcycle. Turns out she's seen you driving around town on that beautiful machine."

"If you're sure it's no trouble."

"No trouble at all."

The two men walked up to the porch and went into a house redolent with the smells of spices and cooking food.

A petite woman with graying hair came out of the kitchen, wiping her hands on her apron.

"Mr. Henry, this is Doris, the love of my life."

Doris smiled.

"I've seen you before, Mr. Henry. At the market and around town. You're staying at the California Gateway, aren't you?"

"Yes ma'am, and it's Burke."

"I hope you're hungry. We've got a lot of food to eat."

After the best meal he had eaten in a long time, he and Ellis went outside. Ellis turned on a floodlight atop a pole next to the driveway. Burke saw that he had loaded the cement mixer onto the flatbed and secured it with chains. Burke pushed his motorcycle to the back of the truck and Ellis showed him how to work the crane and helped him lift and swing the machine onto the bed. Burke chained his bike to the boom post and thanked Ellis for his kindness and hospitality before driving back to the run-down hotel for his last night there.

He lay in his sleeping bag atop the thin mattress listening to the rattle of water in the bathroom pipes down the hall and the sound of an eastbound freight pulling out of the depot. Reflecting on all he had accomplished in the last two days, he felt like he was making progress. He realized he was getting a sense of Smoke Tree.

People were mostly friendly. They certainly kept track of each other. Everyone seemed to know what everyone else was doing. And news about a stranger travelled fast, but that was to be expected. In spite of the fact that highway 66 came right down the main street of town, very few travelers ever got off for more than a tank of gas, a quick meal or a night's sleep. A new person in town was bound to arouse some curiosity.

But so far, it had not been a pushy curiosity. Even though Ellis and Doris had obviously wondered about him, they accepted what little he told them about himself and didn't press for details. It wouldn't be long before people lost interest in him. Which was what he wanted.

He was glad he had returned.

CHAPTER 7

March 1956

The paths of Carlos Caballo and Burke Henry intersected on a windy Sunday afternoon. A call came in to the Smoke Tree Substation of the San Bernardino County Sheriff's Department about a brawl underway at the Sunset Beach Saloon and Grill. The owner of the place, Brenda Rangel, told the dispatcher she was afraid a motorcycle gang was going to wreck her place and hurt one of the tenants from the trailer park. The weekend dispatcher put out a call.

Carlos Caballo, known as 'Horse' by his fellow deputies and just about everyone else in Smoke Tree, was southbound on old 66 heading toward the highway 95 split. In the twelve thousand square mile territory served by the substation, his was the unit closest to town. He took the call. He pushed the pedal to the floor and hit the flasher and siren. In spite of the heavy-duty suspension in his Ford Fairlane, the frame banged off the hardball at the bottom of two of the big dips before he reached 95.

He was turning off River Road into the driveway to the park less than twenty minutes later. He kept the siren on in the hopes it would slow down whatever was going on in the saloon. He pulled the mic from its clip and keyed it.

"Base."

"Go."

"Caballo. I'm turning off River Road. I'll call you when I get a handle on the situation."

"10-4."

In front of the saloon, he saw three Harley hogs toppled onto their sides. He killed the siren and came out of his unit carrying his nightstick. He hustled toward the door.

When he went inside, the jukebox was blaring The Cheers version of *Black Denim Trousers and Motorcycle Boots*. The room was ripe with the smell of beer. There were three men hogtied on their stomachs. One was bleeding from the forehead. All three wore leather jackets with "Outlaws" emblazoned on the back.

Tables and chairs were overturned on the

brushed-cement floor. Broken sugar and ketchup bottles were leaking their contents into puddles of beer laced with shattered glass. The ketchup looked more like blood than the real blood seeping from the man's forehead.

Brenda was in her usual place: on a stool beside the cash register. The hand holding her cigarette was trembling. Horse realized it was the first time he had ever seen her with a cigarette that wasn't in her ebony holder.

The only other person in the room was a man drinking coffee at the counter. He turned his head and nodded at Horse.

Horse reached down and unplugged the juke box. The sound ground down into a distorted, discordant growl. Absent the blaring song, the room was still but for loud groans from one of the men.

Horse turned to Brenda.

"Are you all right, Mrs. Rangel?"

"Yes. I'm sure glad you're here."

The man at the counter stood up. He was tall and slender. His fawn colored skin made an odd contrast with his short, blonde hair and very blue eyes.

"Afternoon, deputy."

His voice was very deep and seemed to fill the room.

Sounds like a drill instructor, Horse thought to himself.

"Afternoon. Please, sit down and drink your coffee while I talk with Brenda."

The slender man sat down without speaking again.

The man who had been moaning was straining to look up at Horse.

"Untie me, Goddamnit!"

His voice was hoarse and scratchy.

"In a minute."

"Now, damnit. That bastard dislocated my shoulder. Hurts like a bitch."

Horse pulled a penknife out of his pocket and walked to the man. He stepped behind him.

"I'm going to cut the piece holding your hands and feet together and cut your hands loose, but don't try to get up. If you do, I'll hit you with my stick. Hard."

"Okay, okay. C'mon, my arm is killin' me!"

Horse cut the piece of rough twine linking the ties on the man's hands to the ones on his feet. When he did, the man's boots thudded to the floor. Horse cut the twine securing the man's hands but left his feet tied.

"Thanks. And thanks for unplugging that damned jukebox."

The man at the counter spoke without turning or looking up from his coffee.

"Just being neighborly. Entertaining our motorbike tourists from Illinois."

The man with the bleeding forehead yelled.

"What about me, deputy?"

"What about you?"

"Untie me."

"Nope."

He walked over to Brenda.

"Need to use your phone."

"Sure."

Horse picked up the receiver of the black, Bakelite phone next to the cash register and dialed the substation.

"Horse here. I'm at Sunset. Everything's under control. I need another unit out here to transport some boys to the lockup. Two of them are going to have to visit the emergency room on the way. Call Zack over at the wrecking yard. I need a tow truck to hoist and haul three Harley hogs to the impound yard."

"I'm on it."

Horse hung up the phone.

The man with the injured shoulder yelled again.

"Hey, Deputy, no need for all that. Just cut us loose, and we'll be on our way."

Horse ignored him and turned to Brenda.

"Tell me what happened here."

Brenda stubbed out her cigarette.

"Burke was in here for a burger and coffee like he is most Sunday afternoons. And boy, he likes it so rare it almost gets up and walks off the bun. Extra big slab of onion and lots of pickles..."

She stopped and shook her head.

"Sorry. I sound like an idiot. I know you don't care how Burke likes his burger, but this shook me up real bad, Horse. My heart is still pounding."

"You're doing fine, Brenda. There's no hurry."

"Anyway, that's when they drove up outside."

"By 'they', you mean the men on the floor."

"That's right. I heard the motorcycles shut off, and the three of them came through the door. They were laughing and cussing. They went over and sat at a table, and the big, smelly one there yelled real loud for some service. He used a whole lot of ugly words, including the "*F*" word.

I went over with my order pad and asked them what they wanted. He said, 'Three pitchers of whatever you've got on tap.' And just like before, there were a lot of bad words mixed in with that. I noticed when I was walking away that Burke had swiveled around on his stool and was looking at them. It wasn't a friendly look. I caught his eye and kind of shook my head. I didn't want him to get hurt trying to stick up for me or anything.

I pulled the pitchers and put them on a tray with the glasses and took them to the table. I told them what they owed me.

Mr. Potty Mouth said, 'Run us a tab.'

'No money, no beer,' I told him, and he said, and

I'll tell you the word he used, he said, 'Listen, bitch...' and I don't know what else he was going to say because all of a sudden Burke was next to me saying, 'Watch your mouth'."

"You know, Horse, I think it surprised these guys. None of them said anything for a minute. Just sat there with their mouths hanging open.

Burke put his hand on my shoulder and told me to go sit down. Believe you me, I was glad to go.

Then Burke said, 'I don't know how it works where you lowlifes come from, but out here men don't use that kind of language around ladies.'

Well, Potty Mouth stood up with a real nasty smile on his face. He's a lot bigger than Burke, and I thought Burke had stepped in it for sure. He said, 'I don't care how you do it here in Cowflop.' And he poked Burke in the chest with his finger.

After that, a whole lot of things happened real fast. Burke got hold of the guy's hand some way and waltzed him around in big circles. Tables and chairs went flying everywhere. That's when I called your office.

Anyway, Burke sort of flung the guy into one of the counter stools. He got up and ran at Burke and swung at him and Burke grabbed his arm and did something to it and put him on the ground. The guy started screaming and cussing a blue streak, but he didn't get back up.

The other two were on their feet by then. They came at Burke. He kicked one guy in the knee. That one's leg went a funny direction, and he went down. Then, the one with the bleeding head there pulled out a knife. Burke got hold of the hand with the knife, and the guy went flying through the air and slammed into the wall. The one with the hurt knee tried to get up, but he couldn't.

And that was it. It was pretty much over. Burke picked up the knife and said to me in an everyday voice as calm as could be, 'Brenda, do you have any cord or twine back there in the kitchen?'

I said I did. He asked me to bring it to him while he kept an eye on the guys on the floor.

I brought the twine, and in nothing flat Burke hogtied two of them. I swear, it was like one of those rodeo riders tying a steer.

He saved Mr. Potty Mouth for last. When Burke pulled his hands toward his feet, the guy screamed and started cussing a blue streak. Burke said, 'I'm not going to tell you again about the language again,' and kicked him in the shoulder.

Well, he stopped cussing, but he started moaning real loud. Burke went over and put seventy-five cents in the jukebox and punched in the same song eighteen times. The one that was playing when you walked in. He came over and asked me if I was okay. I said I was and told him I had called your office.

He walked over to the window and looked out at those motorcycles for a long time. He went outside and pushed them all on the ground. When he was done, he came back in and sat down and asked me for a refill on his coffee."

"And that's everything?"

"Except that my hand was shaking so bad I slopped coffee all over the counter, that's everything I can think of, Horse."

"Thank you, Brenda."

Horse walked down the counter to Burke and sat down on the stood next to him.

"What's your last name, Burke."

"Henry."

"You have any identification on you?"

Burke reached in his back pocket and got out his wallet and flipped it open so Horse could see his drivers' license.

"Thank you. Is what Brenda just told me pretty much what happened?"

"Yes. Summed it up real good. Lady doesn't miss much."

"Do you want to press charges against any of these men who attacked you?"

"Just the one who pulled the knife. The other two, that was a fair fight. But I imagine Brenda would like to get paid for some damages. Kind of messed her place up."

"Brenda referred to you as a tenant when she called our office. You live in the park?"

"That's right. Down at the end of the row."

"You're the man with that English motorcycle, right?"

"Yes."

"I've seen you on it around Smoke Tree."

"I know. I've seen you seeing me."

"Then I'd better introduce myself. I'm Sergeant

Caballo."

"So, that's why Brenda called you 'Horse'."

"That's right. That's what pretty much everyone around here calls me."

"If you don't need anything else from me, I'll be heading home."

"I think that's everything. I'll write up what Brenda told me and have her sign it. Can you come out to the station tomorrow and sign a statement corroborating what she just told me?"

"Be glad to."

"It will be typed up and ready. I'd like to be there when you review it, but I'm rarely in the office. Call ahead so the dispatcher can arrange a time for me to come in and meet with you."

"All right."

As Burke went outside, another deputy was pulling up.

CHAPTER 8

March 1956

Burke called the substation at nine o'clock the next morning and identified himself. The dispatcher asked him to hold for a moment. When he came back on the line, he asked Burke to be at the office at ten.

Burke walked into the substation five minutes early. There were curious glances at the slender man in the Levi jacket who had subdued the three big bikers cooling their heels in the lockup. He was standing at the counter when Horse came down the hallway carrying a Manilla folder.

"Morning, Mr. Henry. Thanks for making the time to come in."

"Glad to help out."

Horse walked over and unlatched the gate that opened into the interior of the office.

"Please, come with me to the break room. We can talk there."

Burke followed him down the hall to a room that, except for the lack of a pool table, reminded Burke of the many day rooms he had seen during his time in the service. Even the smell was the same: cigarette smoke, floor wax and burnt coffee.

"You a smoker, Mr. Henry?"

"No."

"Then we'll sit at the only table without an ashtray."

He indicated a folding chair at the cleanest of the four tables in the room.

"Get you a coffee?"

"Please."

"Cream and sugar?"

"Black is fine."

As Burke sat down, Horse moved to a long counter that held a large coffee urn, a carton of half and half, packets of sugar, a cup full of plastic spoons, a basket of cheap napkins, and a stack of Styrofoam cups. There was a sink at the end of the counter, and above the sink a pegboard with hooks that held coffee mugs.

Horse filled two Styrofoam cups from the urn and brought them to the table.

"I'm sure this is not as good as Brenda's coffee."

"Anything with caffeine works for me."

Horse pushed the folder toward Burke.

"You'll find Brenda's statement on top. It's two pages long. I would like you to review it. If you agree with it, there's a place to sign at the bottom of the second page. It says you concur with her version of the events at Sunset Beach.

Burke opened the folder and started to read his landlord's statement. The room was silent except for the tap of his cup when he put it down between sips and the loud *click* made by the electric clock above the counter each time the minute hand moved. It clicked twelve times before Burke turned the first sheet over and started on page two.

This is a careful man, thought Horse as he watched.

When Burke had finished the second page, he looked up and tapped the second page with his index finger.

"That's what happened. I'll sign."

Horse uncapped an ink pen and pushed it across the table. He watched while Burke quickly reviewed his statement of concurrence, signed it, and pushed the papers and pen back to Horse.

"Thank you, Mr. Henry," Horse said after he signed his own name as witness to Burke's signature.

"Where are the bikers now?"

"In a holding cell. They'll be in court tomorrow morning for arraignment."

"What are the charges?"

"Attempted murder, assault with a deadly weapon, assault with the intent to do great bodily harm, and disturbing the peace."

"So, you're going with everything."

"On the recommendation of the San Bernardino County District Attorney. One of his assistants will be here for the arraignment. Whichever one draws the short straw."

"Bikers have an attorney?"

"Yes. The big one called Chicago yesterday evening, and we had a call this morning from a criminal lawyer in San Diego. Said he'd be here this afternoon."

Burke nodded.

"Figures. The Outlaws are from Illinois. Big in the Midwest. Lots of criminal stuff. Any idea what they were doing in Smoke Tree?"

"The big one's a blowhard. Told me they were on their way to San Bernardino to straighten out some Hell's Angels."

Burke laughed.

"I'd pay something to see that. The Angels would have those boys for breakfast."

There was a momentary silence before Horse spoke.

"Get you another cup of coffee?"

"No, thanks."

"I'd like to ask you something about yesterday."

"Go ahead."

"These are some bad boys. Where did you learn to do what you did to them?"

"Different places. Aikido and jujitsu in Japan. Shorin-ryu karate in Okinawa. Mano mano and Bangkaw in the Philippines."

"What are those last two?"

"Mano mano is grappling. Bangkaw is weapons:

mostly sticks and poles."

"You ex-military?"

Burke nodded.

"All over the Pacific Theater during the big one. Toward the end of the war, fought with the Philippine resistance to drive the Japanese off Luzon Island. After the war, got sent to Japan with the occupational forces. Back to the Philippines in '47, then on to Korea for that nasty business. After the Armistice in '53, back to the Philippines. Then to Viet Nam."

"Where's that?"

"Southeast Asia."

"That's a lot of combat and foreign tours in a row. Weren't you ever stationed stateside?"

Burke shrugged.

"Didn't want to be. Was nothing for me here."

"Where did you serve in Korea?"

"You know much about that war?"

"I was there."

Burke suddenly looked very interested.

"Which unit?"

"Second Infantry Division."

"Indianhead."

"That was us. I was drafted in June of 1950 and got to Korea in time to cover the left and rear flank of the Eighth Army as it retreated to the south."

Burke smiled.

"The official term was 'strategic withdrawal'."

"When you run for your life for two hundred and seventy-five miles, believe me, it's a retreat."

"You were part of a courageous unit. Lost a third of your division in the fighting around Kunu-ri."

"That's right. Where were you?"

"I was on the peninsula for the whole war. Start to finish. With X Corp."

"Were you at Chosin?"

"East side of the reservoir with Task Force MacLean."

Burke stopped talking for a moment and started down at the table, lost in thought. When he looked up, Horse said, "Do you mind telling me about it?"

"Rather not."

"Understood.

Why'd they send you back to the Philippines after

Korea?"

"They were still trying to suppress the Huk Rebellion."

"Huk rebellion?"

"Short for *Hukbo ng Bayan Laban sa Hapon*. That means 'anti-Japanese Army'. Peasant group. Land reformers. Anti-government corruption. They helped the U.S. push the Japanese off Luzon Island. After the war, Harry Truman got a bee in his bonnet about them. Said they were Communists."

"Were they?"

"Not when they were helping us fight the Japanese. But after the war, any peasant group wanting land reform got labeled Communist. Anyway, this new bunch, the CIA, didn't have a clue how to deal with the situation. But in 1948, about a year after I left for Japan, an Air Force Major named Landsdale was put in charge of the operation. He was a smart guy. He understood the local people.

Then Korea blew up. Afterwards, when I was sent back to the Philippines, Landsdale was a colonel by then. He was working with a new President, man named Ramon Magsaysay, on the Huk thing. Magsaysay was an honorable man, unlike the crooks who came before him. Colonel Landsdale understood counterinsurgency. I worked training the scout ranger teams he created to deal with the military side of things while the Colonel himself worked with Magsaysay to bring the Huks out of the jungles and into the political mainstream. The approach worked and the rebellion ended without a whole lot more lives being lost.

The strategy was so good that in '54, after the French got clobbered at Dien Bien Phu, Eisenhower sent Landsdale to Vietnam to try to do there what he had done in the Philippines. I was sent there about six months after Landsdale, but I could tell the Colonel was out of his depth. He did a good job in the Philippines, but Vietnam and the Viet Minh were a mystery to him. We're going to get sucked into that place, inch by inch. It's going to be worse than Korea."

Burke shook his head.

"Sorry about all that detail. I got out just after Thanksgiving. Was in so long I still feel like I'm just on leave."

Horse decided to ask for a favor.

"Excuse me for changing the subject, Mr. Henry, but do you think you could teach me and the other deputies some of those hand-to-hand combat techniques you used against the bikers?"

Burke smiled.

"Got a few years?"

"I'm not asking you to get us to your level. Just some basic stuff."

"I suppose. For starters, I could teach your guys not to use their nightsticks like baseball bats. But why bother? You've got guns."

"We do. But we've also got a gap between no force at all and clubbing a suspect or shooting him. For a long time now, I've been thinking we need a way to control a situation with gradual escalation. Something that takes an officer to the amount of force required, but no more than that."

Burke laughed.

"Sergeant, you sound like Colonel Landsdale. 'Gradual escalation.' 'Appropriate force without excessive force'."

"I'll take that as a compliment.

So, would you teach us?"

"If your guys are willing to get a few bumps and bruises while they learn."

"I'll talk to my Lieutenant and try to set up a time and place. Do you have a phone where I can reach you?"

"No, but you can call Brenda and leave a message for me."

"How much longer will you be living out at Sunset Beach?"

"What do you mean?"

"Well, I know you're building a house on Piute Creek."

"Is there anything the people in Smoke Tree don't know about me?"

"You're a man who has been the subject of a lot of speculation. There's a lot they don't know, so they talk endlessly about the little they're sure of."

"Which is?"

"You showed up in town back in February on a motorcycle. You stayed at the old California Gateway Hotel for a while, and now you live at Sunset Beach in the trailer Kevin Carlton's father lived in while he waited to die."

Horse paused.

"You do know someone died in that trailer, right?"

"Yeah. That's why I rent it so cheap."

"They know you bought the land out near Fort Piute from Billy White. Drove a hard bargain with him for it. Nobody knows how you found that piece of land, and they're real curious about that. There's a lot of people in Smoke Tree don't even know Fort Piute exists."

"How do you think I found it, Sergeant?"

"My guess would be Mr. Stanton told you about it."

"You know Hugh Stanton?"

"I've lived in Smoke Tree all my life, except for Korea. I know almost everybody out this way. When I went to work for the sheriff's department, I made it a point to start learning about everyone I didn't already know. Helps me do my job."

"I can see how that would be.

What else do the locals know about me?"

"Know you have a post office box. Know you have an account at the bank. Know you bought Ellis McCready's flatbed truck to haul the building supplies out to your place. Know Ellis came out and helped you pour the slab and then came back out to help you get your wood burning stove where you want the kitchen. And they know you're buying all your supplies from Keith Halverson over at Smoke Tree Hardware and Building Supply and getting a discount. They don't know how big a discount, and he won't tell them."

"That's a lot!"

"But we both know there are a lot of holes to be filled in."

"I have no intention of filling them."

"You're entitled to your privacy, but I do have one question if you're willing to answer it."

"Ask it, and I'll decide."

"When I look at you, I see Indian ancestry, in spite of your blue eyes."

Burke nodded.

"See some in your face too."

"Mine's Aztec or Toltec or Mayan. One of those. Mind telling me what yours is?"

"I'm Kiowa Apache."

Horse thought for a moment.

"I've heard of Apache, and I've heard of Kiowa, but I've never heard of Kiowa Apache."

"Probably because there are so few of us. Less than four hundred now. Some people call us Plains Apaches because we're associated with the Kiowa, but our language is a lot like Navajo. Like the Navajo and the Arizona and New Mexico Apache, our tribe came down from up around Montana and Wyoming a long, long time ago."

"And the blue eyes?"

"Mother was Kiowa Apache. Father was Ukrainian."

"That would explain it."

"Okay, I've answered your question. I'd like to ask one in return."

"Ask away."

"I saved a lot of my pay during my years in the Army. But I'm burning through what I saved pretty fast."

Horse nodded.

"That's another thing people have been wondering about."

"I've got enough to last until I finish building it, but after that, I'm going to need a job. Any ideas about where I might find one?"

"The biggest employer in town is the Santa Fe. Railroad jobs pay well, but they're just about impossible to get."

"Why is that? I thought times were good."

"They are. Freight traffic is up. The Santa Fe is hiring. But in Smoke Tree, those jobs are passed down from one generation to the next, especially the train crew jobs: engineer, fireman, conductor, brakeman. Those jobs pay really well. They're all held by white men. Those white men are the sons of white men who held those jobs before them.

The yard clerk and rolling-stock maintenance jobs are almost all held by Mexicans. They don't pay as well."

"And the Indians?"

"Track maintenance on the line. The hardest, hottest, dirtiest work. And the least pay.

But all the jobs depend on the recommendation of the local trainmaster, and he knows who is family and who is not. You can go to his office and apply, but you won't be hired."

"Closed system."

"Closed completely.

Here's a possibility to consider. With your Army experience, you could try the Sheriff's Department. There are veteran's preference points for the exam. I'm sure you'd meet the physical requirements. If there's no problem with your background check, you'd be a lead pipe cinch to get hired. Especially if you wanted to work out of the Smoke Tree Substation. Most guys don't want to. They get force-assigned here out of the academy and leave as soon as they have enough seniority to transfer."

"That's why you made sergeant so quick?"

Horse smiled.

"That's it. The Sheriff knows I want to spend my career here."

Burke shook his head.

"I don't think it's for me. Sounds too much like the military. But I wonder, while you're talking sheriff stuff, do you have a reserve posse out here? Guys who ride horses and go out and look for tourists who wander off and get lost in the desert, that sort of thing?"

"Sure do. Would you be interested?"

"I would."

"Do you have a horse?"

"Not yet, but I'm going to get one after I get a job and build a decent corral"

"You have experience with horses?"

"Ever hear of an Apache who couldn't ride? I was breaking horses by the time I was in high school."

"Reason I ask, if you can do hoof trimming and shoeing, you could turn that into something. This area needs a good farrier. Lots of ranches in the New Yorks and the Providence and the Clarks. More ranches around Kingman. And lots of recreational riders and stables in Las Vegas. There's plenty of work. You could be your own boss."

"Any idea how I might get my foot in the door?"

Horse thought a moment.

"Tell you what. I have two horses due for a trim. I've got equipment in my tack room. If you come over and trim them and do a good job, I'll recommend you to the men in the posse. That'll get you started. As you've noticed, word spreads fast out this way. You'd be busy in no time. There's a place in Las Vegas where you could buy your tools and a portable forge."

"I'd like to take you up on the trimming. You can

133

see what you think of my work."

Horse pulled a business card out of his shirt pocket. He turned it over and wrote a phone number on the back and handed it to Burke.

"That's my home number. Call when you've got time to come over."

He stood up. Burke rose with him.

"I'd better get back to work.

Thanks for coming in, Mr. Henry."

"It's Burke, Sergeant."

"And you should call me Horse, like everyone else in Smoke Tree."

Burke had intended to go to his building site on Piute Creek after meeting with Horse that morning, but when he returned to Sunset Beach to pick up his tools, he decided it would be best not to attempt to work in his state of mind. Running an unshielded lumber saw off a power take off to cut two-by-sixes for roof joists required concentration and care if he didn't want to lose some fingers or even a hand.

His meeting with Horse had brought forth a flood of haunting memories that would not go away. He had tried for years to push the events on the east side of

Chosin Reservoir to the back of his mind but had never entirely succeeded: nor did he think he ever would. If he did not face his demons before sundown, they would haunt his dreams that night and for many nights to come.

Instead of loading up his truck, he walked down to the Colorado and sat on a boulder on a promontory that jutted out into the current. For a long time, he just sat and listened to the run of the river and watched clouds of sand swirl up near the shore and dissipate in the channel. He smelled smoke from a fire burning in the farmland across the river. He felt the wind whip the hair that was starting to grow out after all the years of military haircuts.

He breathed deeply and slowed his heart. Then, he leaned forward and put his elbows on his knees. He closed his eyes and let his thoughts return unchecked to those terrible days in the bitter cold of Korea.

As he had told Horse, he had been part of Task Force MacLean. *First Battalion of the Thirty-Second Infantry under Lieutenant Colonel Faith, a great officer.*

General Douglas MacArthur, a man Burke would

despise until he died, had ignored reports that forward units were making contact with multiple Chinese units. He foolishly ordered the task force to go on the offensive and strike out for the Yalu River. The General was, by God, going to teach the North Koreans a lesson and cover himself in glory at the same time.

His boundless ego cost thousands of American and South Korean lives.

The operation was a disaster before it even got started. On the twenty fourth of November, 1950, the Thirty-Second was already taking heavy fire from the Chinese. On the twenty-fifth and twenty-sixth, the battalion moved up and replaced the Fifth Marines on the north side of the perimeter so the Fifth could join the First Marine Division on the west side of Chosin Reservoir to spearhead the drive to the Yalu River.

The departure of the Fifth Marines left the Thirty-Second alone on the northernmost edge of the perimeter with no artillery support. On the twenty seventh, Faith sent out the intelligence and reconnaissance platoon to see what was in front of the unit. Normally, Burke would have been with them, but his company commander was concerned about the lack of artillery support and had Burke supervising the placement of the heavy machine guns and mortars.

The assignment saved his life. The platoon never came back. Not a single man. Contrary to what MacArthur believed in the safety of his headquarters in Tokyo, there were four Chicom divisions in front of Task Force MacLean. That night, the Thirty-Second got hammered by two of them. Over on the west side of the reservoir, the other two hit the Fifth and Seventh Marines head on.

In spite of all that, at around noon on the twenty-eighth of November, General Almond flew into the perimeter to meet with Colonel MacLean and Lieutenant Colonel Faith. He said there was nothing in front of them but "a bunch of Chinese laundry men," and told them they were to attack to the north the next day.

But after midnight, all hell broke loose. The Chinese attacked the Thirty-Second and overran their positions. MacLean and Faith decided to pull back to the south and join the Thirty-First Battalion. They took heavy casualties while trying to load up supplies and wounded. It was five o'clock the morning of the twenty eighth before they could disengage and start south.

What they didn't know was that the Chinese

weren't just behind them as they fled: they were in front of them too. As the Thirty-Second approached the Thirty-First's perimeter, they came under fire. Colonel MacLean, thinking the Thirty-First had mistaken them for the Chinese, ran down the road to tell them to stop. The Chinese opened up on him from both sides of the road and wounded him and dragged him away.

Colonel Faith led a group that drove the Chinese off the bridge they were blocking, and the Thirty Second moved on. But when they finally made it inside the Thirty-First's perimeter, they discovered the battalion was badly cut up. Over three hundred dead. One company, 'L' company, completely annihilated. Dead American and Chinese soldiers all over the ground.

Major General Barr, commander of the Seventh Infantry Division, helicoptered in to tell the task force it was now under the command of General Almond and the Marines. Task Force MacLean was to withdraw to the south and join the Marines there.

There was very little support for the withdrawal. The task force was on its own. It had no radio contact with the Marines. It was pounded by the Chinese and stopped by roadblocks all along the way. The soldiers who survived straggled by dribs and drabs into the

Marine lines on December first and second.

Task Force MacLean had originally had three battalions of infantry, one battalion of field artillery, one heavy mortar company, a tank company, and eight anti-aircraft vehicles with full crews. Thirty-two hundred Americans and seven hundred Republic of Korea soldiers. Less than a thousand of them survived to join up with the Marines, and only three hundred of the survivors were able bodied.

By some miracle, Burke had been one of the three hundred. And able-bodied is a relative term that describes only physical condition.

The newspapers at the time covered the Marine withdrawal on the west side of the reservoir. The papers forgot about Task Force MacLean – just like the generals did. But during the chaotic retreat, the task force battled with great courage, destroying almost the entire Chinese 80th Division. If it hadn't done that, the Marine withdrawal into Hagaru-ri and the eventual break-out would never have been possible. But the journalists covering the war never seemed to recognize that fact. Nor did the military historians after the war ended. Burke didn't think Task Force MacLean would ever get its due.

In spite of all the death and despair, what Burke remembered most was the terrible cold. The temperature at Chosin had hovered at or below zero all through the battle. Along with the fatigue, the intense cold was the enemy, just as much as the Chicoms with their bugles and red flags. Sometimes, men with minor wounds they could have survived just gave up in the face of the cold and lay down and froze to death.

Burke Henry's dreams would be forever haunted by images of men frozen hard to the earth in their own blood.

When he opened his eyes, he was cold in spite of the full sun. He was surprised to see dirt between his feet instead of snow. His field of view slowly shifted from sand and pebbles to the currents of the Colorado and the lands beyond.

The determination to never again be in a place as cold as Chosin Reservoir had been another factor that lead him to return to a tiny town he had glimpsed but briefly through a crack in a boxcar door. It had been the first town he had come to after leaving Oklahoma that bitter Winter of 1942 where the temperature had been above freezing.

CHAPTER 9

April 1957

Burke Henry led his horse down the Old Mojave Road toward the Lanfair Valley on a warm, spring day in 1957. He was now a known quantity in and around the town of Smoke Tree. The brawl at the Sunset Beach Saloon and Grill had brought him unwanted attention for a time, but soon after that event a batch of strangers arrived in town to feed the local appetite for gossip and speculation. A Southern California Gas Company compressor station was being built south of Smoke Tree. The station would recompress gas coming down the pipeline from Texas and boost it on to the cities at the coast.

The workers, and in some cases their families, had filled every trailer park space and rental unit from Topock to the Nevada state line. There were so many of them, some new tidbit popped up every day. Burke was now just another local. Exactly as he wanted.

His house on Piute Creek was finished. It gave him

a surprising sense of accomplishment to have his own home. He had completed his corral and now owned Pepper, a three-year-old gelding. A good horse. It had the stamina for long desert rides. Stamina it would need now that Burke was a member of the Smoke Tree Substation volunteer posse.

An established farrier, he was known for the quality of his work and his way with horses from Kingman to Smoke Tree to Las Vegas. The jobs he sometimes picked up in Las Vegas had once made it easy to drop by a casino or two and break more hundred-dollar bills. But by the spring of '57, the farrier business was doing so well he was bringing in more than enough money to cover the cost of his gasoline and food and clothing, as well as oats and hay for Pepper. Instead of taking money out of the bank, he was now making deposits.

For a combat veteran who had often feared, and with good reason, that he would not live to see the sun rise on another day, he was relatively at peace. His life had begun to take on a satisfying rhythm. On days when he had no farrier work, he roamed the Mojave Desert around Piute Creek. He found the desert fascinating. He usually took Pepper with him. When he did, he led the gelding instead of riding it. He reasoned it was better to exercise both himself and his horse than to make Pepper carry a man healthy enough to walk on his own.

As he led Pepper, the horse's pack saddle carrying food and water for both of them, Burke looked somewhat like an old hard-rock prospector leading a burro. But he was not seeking precious metals. He was seeking the heart of the Mojave. The very essence of the desert. And like all serious desert travelers, serious meaning those who go on foot, the more he explored the deeper he was drawn into the mystery. It was not long before, without realizing it, he himself became part of the mystery. Seduced by the lure of one more set of low, rocky, cactus-covered amber hills. One more desert wash. One more stand of catclaw and desert willow. One more daytime sky with its blazing, relentless sunlight. One more night sky filled with uncountable stars.

On hot, late-spring or summer days, he would seek out shade for the hours between noon and two to eat his lunch and read his favorite book, one he had, for reasons he could not explain, carried and read and reread many times during his military career: The Complete Works of William Shakespeare

If he and Pepper were not bedding down in a sandy wash somewhere, sundown usually found him on his back porch watching the multicolored hues of dramatic sundowns. He often lingered there well into the deepening twilight with his last cup of coffee of the day as he listened to the yips, yowls and howls of the coyote packs in and around Piute Gorge. Since there was no electricity in his house, at nightfall he went inside and read by lamplight: either his Shakespeare or one of the many books he checked out from the Smoke Tree library. But he rarely read too long before turning in.

And some nights he was awakened, usually around midnight, by the sound of voices. Voices so soft they were hardly discernable. Voices that drew him outside. Voices speaking a language he could not understand. But it didn't matter. He knew what the voices were saying. Sometimes they spoke of the corn and squash planted along the creek after it flooded. And sometimes about the harvest soon to come. And other times about the rabbits and mule deer to be hunted and the meat to be jerked in the season of plenty. And about the trips west to the vast and distant ocean to trade for mysterious and beautiful things.

Each day Burke's new life opened itself to him like a cactus flower miraculously blossoming within a forbidding thicket of thorns, inscrutable and nothing more than itself in the wild and deep desolation of the desert. Days upon days of blessed solitude and contemplation. Days that were treasures. Treasures others would have either overlooked completely or described in very different terms.

He would rise each of these new days well before first light and make the morning coffee he drank on his front porch while the pale blue of pre-dawn light slowly leached into the eastern sky. When the sun broke the horizon, he would stand and stretch and shout in his booming voice, "Good morning, desert."

Burke Henry seemed a simple man. But his supposed simplicity was deceptive. When he was at rest, there was a profound stillness to him. When he was in motion, he flowed. Flowed with sinuous balance and dexterous coordination. He seemed to move without hesitation and absent forethought. But that also was deceptive. Burke Henry was thinking all the time.

He had two close friends: Horse and his wife Esperanza. Burke admired Horse for his honesty, dedication and forthrightness. Horse was something unusual in Burke's experience: a law enforcement officer he felt he could trust. Burke admired Esperanza for her intelligence and grace and her unaffected, completely unselfconscious style. For her coherent sense of her own worth and uniqueness and her willingness to unequivocally share that uniqueness with Horse.

The two were completely dedicated to one another, so much so that it was difficult to imagine one having a life without the other. He admired the pair of them even more than he admired them individually.

During his years in the Army, he had subordinates and superiors. He had comrades for whom he would have been willingly given his life. But he never had personal friends.

That changed when he met Horse, and it changed for the most unlikely of reasons: martial arts. When Horse had approached Lieutenant Nelson with his idea of having Burke train the deputies at the substation in the art of gradual escalation, the lieutenant rejected the idea outright.

"Our job here, Sergeant, isn't to handle criminals with kid gloves. We find the bad guys. We arrest the bad guys. If they give as any crap, and I mean any crap at all, so much as a dirty look, we bust their heads. We make sure they never want to be arrested by a Smoke Tree Substation deputy again. We may not be able to stop crime before it happens, but we can damn well make criminals regret they ever got into our crosshairs."

But Horse remembered the three big bikers Burke had so casually vanquished, and he wanted to learn, so he asked if Burke would be willing to train just him.

Burke almost declined.

By nature, he shied away from one-on-one interaction. He was fine with training groups of men. Lord knew, he had trained enough during his years in the Army. But Horse had helped him get his career as a farrier started without any thought of personal gain. And Horse had served in Korea. Burke felt a kinship with him. A kinship he had not felt since his days with his cousin in Oklahoma. So, he agreed to teach Horse some of what he knew. It was a decision he never regretted.

Two weeks after Burke trimmed and re-shod Canyon and Mariposa, he met with Horse at his property on a Saturday morning and told him what was needed before they could begin the training.

"The first thing you have to learn is how to fall. You work to out-maneuver an opponent, but sometimes you can't, and sometimes you get swept or thrown or dropped. If you don't know how to fall when that happens, the battle will be over the instant you hit the ground.

After some training, you'll be able to absorb a fall onto asphalt or cement without being hurt, but you need somewhere soft to land while you learn. The ground here on your property is too hard for that purpose. Do you remember the sand pit they used to teach you some hand-to-hand in basic training?"

"Yes."

"We need to build something like that. Ten by ten will handle the jujitsu throws and be fine for grappling, but some of the aikido maneuvers, especially the self-sacrifice falls, cover more ground and twelve by twelve would be better."

The two men walked the property until they found a spot beyond the corral and adjacent to Esperanza's newly-planted vegetable garden that was level enough for their purposes.

"If this is excavated to a depth of about six inches

and filled with sand, it'll work."

"All right. I'll get back to you once I have it ready."

"It'll go faster if I help."

"But you're building your house."

"Can't hammer nails all the time."

Horse brought tools and gloves from the tack room, and they went to work.

At eleven in the morning, Esperanza came out with iced tea, and they took a break. At one, she called them into the house for sandwiches. When she came out later with more tea, both men were shirtless and glistening with sweat beneath the sunny sky of a windless day. She lingered for a while before returning to the house.

Esperanza first met Burke when he worked her horse, Mariposa. She had been struck by how much Carlos and Burke resembled one another. As she watched them work with their shirts off to build the sand pit that afternoon, her first impression was reinforced. Horse was the darker of the two, but not by much, and he had the high, chiseled cheekbones of an Aztec warrior. The eyes she loved were deep brown, and his hair was jet black. While Burke's hair was blonde and his blue eyes made a startling contrast to his brown face, he had the same cheekbones and slightly Asiatic cast to his eyes as her Carlos.

Carlos was taller by an inch or so. There was more heft to his powerful and well-defined muscles. Burke was leaner, with ropy muscles that rippled and flowed like knotted cords beneath his brown skin as he worked. If there was an ounce of fat on him, it was lurking somewhere it could not be seen. And Burke worked hard. In fact, he seemed to be tireless. She had never before seen a man who could out-work her Carlos. But Burke Henry was that man.

The two were trading off on the pick work. Esperanza noticed Carlos did not slam the pick into the rock-hard ground quite as long as Burke before leaning over to put his hands on his knees to catch his breath. Burke was like a metronome, swinging the pick high over his head and attacking the desert without pause for much longer stretches. And when he did stop, it was only long enough to stretch his back briefly before returning to work.

By sundown of that first day, the excavation work was done. After they returned the tools to the tack room, Burke and Horse walked toward where Burke had parked his motorcycle.

"All you need now is lots of sand."

"Plenty of that in the big wash that runs across 95 just past five-mile road."

"Okay. If you'd like some help, I'll be here in the morning and we can load and haul until we fill the pit."

"Aren't you going to take a day off?"

Burke smiled.

"Some hard work will make my Sunday afternoon burger at the saloon taste even better."

Horse leaned and stretched from side to side.

"Okay. If I can get my sore back out of bed, Esperanza and I will go to early mass. Meet you out here at nine thirty if you still feel like working when you get up tomorrow."

"It's a deal. And if you think you're sore now, wait until I start tossing you around that sand trap."

A week from the day they filled the pit with sand, they started the training sessions that became a Sunday ritual that lasted through the following winter.

April and early May were spent teaching Horse to fall correctly after being swept or thrown. It is not easy for the inexperienced to deal with the disconcerting sensation of being upended and sometimes turned completely upside down before being slammed to the ground. The sensation produces immediate, mid-air panic in the untrained. Learning to overcome that instinctive fear is critical, because fear leads to helplessness, and helplessness leads to serious injury. The new student must learn to orient instantly to the ground and prepare to break the fall and not be injured or stunned.

While the instructor can explain the sequences and techniques in detail, there is no way to learn the correct reaction without being thrown hundreds upon hundreds of times. Being swept, while not as disorienting, requires other skills because the follow-up attack can be more instantaneous and thus deadlier. Once the instinctive panic at being thrown or swept has been overcome and landing without injury has been mastered, the student must learn to recover immediately to a defensive position.

Burke began the process by having Horse fall from a low position. Once Horse knew how to do that, Burke added movement. When Horse could fall and roll in multiple directions, Burke began to throw him from higher and higher positions. Only after Horse was comfortable and confident did Burke teach the final skill: falling, rolling and recovering from over-the-shoulder, feet-up-head-down throws.

Once Horse could do that, Burke moved on to teaching him the self-sacrifice throws that are an integral part of aikido. That knowledge led directly to teaching Horse how to sweep and throw an adversary.

June was devoted to striking. Burke taught Horse the basic punches launched from both agility and power stances in Shorin-ryu karate. The punches were practiced over and over again. Burke also taught him the devastating forearm smashes and heel of the hand strikes to the throat, nose and face. Horse often put in extra hours on his own in the evenings, striking a padded board cemented into the ground in order to be prepared for the next Sunday training session.

In July, they put on fingerless, leather gloves padded with cotton around the knuckles to work on counters to being struck. In that phase, Burke quickly realized that Horse was an exceptional student. As a young man, Horse had boxed Golden Gloves in Las Vegas. In the Army, he fought for his training brigade both in basic and advanced infantry training. He had the size and build of a classic light-heavyweight: flat, hard chest; long, muscular arms; solid trunk; flat, rock-hard stomach; long, powerful legs and quick feet.

The first time they worked at full speed on blocks and counters, Burke learned about the suddenness and deceptive power of an experienced boxer's reactions. When he launched a two-knuckle punch toward Horse's face, Horse not only blocked it but simultaneously countered with a lightning-fast, straight right. A less experienced fighter would have been momentarily stunned by the blow and hammered by the combinations that followed. Instead, Burke's countless hours of training took over. He swept Horse's feet out from under him and put him on the ground. But he came away with tremendous respect for Horse's hand speed and the startling power that had been packed in that short right. He realized if he had to spar with Horse while bound by the rules of boxing, he would be badly outgunned.

Horse, while instantly realizing he had an edge in

154

hand strikes, was amazed at how suddenly Burke had taken him down and locked him into immobility. He understood why the next step in his training involved arm bars and joint manipulation to submission.

August was devoted to kicking and blocking kicks from an opponent. Shorin-ryu, the form of karate Burke practiced, was a product of the island of Okinawa. Okinawans were generally shorter than most Japanese; therefore, the kicks involved were low kicks, mostly to the knees and groin. Shorin-ryu disdained the flashier, higher kicks of other forms of karate because *sensei* thought it foolish to risk exposure to being thrown by getting the kicking foot so far off the ground. Attempting a spinning back kick to an opponent's head was considered downright stupid in Shorin-ryu.

Since Horse had good balance and long, strong legs, Burke taught him kicks above the waist, but never higher than the sternum. As the training in kicking and blocking kicks transitioned from learning the basic moves to execution at full speed, Burke introduced new equipment: cotton padding lashed to the shins with ace bandages.

The training sessions and the coming of summer
moved forward concurrently. When the brutally hot
months of July and August arrived, the starting time
for the sessions was changed to late afternoon. In
addition to padded gloves, boxing headgear and crude
shin guards, the two wore high-top PF Flyers, Levi's,
and heavy, long-sleeved canvas jerseys. Levi's were
tough and could handle abuse, and the canvas jerseys
were strong enough not to tear during grappling and
throwing exercises. Also, the outfits were similar to
the street clothes an adversary might be wearing.

All that clothing magnified the debilitating effects
of the heat. By transitioning the start times to late
afternoon meant that even though the temperatures
were still well over a hundred degrees, at least they
were spared the frightening intensity of the sun
beating down from directly overhead.

When the sessions ended on those hot days, both
men were drenched in sweat. As soon as they pulled
off the padded gloves and removed the headgear, the
makeshift shin guards and the high-top shoes, they
hosed the sand off each other on the cement pad
behind the tack room. Because of the aridity of the
Mojave summer, by the time they stowed the gear and
the training outfits and changed into t-shirts and

shorts, they were completely dry.

On those days, as the light changed from the glare of late afternoon to the softening colors of early evening, Esperanza knew the workout would soon be over. She would prepare a snack and set it on the table on the veranda: two huge pitchers of lemonade, a platter of chips coated with melted cheese, and a bowl of *salsa bandera*.

It was not long before she added a light main course to the menu. Soon, she and Carlos and Burke began to linger on the veranda while twilight tinctured the Black Mountains with multiple, rapidly changing shades of purple. Heat lightning sometimes hugged the eastern horizon, a reflection of the monsoon season thunderstorms over the Kaibab and Colorado plateaus over a hundred miles to the east. And just before the light faded completely from the sky, swarms of bats from the caves and abandoned mine shafts of the Sacramento Mountains would appear overhead, flickering through the heated air as they headed for the insect-rich sky above the waters of the Colorado and the lights of Smoke Tree.

Once darkness had fallen, Esperanza would light the two candles on the table and bring out coffee and flan.

The Sunday supper on the Caballo's veranda was the highlight of Burke Henry's week. It seemed that Horse and Esperanza knew almost everything about everyone in Smoke Tree and the surrounding area. Burke enjoyed having dessert and coffee while hearing about the locals and the colorful history of the little town.

One evening, Horse told of meeting Espernza for the first time on the opening day at Smoke Tree Junior High and how he had decided within minutes that they would marry someday. Esperanza, her eyes glowing in the candlelight, smiled as she told Burke she had reached the same conclusion at almost the same time.

"I didn't even try to play hard to get. It was clear to me that this was the person God had made for me to love."

Burke was taken by the strength and the quality of their bond. He did not envy Horse his good fortune in being married to a woman he loved so much and who loved him equally in return, but he doubted he would ever have such a relationship himself.

On those first evenings, Burke listened far more

than he talked. But as August turned to September and the heat lightning ceased to dance across the desert horizon, he became more forthcoming. He spoke of the history of the Kiowa Apache and shared a few details of his early life on the Kiowa, Comanche, Apache Reservation, known in Caddo County Oklahoma simply as the KCA.

But he never revealed that his first glimpse of Smoke Tree had been at the age of seventeen though a narrow opening in the door of a boxcar bound for Los Angeles. And he never told Horse and Esperanza the real reason he had left the KCA, claiming it was to join the army because of the attack on Pearl Harbor.

Although he respected Burke's privacy and did not pry, the trained investigator in Horse sensed there was more to the story than Burke was telling. Horse simply did not accept that this clearly intelligent man, with his knowledge of Kiowa Apache history and culture and his clear understanding of all that had been taken from his tribe by government, had been driven by patriotism alone to leave Oklahoma behind.

While Burke spoke of riding and hunting on the reservation with his cousin, the only information he revealed about his father was that he was a Ukrainian who had abandoned Burke and his mother and sister when Burke was very young. And about his mother, he said not a word. Nor about his sister.

In late September, Burke began training Horse in the proper use of the nightstick as a tool to subdue an unruly suspect. By the middle of October, Horse had absorbed a truncated version of Burke's vast knowledge, and it was time to move on to the most demanding but important part of the training: sparring. From that time on, the Sunday sessions involved the two men moving at full speed. The sessions were long and arduous and often left Horse gasping for air. Burke, on the other hand, never seemed to be winded or fatigued.

Burke was grateful to have someone to spar with, even if that person could not match his level of skill and expertise. For while he often ran through the basic *katas* of Shorin-ryu karate and rehearsed his jujitsu, mano mano, bangkaw and aikido moves, such practice was an inadequate substitute for engaging with a capable opponent. And Horse was rapidly becoming much more than capable.

While the Sunday training cut deeply into Horse's

free time, he was determined to learn everything Burke was willing to teach. On many occasions, he offered to pay Burke for his time, but Burke always refused to accept compensation. While he had willingly accepted payment for his farrier work he did with Canyon and Mariposa, he would not take money for the martial arts sessions.

"The men who taught me what I know did it for free. It would not be right for me to profit from what was given to me as a gift."

And although he never said it, Burke knew he had already received a gift: the gift of friendship.

As Burke led Pepper across the desert on that April day in 1957, he thought about his progress on the two goals he had set for himself before leaving the army, the only adult life he had ever known, for life as a civilian in the desert southwest.

First, he had been determined never to be poor. Never again to be held captive by a life of grinding, relentless poverty as he and his mother and sister had been on the KCA. The money in his safe deposit box at the Bank of America branch in Smoke Tree guaranteed he had met that goal. He thought of the huge sum from time to time. It was a lot of money, and it comforted him to know it was there. However, there was nothing he needed, so he had no plans to use it. He planned, sometime in the future, to determine what would be done with it in the event of his death. In the meantime, no one in Smoke Tree had any idea that, with the exception of the local mayor, who owned a string of markets across the desert, Burke Henry was the richest man in town

His second goal had been to forge a life on the edge of American society but not be part of that society. To live on the periphery of the modern world and take from that world only that which he wanted and leave the rest alone. And just as importantly, to have it leave *him* alone.

His desire to achieve that second goal was what made his friendship with Horse a paradox. Horse was a law enforcement professional. He was very good at his job. Because of his work, he had access to information unavailable to ordinary citizens. Burke, although he was a naturally reticent man, still had to remind himself frequently not to reveal too much about his past. As long as he remembered that, he could keep his new friends while continuing his day to day life beneath the inverted cerulean-blue bowl of the daytime desert sky and the deep blackness of velvet nights splashed with the countless stars that stretched from horizon to horizon.

Few people who have not lived completely alone and isolated so far off the beaten path can grasp the depth of solitude experienced by a lone, deep-desert dweller. As far as Burke was concerned, that was their loss. He planned to spend the rest of his life watching as the desert around him changed in hue and tone, hour by hour and day after seamless day. Watching as time crawled slowly across the ancient, dusty, worn, volcanic rocks that formed the down-sloping talus field of his life.

Deep Desert Deception

CHAPTER 10

August 9, 1959 Piute Creek, California

A very worried Burke Henry sat on his back porch.
His chair was angled so he could look out over Piute
Creek at the astounding splash of variegated color
splayed across the western sky by the setting sun. In
spite of the beauty of the late-afternoon desert, he was
unsettled and out of sorts.

Earlier that day, at the Whiting Brothers station
on the north side of Smoke Tree, he had caught a
glimpse of Oklahoma plates on a '56 Chevy that
turned off eastbound 66 and drove into the service
island. As he watched, a sturdy woman in a cotton
shift bolted from the passenger side door and took off
running for the ladies' room

As the woman disappeared around the corner of
the building, he heard yelps of anguish and looked
back at the car. Two tow-headed, freckled children
had jumped out of the Chevy in bare feet and landed
on the superheated asphalt that gave off the oily smell
of hot tar. The driver of the car was herding his pudgy,

bleating offspring into the shade of the overhang next to the pumps when he turned his head and looked directly at Burke.

Burke thought he had seen a flicker of recognition cross the man's face before he turned away. After Burke paid for his two quarts of oil and climbed into his truck, he felt the man's eyes on him. He was careful to give no sign he thought he was being watched. He suddenly wished he didn't have the name of his business painted on the door of the truck. When he pulled out of the station, he joined the eastbound 66 traffic instead of turning to head for home.

He glanced into his side view mirror. The heavy set, sandy-haired man was not looking his way, but his stance seemed too casual. Like he was purposely trying *not* to look.

So, what to do? Had he been recognized? Was he overreacting?

His first instinct was to leave the area. Ride into town on his motorcycle, retrieve his money from his safe deposit box and head for the coast and then points north. Leave his house, his horse, his truck and his business behind. That was what a cautious, careful man would do.

As he sat thinking, the color bled out of the western sky. The east-trending evening wind, like a vast and weary exhalation from the earth after the blistering heat of the day, pushed across the landscape and met the cooler air sighing out of the mouth of the canyon carrying the smell of the vegetation surrounding Piute Spring. And still he sat, struggling with his decision. He had built a life here. Built this house above the creek at the mouth of Piute gorge with his own hands. Built a business with his own talent and knowledge. A business that showed the people of Smoke Tree he earned his keep and kept them from being suspicious about the source of his income. A business that allowed him to be around horses for the first time since leaving Oklahoma.

And that brought up Pepper. Even if he had to leave abruptly, he would have to somehow let Carlos Caballo know the horse now belonged to him.

That lead to thoughts about his friendship with Carlos and Esperanza. Kind people. Unselfish people. People who had opened their home and their hearts to him. The first friendships he had enjoyed since losing his cousin and then his sister all those years ago.

Just like that, he made his decision. No

exhaustive list of pros and cons. No logical weighing of the issues and possibilities. He simply refused to give up this life. Refused to be driven away.

At some point in the last two and a half years, he now realized, he had decided he would die in this place. A place that had granted him a degree of peace and serenity he had once feared was forever beyond his reach. A place that had become sacred to him: sacred because of the spirits of the Mojave, Chemehuevi and Paiute who had inhabited this oasis in the desert in times long past and whose presence he felt every day when he walked past petroglyphs painstakingly cut into solid rock by the ancients. Sacred because he believed his own Kiowa Apache ancestors were kindred spirits to those long-departed people.

Whether his death came soon or fifty years from now was of little consequence to him.

It was always possible he just had an overactive imagination, so for a few weeks, he would be wary and vigilant and stay out of Smoke Tree. He would drive to Boulder City for his groceries. Buy his gasoline from Mr. Stanton. Make no visits to Brenda at the Sunset Beach Saloon and Grill to see if any farrier jobs had come in. Climb into the Piutes every morning with water and food and binoculars to the spot where he could glass the Old Mojave Road as it threaded its way both eastward from the broad Lanfair Valley and westward from Highway 95. Spend the days among the desert thistle, desert mallow, range ratany, yucca, cholla and barrel cactus. Spend those days as his own sentry, glassing the approaches to Fort Piute to answer his own silent question: "Who goes there?"

Sleep outside in case his enemies came in the night.

If the man who had locked eyes with him had recognized him, Burke had no doubt the Klan people would come seeking revenge for the killing one of their own: Harold Nevins. They would come soon. But they would not surprise him. He may not survive their coming, but he would make them rue the day they left Caddo and Comanche Counties and came west to hunt the person they had once known as Kyle Sommers.

Because that person no longer existed. The person who had taken his place was deadlier than these men could image.

Deep Desert Deception

CHAPTER 11

August 10, 1959 Anadarko, Oklahoma

The phone hanging low on the wall at Nevins' **Automotive** on West Central Boulevard in Anadarko rang just before four in the afternoon. With a sigh of exasperation at being interrupted, a man in a wheelchair rolled himself away from his task and across the gritty, grease-stained floor of the shop. He flipped the switch on a big, noisy fan next to the phone. It was doing nothing to improve the humid, stifling air in the garage, anyway.

As he picked up the phone, he turned his head away from the blinding glare of the sun pounding down just beyond the open garage door.

"Nevins' Automotive."

"It's Purvis. I saw him."

"Saw who?"

"Kyle Sommers."

Harold Nevins squeezed the receiver with a fierce intensity. His heart accelerated.

"Where?"

"Smoke Tree, California. Crap little desert town.

"What were you doing there?"

"Me and Jayleen took the kids out to Disneyland. Ever since they started watching that Mickey Mouse Club, they been pestering us to go. We finally give in and took them."

"You sure it was Sommers?"

"How many blue-eyed Kiowa Apaches you know?"

"Just one."

"That's the one I saw. Looked right at me with them blue eyes. It was Kyle Sommers all right. Older, but him for sure."

"Where was this?"

"Just told you. Town called Smoke Tree."

"I got that, but where in this town?"

"Gas station."

"He recognize you?"

"Don't know me from Adam, best I recall. He was talkin' to somebody when we rolled in. Walked off and got in a old Ford truck."

"Where'd he go?"

"Don't think he went anywhere. This place is a million miles from any other place."

"I mean when he left the gas station."

"How the hell should I know? Drove off into Smoke Tree."

"You didn't follow him?"

"I was runnin' on fumes when I got there. Gas stations is a long ways apart on that Godforsaken desert. Miles and miles of nothin' and more nothin' out there. Makes Caddo County look like the Garden of Eden."

"Tell me exactly what happened."

"We pulled into the station in the middle of the day. Hotter'n the hinges of hell, and Jayleen was in one of her moods. Yanked open the door and took off for the bathroom before I could even get stopped. Right after that, Tommy and Janice jumped out in their bare feet and landed on a blacktop driveway you coulda fried a egg on. By the time I got them rounded up and got gas and Jayleen come back from the bathroom, Sommers was long gone."

"Damn! I wish you'd followed him."

"Get ahold of yourself, Harold. He's not gonna be hard to find."

"What makes you so sure?"

"Had the name of a business painted on the door of the truck. 'Smoke Tree Farrier'."

"Hot damn! We got him! We can get an address for his business.

Now listen, Purvis. We got a Klan meetin' in Lawton Wednesday night. If we can talk one or two of the boys into going with you, you can go right back out there and kill the bastard."

"Jeez, Harold, I want him dead as much as you do, but I'm tapped out. That Disneyland trip cost me an arm and a leg."

"Can't be that expensive. Shoot on over to 66. Two-day drive there. Kill the half-breed. Two days back. Food and gas. Sleep in the car. I'll put up the money. Purvis, I want Kyle Sommers scrubbed off the face of God's good earth! I want you boys to hurt him real bad before you kill him. I want him to suffer for the way I've suffered all these years.

Purvis was silent for a moment.

"Okay, but when you talk at the meeting, Harold, be real careful about what you say."

"Meanin' what?"

"Don't nobody but you, me, and Scuttler know about what happened with the Sommers girl. Scuttler saw to it the story has always been Sommers robbed you and left you for dead. Just be sure to keep them thinkin' that."

"What kind of fool do you take me for? Of course, I'm not going to bring up the Sommers girl. I've got two whole days to think about what to say. I'll get those boys so riled up, they'll draw straws to see who gets to go."

"If anyone can do it, Harold, you can. You got the fire of the righteous burnin' in you. Always have..."

"Purvis, you done good. I gotta hang up now and go to work getting' that address."

As soon as Purvis was off the line, Harold dialed a number he knew by heart.

"Caddo County Sheriff's Department."

"Get me Dave Scuttler."

"Who's calling?"

"Harold Nevins."

There were a few moments of silence.

"What can I do for you, Harold?"

"Anybody on this line but us?"

"No."

"You can help me find Kyle Sommers."

"We've been over this before. It's been fifteen years. We're never going to find him."

"We just did."

"Where?"

"Town called Smoke Tree, California. Has a business there. It's called Smoke Tree Farrier."

"That makes it easier. Let me put in some calls. I'll get back to you when I know something."

When the call ended, Harold sat in his wheelchair surrounded by the smell of grease, gasoline and parts cleaner. George Jones was singing *White Lightning* on the cheap shop radio. Harold looked without seeing at the flies hanging in the moist air and thought about the night Kyle Sommers had come into the garage when Harold was working late on a brake job for Bobby Swarthout.

Harold had replayed the scene thousands of time.

He knew now he never should have swung on Sommers with that big, heavy wrench when the kid came in screaming at him about rape. Harold had been too slow. He should have remembered how fast that skinny boy could be. He'd seen him on the basketball court for the local high school often enough. Instead of using his speed to jump out of the way like any normal person would have, the breed stepped inside the arc of the swing and shoved Harold with both hands. Shoved him hard. As he tried to regain his balance, his boots slipped on the oily floor and he went over backwards. The back of his head slammed into the concrete and he blacked out.

When he came to, he had been moved. He was lying face down on the dirty floor, his head pounding. His hands were tied behind his back. He turned his head to the side and looked into the blue eyes of Kyle Sommers. Blue eyes he would never forget.

He could make out something above the boy's head. He blinked several times to clear his blurred vision. The underside of the hydraulic lift suspended above him swam into focus. The lift he was always careful to keep flat on the floor unless there was a vehicle on it.

Kyle got to his feet and walked away. Harold watched as the boy closed the garage door before returning to kneel down again. He was silent for a long time. Then, he took a deep breath and began to talk.

He told Harold about coming home from school that day and finding his sister crying in her bedroom. About his sister telling him she had been raped earlier in the day by Harold and two other men: one man she had never seen before and the other a sheriff's deputy. She didn't know the deputy's name, but she had seen him around Anadarko in his cruiser.

When Harold protested that her story was a lie, Kyle grabbed his long, greasy hair and slammed his face into the concrete. Broke his nose. Told him to shut up and listen. Said he had left the house to search the bars in Anadarko for their mother but couldn't find her. When he returned home, he found his sister hanging from the catalpa tree out back.

The breed was crying by then. Tears were running down his face. Tears for some no-account little Apache slut.

When Harold spoke again, it was to complain.

"Can't move my hands or feet."

"That's all you got to say?"

"Yeah."

"I'll untie you if you tell me the names of the two men who were with you."

"Piss off! I'm not giving you any names. You're in some deep shit, boy. You've gone and messed with a member of the Klan. I'll give you some free advice. Start running!"

"Not before I fix it so you never rape anybody again."

Kyle got to his feet and disappeared from view. A moment later, Harold heard a horrible sound. The sound of air bleeding from the hydraulic lift.

He was screaming before the lift ever touched him. Screaming while Kyle walked over and turned the radio to full volume and disappeared into the night, pulling the garage door down as he left.

If Bobby Swarthout hadn't stopped by a short time later to see if his emergency brake job was finished and found Harold unconscious beneath the lift, his legs smashed into something that looked like pomegranate jelly, something Bobby Swarthout would never eat again, Harold would have died that night. As it was, he survived. Survived to have his legs amputated above the knees. Survived to live the rest of his days in a wheelchair, suffering endless, agonizing bouts of phantom nerve pain.

But now, he considered himself lucky to have survived to live even so diminished a life. If he had died, he wouldn't have been able to dream of revenge. A dream that might now come true.

He wheeled his chair over to the garage door and pulled the chain that rolled it down. In the office, he rotated the sign in the window from 'open' to 'closed.' Locking the door, he wheeled back into the garage. Snapping off the radio, he sat in the gloom of the stifling-hot, darkened shop and thought about how to convince one or two men to go with Purvis.

He decided he would start by talking about the klaverns in the South. Like in Mississippi, where they had taken care of Emmett Till just for remarks to a white woman. And took care of the un-Reverend George Lee and Lamar Smith, too. And in Alabama, where Klan Wrecking Crews took out Woodrow Wilson Daniels and Willie Edwards. How it was only a matter of time before the southern klaverns got rid of Medgar Evers and Martin Luther Coon.

When he had their blood-lust ramped up, he would slide right into the Indian problem in

Oklahoma. After all, Caddo County had the highest percentage of Indian population of any County in the state. Explain that those Indians were starting to think they were the equal of white people. How that could lead to problems like what had happened last year in North Carolina where a bunch of Lumbee Indians got so bold they raided a legitimate Klan rally in Robeson County. How the government, instead of prosecuting the savages, had put James Cole, a Grand Dragon, in jail for two years.

End up with what had happened to him in nineteen forty-two. Robbed and crippled by a Kiowa Apache. Condemned to a wheelchair for the rest of his life by a mud person. And him a white man. Not only a white man: a Citizen of the Ku Klux Klan. How that could be set right after all these years. Set right by killing Kyle Sommers and letting the word get around that the Indian who had crippled a Citizen was dead. How his body would never be found.

He smiled a satisfied smile.

The time for sweet revenge has come, he thought.

Deep Desert Deception

CHAPTER 12

August 10, 1959. Smoke Tree, California

The intercom on Oscar Rettenmeir's desk crackled to life.

"Chief."

He opened his eyes and lowered his boots from the corner of the desk and pushed the toggle switch.

"Yeah."

"Guy on line one for you. Says he's a sheriff's deputy from someplace in Oklahoma."

"Okay."

He punched up the call.

"Chief Rettenmeir speaking."

"Good afternoon, Chief. This is Deputy Dave Scuttler, Caddo County Sheriff's Department in Oklahoma. I'm hoping you can help me with something."

"Be glad to, Deputy, if I can."

"A man was seen in your town by one of our residents who was passing through. This man is someone we'd really like to talk to."

"In connection with...?

"An old, attempted murder case."

"How old?"

"I'm embarrassed to say. It's been on our books since 1942."

"I'm surprised anyone remembers it."

"The guy who saw the person we'd like to talk to was a close friend of the man who was the victim."

"Still, pretty unusual for your department to still want to pursue it. The damage must have been pretty severe."

"Put him in a wheelchair for life."

"This person you're looking for, what's his name?"

"Kyle Sommers."

Chief Rettenmeir was silent for a moment.

"Can't say that name brings a face to mind, and I know most of the people in this little town. Maybe this person wasn't from Smoke Tree. Maybe he was passing through just like the man who saw him."

"Our resident says the guy was driving a truck with the name of the business on the door."

"That would go a long way toward solving the mystery. What was the name?"

"Smoke Tree Farrier."

The Chief sat up a little straighter.

"I've seen that truck around. But the name you gave me is not the name of the man who owns the business."

"Maybe Sommers works for him. What's the owner's name?"

Chief Rettenmeir took the receiver away from his ear and leaned forward and toggled the intercom.

"Mike, what's the name of that guy got in a tussle with those bikers out at Sunset a couple years back?"

"Henry, Chief. Burke Henry."

The Chief put the phone back to his ear.

"The owner's name is Burke Henry."

It was Deputy Scuttler's turn to be silent. So that's how he did it, he thought. Took his cousin's name and ran. His dead cousin. No way to squeeze the Henry boy's parents now. They were both dead. He quickly considered how best to manipulate this hick town police chief.

"That's also a name I'm familiar with, Chief. Cousin of the guy we think is guilty of the attempted murder. He may be a material witness in this case. We'd really like to talk to him."

"I thought your resident told you he had seen Kyle Sommers."

"He did. But like I said, Kyle Sommers and Burke Henry were cousins. Looked a lot alike. After all these years, be easy to confuse one for the other."

"Well, I suppose I could ask him to give you a call."

"Not a good idea, Chief. Give him too long to think up a story to cover for his cousin. Rather put it to him face to face. See how he reacts."

"Understood. But you'd come all the way out here from Oklahoma to do that?"

"Not me. Our sheriff is going to be in Las Vegas later this month. That's not too far from you, right?"

"A little over a hundred miles."

"He'd really like to get this cleared up. He could swing down your way and look this Burke Henry up.

Can you give me an address for him?"

"Can't say he exactly has one. Lives outside of town down a dirt road."

"How far out of town."

"Let's just say it's a fair piece. No mail service. No phone. No electricity. Has a little place at the mouth of a canyon. Lives rough, you might say."

Perfect, thought Deputy Dave. Completely isolated! We can send some boys out there who will get the job done and leave no trace they were ever there. No trace of Sommer's body, either.

"Think you could tell me how to get there? I'll pass the details on to my Sheriff."

The sudden eagerness in the Deputy's voice, the confusion about the name of the man who had been seen in Smoke Tree, the seamless shift in interest from the name Kyle Sommers to the name Burke Henry, all made Chief Rettenmeir a little uneasy. He thought for a moment and then dropped the receiver on the desk and walked to his door. He opened it and slammed it shut before walking back to his desk and picking up the phone.

"Deputy, sorry to interrupt our conversation. We've got ourselves a little emergency out here. Give me your phone number, and I'll call you back after I deal with it."

"Sure."

The Chief wrote down the number the man recited.

"I'll call within the hour."

"Thanks. I'll be available."

Chief Rettenmeir hung up sat quietly at his desk for a few minutes. Then he got up and walked out of his office.

"Mike, I'm going to go around the corner to the library. Won't be long."

Twenty minutes later, he was back in his office with the name of the county adjacent to Caddo County in Oklahoma. He dialed the operator.

"This is Chief Rettenmeir. I need a phone number for the Comanche County, Oklahoma, Sheriff's Department."

When the operator gave him the number, he asked her to make the call for him.

It was answered on the first ring.

"Comanche County Sheriff's Department. Dispatch."

"This is Chief of Police Oscar Rettenmeir in Smoke Tree, California. I'm trying to locate a Deputy Dave Scuttler. Is he available?"

"Sorry, Chief. You've got the wrong department. Scuttler works over in Caddo County."

"Can you give me the number over there?"

"Sure."

The number the dispatcher provided was the same as the one given to him by Deputy Scuttler. While there was something a little hinky about the man, he was apparently who he claimed to be.

The Chief dialed the Caddo County number and asked for the deputy. When Scuttler came on the phone, Chief Rettenmeir gave him very detailed directions that would get him to the service station across the Santa Fe Tracks just beyond Klinefelter on Highway 95. He told the deputy the sheriff would have to stop at that service station to get exact directions to the turn off for the Old Mojave Road. That road would take him to Piute Creek. He also explained how far the deputy's boss would have to drive down that badly eroded dirt road after leaving the highway before arriving at Burke Henry's place. The chief added he hoped the sheriff had a pickup truck at his disposal because a passenger car was not going to get over that road.

After he hung up, he made a mental note to mention the call to Lieutenant Ron Nelson, commander of the Smoke Tree Substation of the San Bernardino County Sheriff's Department, the next time he saw him. Technically, Burke Henry was in Nelson's area of responsibility, not his, so a heads-up would be in order.

But one week later, he still had not bumped into the Lieutenant. And he never would. Because one week later, the world of Smoke Tree had turned upside down, and Ron Nelson was dead.

CHAPTER 13

August 15, 1959 The Mother Road

They began bickering not long after they crossed the New Mexico state line. Although Purvis Davis, Darryl Vogel and Gene Wexler were old friends and long-time members of the Lawton, Oklahoma klavern of the Ku Klux Klan, three beefy men in the confined cab of a 1956 Dodge pickup was one beefy man too many. They had left Caddo County before dawn, and being on the road for hours in cramped quarters was making all three of them irritable.

They had agreed they would drive all the way to Arizona before stopping for something to eat, but Darryl started bitching about being hungry before they were halfway across New Mexico. Purvis tried to hold out, but Darryl's whining was making him crazy. He pulled off in Gallup. Although it looked too pricey for their budget, the three went into the restaurant at the El Rancho Hotel for a late lunch. Darryl went heavy on the refried beans and fiery-hot salsa washed down with several beers.

They drove on beyond sunset and into the dark of night before stopping for another meal at a greasy spoon in Flagstaff. Back on the road, they drove for another hour before passing through the tiny town of Ash Fork. Purvis had made it clear before they started that he would be the sole driver of his prized pickup, so when he thought he could drive no farther, he turned off 66 onto a secondary road and stayed on it until he found a dirt road that angled off to the northeast. A few miles down the deserted two-track, he pulled off. He and Darryl and Gene spread their blankets on the ground. Although they had only one thin blanket apiece and the temperature was in the low 50s, they were so tired they drifted quickly off to sleep.

They awoke in a drenching rainstorm. They picked up their blankets and scrambled for the truck. After some general grousing and jockeying for position in the cramped cab, they were finally drifting off to sleep again when Darryl farted.

All three men were now wide awake.

"I told you to lay off those beans and salsa," said Gene.

Before Darryl finished apologizing, he let loose another one. It was a wet, syrupy monster that rushed out from deep in his bowels. It was of such magnitude and intensity it drove Purvis and Gene out of the truck into the pouring rain.

Darryl rolled down the window and said, "Sorry. Couldn't help it."

After huddling outside wrapped in their blankets until the cab aired out, Purvis and Gene climbed back inside.

Darryl farted again. It was worse than the one before.

"That's it," said Purvis, rolling down his window and starting the truck. They were soon back on 66, barreling down the highway with both windows down and the wing windows open.

Purvis now had a headache. The glare of oncoming lights was making it worse, but he was determined to drive until he couldn't drive anymore. They went through Seligman, Peach Springs, Valentine and Hackberry before beginning their descent into the Lower Colorado River Basin at Kingman. Although it was growing later with each passing mile, the temperature had been slowly rising since Seligman, and when they rolled through Yucca Flats, it began to rise much more sharply. That didn't seem right to three men from Oklahoma. It was supposed to get cooler as the night went on. Rolling down the windows didn't help: the terrible heat just blasted though the cab.

Bugs began to splatter on the windshield. Not a few bugs. Hundreds of bugs. Each one left a smear of yellow.

"What are them things?"

"Some kind of grasshopper, I think."

At the bottom of the grade, they were approaching the bridge that spanned the Colorado River at Topock. They had been on the road for over twenty hours.

Purvis saw a narrow blacktop road leading off to the north.

"Eyes feel like they's full a sand. I can't drive no further. There's so many squashed bugs on this windshield I can't hardly see. We'll cross into California in the morning."

He steered the truck off of 66 and onto the side road. On the west side of the road, the black waters of Topock Slough gleamed in the headlights. Purvis kept looking for a place to pull off the road, but the shoulders were very narrow. Finally, after a few miles, they reached the parking lot of a place called Catfisherman's Paradise. He pulled in. As he did, the headlights picked up a row of picnic tables under the aethel trees on the north side of the lot.

A little bait shop sat thirty yards from the road, but it was closed. There were no lights on anywhere. They decided the best place to sleep would be on the tables. They locked up the truck, leaving their blankets behind. Intense humidity had been added to the terrible heat. They were all exhausted, Purvis most of all, but he could not sleep. When he turned onto his side atop the redwood table, he felt like he was still driving. Felt like the table was in motion and the endless headlights of oncoming traffic were still flaring in his eyes across the two-lane blacktop.

He was finally starting to doze when he heard the first mosquito. Then he heard another. And another. Then one bit him on the arm. Cursing, he sat up and looked around, flapping his hands around his face to drive away the mosquitos and their irritating, high pitched whine.

He looked at Darryl and Gene atop the other

tables. They were both asleep, oblivious to the steadily increasing cloud of blood suckers. Purvis climbed down off the table. He heard some kind of fish flopping heavily in the black waters across the road. He walked to the truck and unlocked it. Climbing inside, he climbed in and rolled up the window to keep the mosquitos out. He struggled to get comfortable on the vinyl seat. The temperature in the cab was in the high 90s. He was soon drenched in sweat, but he was too tired to care. He was almost asleep again when he discovered that one of the mosquitos had come in the truck with him.

He held very still until it bit him on the neck. Then he slapped it, wiped the blood off his hand, and went to sleep.

CHAPTER 14

August 16, 1959 Topock Slough, Arizona

Purvis Davis woke up the next morning with his sweaty torso glued to the vinyl seat. The blazing July sun was superheating the cab and magnifying the stink of his rank body. He unstuck himself and moved to the picnic tables that were shaded by the ancient aethel tress. Darryl and Gene were still asleep. Both men had taken off their t-shirts the night before and were covered with mosquito bites.

He was about to rouse them when the screen door to the bait shop banged open. A red-faced man stormed across the lot toward him.

"Hey! Mister! You can't just pull in here and sleep on our tables. There's a fee for using this place. You owe me five dollars."

Purvis was not in the mood to be yelled at. He turned to face the man, who was now just steps away.

"Shut your face, Goddamnit."

The man stopped in his tracks. He stared at the ss death's head insignia and ss *Siegrune* tattooed across the bare, broad chest of the huge man in front of him. He lifted his eyes and looked into a pair of small, blue eyes that had neither pupils nor bottom.

His mouth was suddenly dry. He snapped it shut and turned and walked briskly back to the bait shop. The screen door banged again as it closed. He shut the interior door. Purvis saw the *open* sign in the window rotate to *closed.*

When he turned around, Darryl and Gene were on their feet, scratching vigorously.

"Let's get out of here," said Purvis as he moved to the truck.

"I'm going across the road to splash some of that water on these bites."

Purvis and Gene followed.

They reached the other side just as Darryl removed his boots and waded into the water. He promptly sank up to his calves in the black muck of rotted vegetation on the bottom of the slough. He tried to pull his legs out of the stinking mess and turn around at the same time.

It didn't go well. He fell heavily and was completely submerged for a moment. He rose cursing and spitting, the foul water clogging his nose and mouth.

Three quarters of an hour later, the three men were in a booth at the Bluebird Café in Smoke Tree having breakfast. They stunk of the slough and their own sweat. The booths on either side of them were empty: the regulars who usually sat in them each morning instead perched on stools at the counter. The stools that were the farthest from where the three huge men huddled.

The crude map Deputy Dave had made them was spread out on the table as, in low voices, they planned their day.

"We stay on 66 to the 95 cutoff. Across some railroad tracks, we come to an old service station. The man who owns the place can tell us how to find this Old Mojave Road to Fort Piute."

"Then what?" asked Gene.

"Find the road. Drive it a couple miles. See if it's as bad as this local cop told Scuttler. Come back and find a motel with a swimming pool. Cool off by the pool for a while. Get to bed real early. Be at the Sommers place with the light behind us at sunrise."

He looked around the café to see if anyone seemed to be listening to their conversation before he leaned forward and whispered to Gene and Darryl.

"We walk him out into the desert and hurt him bad for a real long time before we kill him. Cut him into eleven pieces with cleavers and game saws. Bury the parts eleven different places. No one will ever find him."

It was nearing noon when they pulled into the parking lot at the gas station. They got out and walked toward the screened-in porch attached to the old building. The Pepsi Cola thermometer under the overhang read one hundred and fourteen degrees. They climbed the steps that led to the office.

As Purvis pulled open the screen door, they could feel the damp breeze from a swamp cooler. They stepped inside. An old man wearing a green t-shirt and canvas pants cinched tight by a belt notched at the final hole stepped through an open door from a darkened room behind the counter. The long tongue of leftover leather dangling from the belt buckle swung as he moved. He was incredibly thin and had a head of thick, black hair. His face was mostly unlined. Only his arthritic hands, knotted and battered by decades of work, spoke to his true age.

There was a Santa Fe calendar tacked to the wall beside the door. It showed an eagle dancer against a desert backdrop. Discounting his age, the old man's face bore a remarkable resemblance to the face of the figure in the painting. He stopped next to the calendar and peered past the three men toward the service island outside, searching for a vehicle.

"Hep you gentlemen with something?"

"We're looking for the Old Mojave Road."

The man cocked his head and ran a hand through his hair before he spoke.

"Not many people come by lookin' for that one. But it's not hard to find. Just go north on 95 about nine miles and start looking for rock cairns on both sides of the highway.

If you don't mind me askin', why you lookin' for it?"

"We're big fans of western pioneer trails. Already been to the Santa Fe and the Chisolm. Want to travel the road them pioneers took across the Mojave. Want to see Fort Piute and the other old army outposts."

"Well sir, you've already missed the first one. Fort Mohave is on the Arizona side of the river. But if it's Fort Piute you're a-lookin' for, then turn west off the highway. Once you visited Fort Piute, the old road will take you on to Camp Rock Springs and then Government Holes. It goes on to Marl Springs and Soda Springs after that, but I'm afraid your journey will end before you get that far. No way you can make it all the way to the Marl Springs redoubt unless you have something with four-wheel drive, like a army jeep or a Willy's or something of that kind.

In fact, let me have a look at what you're driving, and I can tell you whether it'll get you as far as Fort Piute and Government Holes and then on to the Cima/Kelso Road."

He reached under the counter and retrieved a long-billed, green cap and clamped it firmly on his head. He and the three Klan members went out the door and down the rickety steps. As they moved across the parking lot, the old man in the lead, they made an unusual parade: three hefty, heavily-sweating, red-faced men and one ancient man who seemed completely unfazed by the scorching noonday sun.

Any of the large men would have made two of the one who halted short of the pickup.

"C-Series '56 Dodge, huh?"

"That's right," said Purvis.

"She got the power dome V-8 or the old L-head 6?"

"The V-8."

"Run good?"

"Got us here."

The old man looked at the license plate.

"Oklahoma, huh? That's a right fur piece."

Gene started to speak, but Purvis interrupted.

"No sir, Illinois. Chicago. Me and the boys had a car, but we blowed a head gasket coming into Oklahoma City. Should have stopped, but I thought I could nurse her into town. Engine seized right up. Had to leave the car. But we was determined to come out here. Bought this truck off a used car lot in OKC."

"Sorry to hear about your automobile, but maybe that's for the best. I can flat out guarantee you the car hasn't been made that could drive the road you boys want to take."

He walked around the truck.

"Got pretty good clearance around the front wheels. I think you can just about make her if you're real careful. Got extra oil in case a rock punches a hole in your oil pan?"

"Couple quarts."

"Okay. Teach you a old desert trick. If you get a leak, cut you a piece of a creosote bush and pound it into the crack. Slow the leak down enough your extra oil might get you on through.

Got a shovel?"

Got three of them, thought Purvis. Three spades to bury the man who lives down that road you're helping us find. But that's not what he said.

"Yessir."

"You'll need it. You'll be driving through lots of washes full of sand. If you get stuck, you'll have to dig yourself out. And here's another desert trick. If you dig and dig and still can't get her out, let about half the air out of the tires. Spreads the load, you see. Gets you some extra traction. I got a couple old boards out back I'd be glad to give you. Dig them in under all four tires. That and the low air pressure should do it.

Speaking of tires, got plenty of patches for them

tubes? Cholla cactus out there is sure to punch a hole or two in them."

"Got patches and a pump."

"How much water you got?"

"Couple canteens."

The man shook his head.

"Not enough if you get in trouble. Day like today, you get stuck or broke down out there without at least a gallon each, you'll die before you can walk out."

"What about radiator water?"

"Kill you to drink it if there's anti-freeze in it.

Get you a couple of them desert bags. Made of canvas. Fill 'em with water and hang 'em on the truck. Evaporation helps keep the water from getting too hot to drink.

Now listen, there are springs across the Mojave. Piute Creek next to the fort, Rock Springs and Government Holes. Make sure before you leave Piute you fill up your containers. At Rock Springs, I'd leave that water be. Cattle get in it and foul it. But Government Holes is good water. Fill up at the cement cistern there.

Like I said, you won't reach Marl Springs, but you

can take the Cima road to Kelso. That's the first paved road you'll come to after you turn off 95. At Kelso you can take Kelbaker road on to Baker. You can get gas and more water there and put the air back in your tires if you had to let some out."

"That's good advice."

"Here's some that's even better. Don't go out there. Come back in the winter. That way, if you get stuck you'll have a long walk, but you'll live to tell the tale."

Purvis took off his Caddo Grain and Feed cap and scratched his head.

"Old timer, I do believe you're right. Never seen heat like this before. Don't think I could walk a long ways in it, water or no water. Better not push our luck. We'll drive on up the highway and find the road.

After we have a look, we'll turn around and head on home. Maybe take a big detour and stop at Tombstone along the way. Always wanted to see that there O.K. Corral."

The three men moved to the truck. Darryl grabbed the passenger-side door and then yelped and pulled back his hand.

The old man smiled and pulled a shop rag out of

his back pocket and opened the door for him.

When the truck pulled onto 95 and turned to the north, Hugh Stanton stood watching until they were out of sight.

If them's city boys from Chicago, he thought, I'll eat my hat. I know a Oklahoma accent when I hear one. Got one myself. And if they was real fans of the old west, they would know pioneers didn't go down the Old Mojave Road. Mostly the Army and freighters and the U.S. mail on that road.

CHAPTER 15

August 16, 1959 Arrowhead Junction, California

"You think he bought it about us being from Chicago?"

"Hell, that old man is Chickasaw or Choctaw," said Purvis. "Must'a moved out here from Missouri or Arkansas. Just another ignorant savage don't know his ass from a hole in the ground. Course, he bought it."

A few miles down the road, a sign appeared showing it was ten miles to the town of Searchlight.

"Hey," said Darryl, "We're almost to another state. That Searchlight place is in Nevada."

Just beyond the mileage sign, they saw the rock cairns on both sides of the highway that marked the Old Mojave Road. Purvis turned off 95 and headed west.

It took a little shovel work to get across the first broad wash. After that the road seemed passable enough for a while. But then, it began to rise and meander in and out of more sandy washes that ran perpendicular to the road. The gullies were lined with scrub plants none of the men could identify, although Gene said he thought some of them looked like willows.

"Willows grow where there's water," said Purvis. "You see any water?"

Many times, when they entered one of these washes, the location of the road on the other side was unclear. When that happened, Purvis just aimed the Dodge toward the lowest part of the bank and gunned the engine and hoped for the best.

After five miles of increasingly slow going, he stopped the truck on a level spot. The three men got out and surveyed the terrain.

"Damndest place," said Purvis. "Looks flat from the highway, but it's all chopped up by these gullies. Sometimes you get one back wheel on hard pan and one in the sand. Been lucky so far the sand-side wheel ain't buried itself when we was hanging ass-catawampus coming out of a gully.

This is far enough. Don't want Sommers to know someone's on his road. We'll come back before daybreak. Drive right up on top of him while his worthless, lazy, blanket ass is still in bed. Tomorrow is the last sunrise that half-breed will ever see."

"Why would he live out here on this Godawful desert?" asked Darryl. "Place looks like somebody dropped a bomb on it."

"He's scared. Scared the Klan will find him and kill him for what he done to Harold. And, by God, the Klan has found him. He's about to reap the whirlwind!"

They climbed into the truck. Purvis made a three-point turn and headed back toward the highway.

Deep Desert Deception

CHAPTER 16

August 16, 1959 Piute Mountains

From his perch high in the hills, Burke watched the three men next to the green pickup through the Nikko 10x70 combat binoculars he had liberated from a Japanese officer in the South Pacific.

His visitors had arrived. They were big men, but running to fat. Although he couldn't make out the writing on the truck's license plate at this distance, it was white on a black background. The same as the plate on the Chevy that had pulled into the Whiting Brothers station a week ago.

So, unfortunately, he had been right to be alarmed after he had locked eyes with the driver. The same driver had just climbed out from behind the wheel of the pickup. He was probably one of the three men who had raped his sister. He wondered if the deputy who was the third rapist was one of the men in the truck. Burke could only hope he was that lucky.

After conferring for a few minutes, the men got into the truck and turned around and headed back toward 95. But they would certainly be back. Probably the following day. Probably before sunrise. That's the way he would do it.

CHAPTER 17

August 16, 1959 Searchlight, Nevada

They were almost back to 95 when Darryl brought up Searchlight again. He tried to be off-hand about it, but his companions could hear the eagerness in his voice.

"What do you say we drive on up to that Searchlight place? I bet they have a casino. I hear all these Nevada towns have casinos, not just Las Vegas."

"Don't have no money to gamble," said Purvis. "Got just enough for the trip. Shouldn't even stay in a motel tonight, but we got to get a good nights' sleep."

Darryl was quiet for a while as the Dodge crawled along the dirt road.

"Okay, I gotta admit something. I knew this place was close to Nevada. Brought some cash I've been squirreling away. If that town has a casino, I'll share the money. We can play a little blackjack or some of them slot machines. Have ourselves some fun and not eat into our travel money at all.

Always wanted to go to a casino. What about you, Gene?"

"Sounds okay to me. As long as you're flat-out sharing this money and not saying it's a loan of some kind."

"Free and clear, boys. Free and clear. Anything you win, you keep. Only thing I ask is, if you win big, you give me back my seed money. But if you lose, it's on me."

"What do you think, Purvis?" asked Gene.

Purvis stopped the truck and turned to stare at his companions.

"I don't like it. We come here to do a job. We need to get 'er done and clear out. That half breed crippled a white man. And not just any white man. A Citizen of the Lawton Klavern of the Ku Klux Klan."

"Yeah, but..."

"Yeah, but nothing! We're a Wrecking Crew."

"No, we're not," said Darryl. "If we was, there'd be at least five of us, or maybe even seven or eight. And sanctioned by the Grand Dragon of the Oklahoma Realm."

"There wasn't time. Harold was scared this guy might pull up stakes. I say we're a Crew, and Harold Nevins appointed me Nighthawk to lead it."

"He don't have no authority to do that," said Gene. "Far as I'm concerned, we're just Citizens, out here to help a fellow Citizen. It's not a Wrecked. It's not official. And you're not Nighthawk."

No one said anything for a while. In the stationary truck, the terrible heat of the desert roasted the three men in their own juices. Salty sweat poured off them.

Then, Darryl spoke again.

"Since there's no sanction, and there's no Wrecked, and we're not a Wrecking Crew, this is a democracy. I say we vote.

Those in favor of going to the casino, raise your hand."

He raised his hand. Gene raised his.

"Majority rules, Purvis. You don't think it does, maybe you can take care of that breed on your own."

Purvis was so angry he didn't trust himself to speak. He said nothing for a while. Just sat there, sweating, with his eyes closed.

Finally, he opened them.

"Fine," he said, bitter and tight-lipped. "I know when I'm whipped. We'll go see if there's a casino. But if there ain't, I'm drivin' back to Smoke Tree. Don't you two be thinkin' about goin' to no Las Vegas!"

They pulled into Searchlight and discovered there were actually three casinos in the tiny town. The best-looking one was the El Rey Club. That's where they went.

Their luck was surprisingly good. Purvis was playing blackjack and doing the best: doubling down on hands and hitting twenty-one on four and five cards. And the dealer kept busting. Since it wasn't Purvis's money, the more he won the bigger he bet. Before long, he was up over two hundred dollars.

Then that damned Darryl was beside him, jawing in his ear.

"Purvis!"

"Don't bother me."

"Purvis, they got whores here!"

"I said, 'don't bother me'."

"Real purty ones, Purvis. Work out of those motels across the street."

"Clear out of here!"

"Listen Purvis, we'll never get a better chance than this. Our wives will never know we got ourselves a little strange out here."

Purvis, who already had two cards up, signaled the dealer to hit him.

The dealer dropped a face card on him.

Busted!

The dealer took his money.

"Damnit Darryl, you're makin' it go away."

The dealer set out another hand. Purvis had two face cards. He was feeling good again.

"Come on, Purvis. Peel off some of them winnin's and let's go have some fun."

The dealer had a king and a six. He dealt himself another card. A five!

The dealer took his money again.

"Damnit, that's the first time I've lost two hands in a row since I sat down. Why'd you have to come creepin' over here?"

"C'mon, Purvis. Deck's cooling off. Let's go get our ashes hauled."

"You'd better hope it ain't, 'cause I'm gonna make you a deal. I go up another two hundred dollars, we'll get us some wimmin. Meantime, get your sorry ass away from me."

Darryl smiled.

"You're on. Your luck's going to run hot again, starting right now. We'll be across the road in no time."

And it did and they were.

Then, they all wanted to gamble some more. Especially Purvis. So, they went back to the casino and started playing. The cocktail waitresses kept bringing them free drinks. They hadn't known casinos served alcohol twenty-four hours a day.

By four o'clock in the morning, they were unbelievably drunk, flat broke, and back at the truck.

"Oh well," slurred Darryl, "we got laid, and our gambling money lasted a long time. That was something I'll never forget."

"Yeah," said Gene, "that was fun. Now we can get on with what we come out here to do."

"We got us a little problem, boys."

"What problem's that, Purvis?"

"Didn't just lose the money I won."

"Like I told you, the gambling money was my treat. You don't owe me nothin'."

"I don't know what come over me in there. Thought I couldn't lose. But I did. And not just the gambling money."

"Whoa down a minute," said Gene, suddenly more alert. "You sayin' what I think you're sayin'?"

Purvis couldn't look either of them in the eye.

"Yeah. The trip money, too. We don't even have enough for gas. And we damn sure don't have enough for no motel room."

The three men leaned against the truck in silence, Darryl and Gene absorbing that last bit of information. Then Purvis pushed off and walked away. He shoved his finger down his throat and vomited in the dust. Wiping his mouth with the back of his hand, he leaned forward and swayed from side to side before he forced himself to throw up again.

He turned away from the mess at his feet to face the others, saliva drooling from his mouth.

"Gotta get sober to drive."

He went back inside the El Rey and rinsed his

mouth at a bathroom sink. He splashed water on his face and stared bleary eyed at himself for a few minutes before shaking his head, patting his face dry, and going back to the parking lot.

"Don't fret it, Purvis," said Gene. "I bet that Apache's got money. And got guns and other stuff we can sell or trade for gas. We'll do the job and get ourselves home."

They got into the truck and drove into the desert night to find a place to sleep. The nearly-full, gibbous moon was approaching the western horizon. The stars that had not been obliterated by the pale luminosity of the moonlight were dying behind the distant mountains when they turned away from town onto a secondary road that led to a place called Nipton. They drove a few miles down that road before Purvis guided the truck onto a barely-discernable two-track snaking up the side of a hill.

At the crest, he turned off the engine. The eastern sky was glowing with the approach of dawn when the men climbed out and spread their blankets on the ground.

CHAPTER 18

August 17, 1959 Piute Creek

It was past noon when the Dodge truck appeared again, grinding slowly out of the rough terrain to the east. Although the sun was slightly behind him, Burke shielded the deeply inset lenses of his binoculars to be sure no reflection would warn the men in the vehicle they were being watched. All three were in the cab. He had expected to see two of them standing in the bed, elbows on the roof, glassing the area in front of them. But there was no one. They were all inside.

Sloppy. Or ignorant. Or both.

Before he crawled away from the crest of the hill, he noticed the flanking edge of a massive, snow-white pile of cumulonimbus clouds to the east was in motion. Giant scoops of vanilla ice cream. Monsoon weather, up from the gulf, forming and dissolving and re-forming and fanning out above the far-distant Kaibab and closer Colorado Plateau. Such clouds often appeared on the eastern horizon in August, but they usually evaporated before they could bring rainfall to the Mojave. Even when they did stay together, they usually produced only virga: ephemeral precipitation that tantalized and then disappointed the parched desert by evaporating before it reached the ground.

And yet, these seemed different. Faster-moving than usual. Billowing ever higher, darker now on the bottom. Vanilla ice cream in chocolate sauce.

Once he was well below the crest, he stood and climbed down the hillside and into Piute Gorge. He moved out, canteen and binoculars slung over one shoulder, his scoped .308 Remington over the other. As he traversed down into the steep gorge, he thought about how easy it would have been to take out all three men as they drove in. But he was going to have to dispose of the truck after he eliminated its passengers. A windshield riddled with bullet holes and seats covered with blood would lead to questions, no matter where he dumped the vehicle.

As he moved, he thought about the clouds again.

Ominous. Perhaps even dense enough not to disintegrate now that they were over the Black Mountains. Perhaps thick and heavy enough to spread out over the desert floor and produce heavy rain. Although he had seen such storms form and break apart many times before, he remembered the sudden storm produced ten days previously by clouds similar in appearance to the ones he had been watching. A storm that had dropped three quarters of an inch on the Piutes. A flash flood, the likes of which he had never seen before, had spewed from the mouth of the canyon.

It wouldn't do to be caught up inside the gorge if those clouds held together long enough to bring a rainfall as heavy as the one of August seventh. Especially not in the section where the sheer rock walls of the canyon narrowed. He wondered if the men in the green Dodge knew that. He doubted they had any idea such a thing could occur out on the desert in the middle of summer.

He picked up his pace.

When he was in position south of the mouth of the gorge, he could see Pepper in the corral on the far side of the creek. The horse's ears went up and he began to pace the perimeter of the enclosure. He had probably picked up the sound of the approaching truck.

Then Burke heard it, too. A few minutes later, it came into view, moving as fast as the rutted road would allow. No attempt at stealth. Two of the men were now standing in the bed, elbows propped on the top of the cab, outstretched hands pointing pistols, ready to shoot if Burke came out.

Give them a tenth of a point for some kind of readiness.

The truck slid to a stop behind his flatbed. The driver jumped out and assumed a shooting stance behind the door.

"Hello in the house!"

Pepper nickered in his corral.

"Mr. Henry? We've come to see you about getting some horses shod."

The world had gone still. No birds called. Even the cicadas in the mesquites had ceased their sibilant shrieks. The wind, which had been quartering from the northeast, suddenly stopped. There was a dense, ominous feel to the air, and the quality of the light had changed.

The two men in the back of the truck climbed over the tailgate and stepped off the bumper onto the ground. Through the binoculars, Burke could have counted the hairs in the rough stubble on their faces. The close-up view explained why they were so late in coming. They were hungover. It made him smile. It meant they were not only careless but more than a little stupid. It also meant they were not well-rested. They were irritable. Dehydrated. Primed for making mistakes.

The two joined the man behind the open door of the truck. There was apparently some kind of a conference. Burke didn't know exactly what they were discussing, but it didn't matter. He was pretty sure about what was going to happen next.

They stepped to the front of the truck. The two who had been in the bed walked to the rear of his house. They eased cautiously onto the back porch, their pistols extended, and positioned themselves on either side of the door.

The driver headed toward the front. Soon, Burke could no longer see him. Then, he heard the man's voice again.

"Mr. Henry? We've got some work for you. Big job."

After a few minutes, he heard the man yell, "Go!"

The one on the left stepped quickly in front of the door. Raising his right leg, he slammed his boot into a spot just below the doorknob. The frame splintered. The door flew open and banged against the wall inside the house. Burke heard a second loud crash as the driver apparently kicked in the door at the front of the house.

Stupid is as stupid does, thought Burke. Both those doors were unlocked.

The three men stayed in the house for a long time, but Burke could hear no loud noises. He thought they were probably looking for anything of value that might be inside. Money, if there was any. Anything they could sell, if there was no money to be found.

By now, the clouds he had seen earlier in the east were directly to the north. They were darker and lower. He saw several flashes of lightning, arcing like jagged, crooked legs that were trying to walk the clouds toward the gorge. Volleys of thunder rolled down the canyon. The smell of ozone filled the air. The temperature dropped. The wind picked up again and rapidly increased in velocity.

Just stay in there a little longer, boys, thought Burke. Make yourselves to home. Look around all you want. Steal everything you can carry.

When the three came out the back door, they seemed uncertain about what to do next. Magnified by the binoculars, they looked like they were standing right in front of Burke. All were blue eyed. Snuff or chewing tobacco had left brown stains on the blonde beard of the one who had been driving. He cupped his hands around his mouth and shouted again. His teeth were stained the same color.

"Mr. Henry! Burke Henry!"

There was another peal of thunder.

Burke turned his binoculars to the north. Dense sheets of rain were pouring from the black clouds that were now above the Piutes. He put the binoculars, his canteen and his rifle on the ground at the base of the rock where he had taken cover. He stood up so he could be seen.

"Who is that over there?" he boomed in his deep voice.

All three men looked toward the sound.

"We need some work done on some horses. A lot of work. Lots of horses."

"I don't see any horses."

"They're over by Kingman. We came to talk about prices."

"Sorry, got all the work I can handle right now."

Burke dropped behind the rock and scrambled away to the northwest, staying under cover.

"Come on over here so we can talk about it. When we tell you how much we're willin' to pay, I bet you'll want the work."

Burke moved into view again.

"I see you've busted my back door. I want you the hell off my property."

There was no immediate response.

Burke dropped into cover and moved again. When he showed himself after a few minutes, all three men raised their pistols and began to fire. He saw smoke and heard bullets hitting the ground and ricocheting off rocks before he heard the reports. The fact that all the rounds had fallen short gave him confidence. These men were apparently not adept at compensating for distance. The chances of one of these clowns hitting him with a pistol at this distance were somewhere between slim and none. It was a chance he was willing to take to put his plan in motion.

He crouched down to present a smaller target but did not immediately seek cover again.

"What the hell is wrong with you people?"

He tried to sound panicked before turning and running toward the mouth of the canyon. The men continued to shoot.

After a long, zigzagging sprint, he ducked down and looked back. The men had been reloading their pistols and were just beginning to move into the wash. The delay meant they did not have speed loaders or extra magazines, which could prove to be important. Because he did not yet know whether he might be forced to shoot them before the day was done, the fact they were undisciplined enough to empty their guns at the same time was of even greater significance.

He watched as they started toward him. They were not making good time in the rock and brush strewn bottom of the wash. These were men who weren't used to running. Beer-guzzling, good old boys whose idea of exercise was leaning forward in their chairs to spit gobs of tobacco juice as they sat on a porch and talked about how superior they were to the non-white people of the world.

He let them get much closer before he ran again, determined to lure them ever onward. As soon as he was visible, they began shooting again. The sound rolled through the wash, but not as loud as the peals of thunder coming down. Burke knew they had an even slimmer chance of hitting him now that they were breathing hard.

He moved farther into the gorge. The rocks were bigger and more difficult to navigate. That suited his purposes. He was more interested in the storm to the north of him than he was in the struggling, out of shape men behind him.

As he came closer to Piute Spring, the rain began to fall. There was no gradual transition. No sprinkles. No spattering. One minute it was not raining. The next it was. Rain in sheets. Rain by the bucket.

Burke turned to face his pursuers again, water streaming down his face. He wanted to make sure they didn't lose sight of him as the sky opened up. If the rain was giving them pause, they didn't show it. They were too busy trying to breathe. One, and then another, would stop and bend at the waist to suck in big gulps of air.

He made sure he was visible before he set off again. As he moved, he feigned a limp.

"He's hurt," yelled one of the men.

"We hit him," screamed another in atavistic delight.

"Get closer before we shoot again."

Burke came to the heavy stand of willows that marked the location of Piute spring, the water source for Piute Creek. He moved quickly through the lucent cottonwoods and willows and the arrowweed and chuparosa. He avoided the honey mesquite and catclaw acacia. He was sure the men behind him lacked experience with catclaw. They would soon discover why locals called it "wait-a-minute bush".

Inside the dense, clogged thicket, the understory filled with California bulrush, narrow-leaf willow and mule fat, he was no longer visible to the would-be killers. The rain was now slamming down so hard it continued to soak him even through the dense foliage. His olive drab t-shirt was plastered to his torso. A covey of Gamble's quail exploded from the brush.

A call came from behind him.

"Hurry. Don't let him get away."

As Burke came out of the willows and the canyon began to turn ever more westward, he broke into a sprint. Two hundred yards and two more bends of the canyon brought him closer to the place where he intended to climb out. He slowed to a steady run. This far inside the gorge, the walls were solid rock. He slowed just beyond the huge ball of rocks that had washed onto the canyon floor from the cliffs above in times long past.

He arrived at the forty-foot rock face where he intended to climb out to the south. The face required carefully selected hand holds. As he began his ascent, the increasingly heavy rain sent streams of water cascading down the rocks into his face, making the climb even more of a challenge. As he clung to the rock and climbed higher, he knew if he slipped he would be seriously injured. To fall in the face of what he now knew was coming would be an even greater disaster. To fail to get high enough quickly enough would be just as bad.

Burke was sure there was no way the out of shape and overweight men pursuing him could ever climb out of the canyon once they reached the spring and moved beyond it. They were already trapped. They just didn't know it yet.

The muscles in his arms and shoulders were trembling with effort by the time he reached the top of the vertical face. A volcanic-rock-covered hillside titled away in front of him at a less-challenging angle, leading southwesterly out of the gorge and to the hills far above. His ascent changed from a technical climb to a difficult and demanding scramble.

He was still working his way up the rugged slope when he heard it. A roaring sound, like a steam locomotive careening down a straight stretch of track under full power. A train in a place where there had never been tracks nor trains. The steep hillside trembled beneath him. He could hear the stony clatter of rolling boulders clashing together farther up the gorge. He climbed faster. The rumbling noise grew louder. When he turned to look, the flood emerged from around a bend west of his position like the obscene, probing tongue of a giant, hungry beast.

It not only did not sound like water. The thing that came roaring into view below him didn't even look like water. A dense, red and gray, dirty froth with brush on top. Rocks and mud and spewing liquid. More like a nightmarish kind of pudding than a flood. Thick and viscous and murderous and alive. Intent on consuming everything in its path. It reminded him of the thing in the silly "Blob" movie.

As the flood rushed through the narrow canyon below and rose above the rock face he had just climbed, it began to rip and ravage the bottom of the hill he was on, tearing out huge chunks of soil and rock. Had he still been on the face, or even lower down the hill, he would have been swept away.

The flow behind the crest was heavy. Implacable and undiminished, it completely filled the bottom of the canyon from rock face to rock face.

If any of the men had cried out, Burke could not have heard the sound above the roar of the flood. He estimated that when the beast descended upon them, they were a little over a hundred yards above the spring. But whether they shouted or simply turned and ran, spurred on now more by self-preservation than they had earlier been spurred on by hatred, was of no consequence. Either way, they were swept to their deaths. Killed by a flood in one of the driest months in one of the driest places in all of North

America.

There would be no survivors. No bullet-riddled bodies to bury. Perhaps no bodies to be found at all.

Burke turned back to his climb, picking his way up the steep hillside in the face of torrents of water coursing toward him. Pelted by heavy rain, he struggled with the difficult footing as he moved carefully upward through the desert garden of Mojave Yucca, bayonet yucca, buckhorn, staghorn and pencil cholla, reddish barrel cactus and blackbush and creosote scattered throughout the volcanic rock.

Burke finished his climb out of the gorge near the OX Cattle Company Corral, well to the south of where he had begun. He then turned north on the plateau. It was still raining hard throughout the Piute Range, but the bulk of the storm was moving over the broad Lanfair Valley, the huge clouds like giant black crabs hulking across the landscape on wicked-looking, flashing and stabbing legs.

A flood even heavier than the one he had just left behind in the gorge was already coursing through Sacramento Wash to his west. The fifty-yard-wide wash was the conduit for all the rainfall now lashing

Lanfair Valley, from Carruthers Canyon in the New York Mountains southward toward Hackberry Mountain and Von Trigger Wash. That massive outpouring would eventually hit the Santa Fe line just west of Homer. When it did, it would cut the main east-west line, destroying the low bridge that spanned the wash and washing away big chunks of the embankment on either side of the span. A crew from Smoke Tree would have to come out and build a shoofly before any trains could move through the area.

After it took out the bridge, the flood would destroy part of Old 66 before turning southeast to join the flood already rampaging down Piute Wash and into which the floodwaters from Piute Gorge and Piute Creek were emptying. There would be a confluence of all those furious waters just north of Klinefelter. Burke was sure the double deluge from the two major drainages would cut Highway 95 and then destroy another section of the Santa Fe line before taking out new Highway 66 and more Santa Fe railroad tracks northeast of Smoke Tree.

Travelers were going to be stranded all across the Mojave.

Burke traveled north along the eastern flank of

the Piutes before crossing the range just north of Piute Gorge and turning south again toward Fort Piute. By the time he made it back to his property, it was late afternoon. The rain was no longer falling. All that remained was the perfume of wet sage and damp creosote. The water that had not sluiced off the hardpan was already being sucked into the air so rapidly that the steaming, ephemeral moisture rising into the sky looked like a London mist. But a mist that rose only a few feet off the ground before it evaporated entirely, creating a temporary, ground level humidity so dense it reminded him of the jungles of the Philippines and Viet Nam.

There was nothing either cool or refreshing about the aftermath of the rainfall.

He walked past the Dodge pickup. The driver-side door was still ajar. The interior was soaked. Before going into his house, he walked to the corral to calm his agitated horse. Pepper was circling the enclosure, rolling his eyes in alarm at the heavy rumble of the water rushing hard down the creek bed. And although a temporary river was rolling past not many yards from where Pepper ran, his hooves were already kicking up puffs of dust from the ground upon which heavy rain had fallen just a short time before.

Burke went into his tack room. It showed no damage from the rainfall. He took a large scoop of oats and used it to coax Pepper under the cover of the roof he had built over the southwest corner of the corral to shelter the animal from the terrible summer sun.

As Pepper ate his oats, he began to settle. When he seemed calm, Burke walked to the edge of what a few hours before had been the trickle of Piute Creek. He watched as tons of mud, rocks and shrubs rumbled past. A big willow twisted and turned in the current. Snakes, lizards, woodrats and ground squirrels shared the sanctuary of its trunk and branches. A jackrabbit swimming in the flow was overtaken by the root ball of a big tree and disappeared under the water. Burke watched for a long time, but the rabbit did not reappear.

A portion of his five acres was gone: washed away. The bank he had often stood on to look at the creek was now downstream somewhere, headed for the far-distant Colorado River and eventually the Sea of Cortez. On the other side of the creek, several giant cottonwoods were gone: trees that had stood for decades, suddenly undercut, uprooted and carried off on the flood.

While the water had run hard after the rain of August seventh, it had been nothing like this.

Burke walked up to the house and entered through the ruined front door. He could smell the stink of the men who had been inside. His possessions were strewn about the floor in every room. His books had been yanked from their crude shelves. The door of his little propane refrigerator was open. The interlopers had helped themselves to his supply of Nehi Grape. One of them had even made a cheese and salami sandwich, leaving the meat, cheese, mayonnaise and whole wheat bread on the counter. In the intense heat inside the house, the exposed slices of bread had already begun to turn into something resembling toast.

The single shot .22 he used to hunt rabbits had been removed from its rack and thrown across the room. If the men had taken it with them, it might have altered events. Leaving the rifle was not their only mistake. They had also failed to fill his spare canteen with water and take it along. It still hung by its strap from the coat rack on the wall. Since his other canteen was still on the far side of the raging torrent, Burke pulled the spare off the peg and filled it from the tap in the sink before going outside to look for the bodies of the men he was sure had drowned.

He walked east along the bank of what was now Piute River all the way to where it emptied into Piute Wash. He found no trace of the three men who had come from so far away to kill him. As he retraced his steps toward home, he stopped every ten feet or so to look again for any signs. There were none. No bodies. No clothing. No shoes. He didn't think the corpses would ever be found. Even if they were, it wouldn't matter. He remembered instances in Oklahoma where floodwaters had stripped bodies of their clothing. No clothing meant no identification. The three members of the Ku Klux Klan were now just anonymous casualties of the whims of the weather on the vast, unforgiving and often hostile Mojave.

When he got back to his property, the sun was on the horizon above Piute Hill. The storm had moved well to the west, creating a sunset the likes of which he had never seen. It sprawled across the western sky like spilled mercurochrome laced with molten silver and flecked with shimmering gold dust. Radiating shafts of purple light, spread like the open fingers of God's hand, shot through the other dazzling colors.

Bats and nighthawks flitted above him in the

dying light of day, feasting on clouds of gnats that had already hatched in the waters of the departed storm. Before the last vestiges of the miraculous sunset had completely faded, the full moon rose behind him, replacing the opalescent oranges, reds and purples of the diminishing spectacle with a milky, luminous and mysteriously pearlescent glow.

He decided to see how badly the Old Mojave Road had been damaged. A demanding and unforgiving road at the best of times, Burke was sure the storm had not improved it. In the tack room, he got a desert bag and went to the house and filled it. He also refilled his canteen. Back at the corral, he retrieved a sawbuck packsaddle, a rope halter, a lead rope, and a small bucket. He saddled Pepper and hung the desert bag, his canteen and the bail of the small bucket from the crossbars. Attaching the halter and lead rope to Pepper, he opened the corral. Leading his horse through the perfume of sage and creosote in the soft, purple, moonlit twilight, he set out at a run past the green pickup and onto the Old Mojave Road. Although the sun had set, the August heat was still intense, and he stopped frequently to drink from his canteen and fill the bucket with water for Pepper.

The first four miles of the road leading eastward

toward Highway 95, always the worst part of the road, had been further damaged by the rainstorm. As bad as the road was, he saw nothing in those four-miles he could not get the truck across with some boards and a shovel, given sufficient time. The last five miles of the road to the highway would be in better shape, except for where it crossed Piute Wash.

He turned and headed home beneath the rising moon.

As he ran, Pepper close behind him, Burke felt a surge of satisfaction. He had vanquished his would-be killers without firing a shot. Should their bodies ever be found, there would be no evidence of his complicity in their deaths. He slowed and then halted as the next thought crept into his head. Pepper, surprised by the sudden stop, nuzzled Burke between the shoulder blades with his velvety nose as they stood on the now-dusty road under the full moon. Would others now come to attempt the mission the three dead men had been unable to accomplish? He had no way of knowing, but if they did, he would be ready.

He began to run again, thinking now about obliterating any evidence that the three Klansmen had ever been at Piute Creek.

The full moon was far above the eastern horizon, and the flow in the creek had subsided by the time Burke wrapped his gloved hands around the steering wheel of the Dodge pickup. His motorcycle, tightly secured by stout ropes at four points, was on its kickstand in the bed. It would not fall, no matter how rough the ride to come. Four two by sixes left over from building the joists for his roof were next to the motorcycle. Cranking the ignition, he turned the truck around and headed for Highway 95.

Behind the bench seat of the truck, he had found three spades, two meat cleavers and a game saw.

Optimistic about their chances, those boys, he thought.

It took him over three hours and a lot of digging and putting boards beneath the wheels of the truck to get to highway 95. Getting across Piute Wash was much more difficult than he had anticipated. When he turned north, he had a completely deserted highway all to himself.

At the bottom of the deepest dip south of Searchlight, the road was closed on the Nevada side. There was no longer water running in the wash, and there was no barrier on the California side. That meant 95 was cut where it crossed Piute Wash at Klinefelter, and no highway patrol or department of transportation vehicles had been able to come this far north. There were two barriers on the Nevada side, but there were no State of Nevada law enforcement vehicles present on the other side of the barriers.

Typical of the Clarke County Sheriff's Department, thought Burke. Not much interested in anything that happened outside of the tight little world of Las Vegas, Henderson and Boulder City. Still, on this night he was pleased about their indifference. It meant he could get across without any interference.

Burke climbed out of the truck and surveyed the situation by the light of the moon almost directly overhead. The broad wash was filled with mud and debris. Chunks of asphalt that had once been the highway were visible in the mud on the east side of the wash. They looked like chunks of chocolate bar discarded by a childish giant. He went back to the truck and got the two by sixes and one of the spades and began the laborious process of getting the truck through the washout.

It took half an hour to get the truck across the no-longer-existent section of Highway 95. It was mostly a matter of putting the boards on top of the mud and moving seven feet at a time until he finally reached the pavement on the far side. Once there, he moved the barriers out of his way. He drove forward a few yards and returned to replace them before driving on

It was nearly midnight. He turned on the truck radio and fiddled with the dial until he picked up the fifty-thousand-watt signal from KFI in Los Angeles. He turned down the volume as he waited for the midnight news.

It came on as he was passing through Searchlight. The lead story concerned a tiny desert community on the banks of the Colorado River that had been isolated from the outside world by a massive flash flood, described by the breathless announcer as a twenty-foot wall of water. Highway 66, Highway 95, and the Santa Fe Railway line on both sides of the Colorado River had been cut in a number of places. Hundreds of motorists were stranded between the cut sections of the two highways and would remain stranded for up to twelve hours until detours could be created around the washed-out bridges and sections of highway.

247

Hundreds of other tourists were stranded in the town itself, which lacked enough motel rooms to house them all. The Smoke Tree Traveler's Aid Society had opened the high school gymnasium and citizens were arriving with prepared food as well as blankets to spread on the gym floor for the motorists.

Lieutenant Ronald Nelson, commander of the Smoke Tree Substation of the San Bernardino County Sheriff's Department, had suffered a brain aneurysm while arguing with a motorist who was determined to cross a flooded section of Highway 66 just north of the city limit. After the Lieutenant collapsed, the motorist with whom he had been arguing attempted to cross the flooded section. His car had been swept away, but the motorist was rescued by members of the volunteer fire department. Burke thought he detected a note of regret in the announcer's voice when he read the part about the rescue.

Fifteen miles north of the town, in a broad wash, the Santa Fe Railroad tracks had been damaged by a smaller flash flood earlier in the day. A track crew dispatched to assess the problem and plan for repairs had been caught in a second, much larger flood, which arrived without warning after over an inch and a half of rain fell in less than an hour in the distant desert mountains. The track foreman and one other man had been found and taken to the local hospital, but four other workers were missing and presumed drowned in the swirling waters. The search for their bodies would resume at dawn.

Burke was thinking about the kind of a night his friend Carlos Caballo must be having when the announcer stopped in mid-sentence. The open microphone picked up the crinkle of paper.

"This just in. United Press International reports a huge earthquake struck near Yellowstone National Park in Madison County, Montana fifteen minutes ago. A number of people who were camped near the park are missing. It has been reported, but not yet confirmed, that a family of seven was buried under a huge mudslide.

Stay tuned to KFI, 640, your source for news. We will bring you more details as soon as they are available."

And so, thought Burke, a new story replaces the Smoke Tree story. And the world moves on. A light-hearted show tune, came from the speaker.

Burke turned off the radio and continued north. He drove very slowly because he was unsure of the condition of the road, but there were no more washouts between the town and the Boulder Highway. He picked up speed after Railroad Junction and was in Las Vegas by two in the morning.

Sin City was open for business. It would take more than some floods to shut that place down. He drove out to the Dunes at the southernmost tip of the strip. He parked the truck in an empty corner of the parking lot and quickly unloaded his motorcycle. The lot was dry and it did not smell like rain had fallen. When he was done, he coiled and stowed the tie-down ropes in his panniers and lugged the two by sixes to the bordering oleander bushes and tossed them over.

Back at the truck, he was about to unscrew the license plates when he saw headlights coming his way. He had no idea whether it was a gambler or casino security, but he knew it would be best not to be associated with the truck in any way.

He tossed the screwdriver into his saddlebags and kicked the Royal Enfield to life. A short time later, he was in line at the Silver Slipper for the fifty-cent breakfast buffet.

By four thirty in the morning, he was southbound on 95. Faint traces of the purple twilight that presaged the rising of the sun were showing in the east. His motorcycle made short work of the washed-out section south of Searchlight. When he turned left off 95 and began to navigate the Old Mojave Road, the impending sunrise was brightening the horizon behind him. Traveling the damaged road was much easier than it had been in the pickup, but it was still a long, slow trip.

By the time he reached home, the molten sun was well up in a sky that was cloudless from horizon to horizon. He went into the house and got some carrots out of the refrigerator before walking to Pepper's corral. He stood their feeding the carrots to Pepper and enjoying the crunching sounds from his horse as he reviewed the events of the previous fifteen hours.

It had been a busy time.

He walked to the house and climbed into his own bed for the first time since he had seen the burly man from Oklahoma at the Whiting Brothers station in Smoke Tree.

Deep Desert Deception

CHAPTER 19

August, 1959 San Bernardino, California

Lieutenant Ron Nelson had been a veteran of World War Two. As his wife, Carolyn, wished, he was buried with full military honors at Mountain View Cemetery in San Bernardino, the town where he had been born and raised and met and married Carolyn. The local American Legion Post provided the honor guard.

Horse and several other deputies from Smoke Tree were there, as were many other deputies who had worked with Ron Nelson during his career. The Sheriff and Undersheriff of San Bernardino County sat in the front row, flanking Mrs. Nelson, her son, Daniel and her daughter, Tanya.

Horse stood at the rear of the gathering. He thought he was going to be all right, but then came the rifle salute and the playing of "Taps". As the notes poured over the cemetery, competing with sounds of traffic from nearby Waterman Avenue, tears came unbidden as he recalled comrades who had never returned home from Korea.

Few noticed the tears streaming down his face. Those who did thought they were for Ron Nelson, but Horse had never felt much connection with the man. He was Horse's boss: nothing more. He and Esperanza had never been invited to the Lieutenant's house. The Lieutenant and his wife had twice been invited to the Caballo's home, but they had begged off both times, claiming unspecified, last-minute emergencies.

To Lieutenant Nelson, Horse had been an annoyance. He knew the man had opposed his promotion to sergeant, arguing that Horse had not had enough time in uniform to deserve such advancement. But Horse believed there had been more to it than that. He suspected the Lieutenant didn't think a Mexican should be promoted into a position where he supervised other officers. In fact, Horse thought, the Lieutenant probably didn't think Horse should have been hired in the first place.

When the services ended, the Undersheriff told Horse to stop by headquarters before he returned to Smoke Tree. Horse assumed he was going to be introduced to Lieutenant Nelson's replacement and tasked with orienting the new man. After all, there were special difficulties involved in commanding the most remote substation in the department.

He was wrong.

Horse walked into headquarters as the youngest sergeant in the department. He walked out as the youngest lieutenant and the new commander of the Smoke Tree Substation.

His first act as commander was to drive to the nearest pay phone and call Esperanza with the news.

Deep Desert Deception

CHAPTER 20

August, 1959 Smoke Tree, California

The day after Carlos Caballo was promoted to Lieutenant, Oscar Rettenmeir had another call from Deputy Dave Scuttler of the Caddo County Sheriff's Department in Anadarko, Oklahoma.

"Good morning, Deputy."

"Good morning, Chief. I've got a couple of questions if you have a minute."

"Go ahead."

"We're missing a citizen who was out your way on the sixteenth or seventeenth."

"We're missing a few ourselves. Had a big flood out here that day."

"Yeah, heard about that."

"You think this person you're missing might've got

caught up in it?"

"Not exactly. Look, Chief, this is kind of hard to explain. The man was headed to Smoke Tree, but his truck was found in a casino parking lot in Las Vegas."

"Then you should be talking to either the Clark County Sheriff's Department or the Las Vegas police, not me."

"It was the Las Vegas police department that called here about the truck."

"Why call me, then?"

"Because there was no sign of the owner of the truck."

"I still don't see what that has to do with us in Smoke Tree."

"You remember our conversation the last time I called?"

"Yes. You said your Sheriff was going to pay Burke Henry a visit and ask him some questions about an old case."

"That's right. Except the Sheriff didn't make the trip. The man who is missing was going to talk to Mr. Henry."

"He worked for your department?"

Deep Desert Deception

"Not really."

"You're losing me here, Deputy."

"The man's name is Purvis Davis. He was on his way to L.A. Since he was going to be out your way, I asked him to stop by and visit this Burke Henry as a favor to the department."

Chief Rettenmeir was silent for a moment before speaking again.

"You're telling me you sent a civilian, a man with no official connection to your department, to interview a man who might be a material witness in a felony attempted- murder case?"

"I know, it sounds a little unusual."

"Unusual? Unusual is not the right word. The right word is 'stupid'."

The Deputy's voice suddenly lost its folksy, easy-going timbre.

"Climb down off your high horse, Chief. I represent a law enforcement agency that's asking another law enforcement agency for a little cooperation."

"I think there's something else going on here."

"What are you saying?"

"I don't know what you're up to, but what you did was very unprofessional. I don't intend to get pulled into it. The hole you've been fishing in with these calls has just dried up."

"I see."

"One more thing, and I should have told you this the first time you called. The place where Mr. Henry lives is miles and miles beyond the city limits of Smoke Tree. That's really not my bailiwick out there. In fact, I'm not sure whether that place is in California or Nevada. The state line cuts through somewhere out there. So, it's either the responsibility of the San Bernardino County Sheriff's Department or the Clark County, Nevada, Sheriff's Department."

"And if it's in California, who's in charge at the Sheriff's Department out your way?"

"The substation commander had a brain aneurysm and died during the flood emergency. A new fella, Lieutenant Carlos Caballo, just took over. He's very busy right now, with the new job and all the damage from the flood. I wouldn't be bothering him anytime soon if I was you."

"Caballo, huh?" Deputy Dave's pronunciation came out as 'Cah-bow-yo.'

"What kind of name is that?"

"It's a Mexican name."

It was Deputy Dave's turn to be silent.

"You mean to tell me y'all got yourselves a Mexican runnin' a law enforcement office?"

"We do."

"Lordy, if that don't beat all! And you've got the nerve to tell me *we're* unprofessional? I heard things was screwy in California, but I never believed they were this bad.

A Mexican, huh? All his deputies Mexican too?"

"Of course not."

"A Mexican is in charge of white deputies?"

"Deputy Scuttler, this call is over. Don't call here again. And if you're ever in Smoke Tree, don't drop by to say hello."

"Now just one damn minute..."

But Chief Rettenmeir had hung up.

Deep Desert Deception

CHAPTER 21

August 1959 Anadarko, Oklahoma

Deputy Dave Scuttler parked his cruiser in front of Nevins' Automotive in the middle of a very hot day. A dust devil was swirling trash in a vacant lot on the other side of the street, funneling the debris high into a cloudless sky. He got out and walked toward the garage door, carrying a paper bag stained with grease.

His chiseled face was edged with squint and frown lines. The squint lines were the result of never wearing sunglasses beneath the fierce, Oklahoma summer sun. The frown lines were of his own making; the result of a bitter, vindictive attitude and a vituperative, hostile personality. Even though his skin was sun-damaged, it stretched tightly over his jaw and cheekbones. His short sleeved uniform shirt displayed biceps and forearms corded with sinew and well-defined muscle. His stomach was flat, his shoulders broad. His waist was the same size it had been in high school.

He did not look or move like a man of fifty who had spent his adult life as a bachelor, never cooked at home, and ate the kind of food inside the greasy bag three times a day.

Genetics had been kind to Deputy Dave.

When he walked into the garage, Harold Nivens was re-assembling a carburetor at a modified bench set low to allow him to work from his wheelchair. The sharp odor of parts cleaner filled the air. A cheap radio on the bench was quoting hog belly and grain futures.

"Hello, Dave," Nevins said, without turning around.

"How'd you know it was me?"

"Hydraulic lifter sticking. Been sticking for two months now."

"I'll bring it by. You can fix it."

"Add a pint of Marvel Mystery Oil. Should do it."

"You add it for me. Write up a repair bill for a tear down job. I'll get the County to pay for it. Consider it an act of kindness from a fellow Citizen."

Harold wiped his hands on a shop rag and clicked off the radio. He pivoted his chair and pointed at the bag Dave was holding.

"Bertha's Breakfast &Lunch Box?"

"Today's special. Fried pork chops, mashed potatoes with meat gravy, butter beans and French fries."

"I have to wash up. Roll down that garage door and meet me in the office. Get a couple Cokes out of the refrigerator."

The two men ate lunch silently. When they finished, Dave gathered the remains of the meal and carried them out to an overflowing trash can.

When he came back inside, Harold was alternating toothpick work with sips of Coke.

"Got more news about Purvis and the others?"

"Not Purvis and the others. Just Purvis. And the news is there's no news."

"You didn't tell the police about the two other men?"

"Think it through, Harold. The Las Vegas police run the plate on the truck. They call our office because it turns up the name of a man who's from Caddo County. You with me so far?"

"Yeah."

"If I pop up with, 'what about the two guys who

were with him,' what's their first question going to be? It's going to be, 'How do you know there were two other men with him?' And then, 'Do you know why they were out here?' Followed by, 'What's your connection to these men?'

Come on, Harold, use your goddamned head!"

"Okay, okay. Don't have to go on and on. Nothin' new about Purvis?"

"Harold, Purvis and the others are dead. Nothing else makes sense. And there's more. They're asking me if I knew why the owner of the truck had three shovels, three meat cleavers, and a game saw behind the seat."

"What'd you say?"

"Told them I had no idea why that stuff was there."

"How about that police chief in Smoke Tree?"

"Bastard hung up on me. Told me not to call him again. I think that well's run dry."

"That's it?"

"No, Harold, that's not it.

You and I still have to go to the next meeting of the Klavern and tell the boys that Purvis, Gene and Daryll won't be coming home. Gene was single, so there's no problem there, but Purvis and Darryl were married. The Klan is going to have to tell their wives something."

"The Klan will tell them there's danger for Klan members who fight for the integrity and purity of white men and their white women."

"Think they'll accept that?"

"If they know what's good for them. The sharp sword of the Ku Klux Klan cuts both ways.

Let's get back to the man who put me in this wheelchair, since Purvis and the others didn't get the job done."

"I'm going to take care of that situation myself. But not just yet."

"When?"

"It's going to have to wait until I retire. I want to be sure my pension is secure and in place if there's any blowback."

"When's that?"

"Nineteen and sixty-two."

"That's three years!"

"It is, but that's the way it's going to have to be."

"Send somebody else!"

"Amateur hour is over, Harold. Anyway, I don't think guys are going to be lining up for this one after the first three didn't come back."

"Any idea happened out there?"

"Either those boys were careless or this Sommers is something more than what we thought he was. Or some combination of those two things."

"I don't want to wait three years."

A different look came into Dave Scuttler's eyes. A look Harold had never seen before, but a look a number of men in Caddo County had seen just before their lights went out.

When he spoke, he didn't raise his voice, but his tone was harder. More brittle. Any hint of comfort and friendship was gone.

"You were the one who suggested having fun and games with the Sommers girl back in forty-two. So why don't you just drive yourself on out there in that special van of yours and roll over that stony desert in your wheelchair. See how you make out with the man who just eliminated three big, nasty boys."

Harold should have had enough sense to be

afraid, but he had a short fuse. It was his turn to get angry.

"You and Purvis were all for climbing her!"

"That's right, Harold, we were. And I'll give you this, when the shit came down, you had the sand to keep your mouth shut and not tell Kyle Sommers we were with you."

"And don't you forget it."

When Dave replied, that discomfiting look was still in his eyes. He spoke slowly and quietly but with hostile intensity.

"Harold, now that Purvis is gone, you're the only one who knows I was there. I'm the man with the gun and the badge. A man who has eliminated many a problem in Caddo County. A lot of them the Sheriff doesn't even know about."

Harold held up his hands, palms facing the deputy.

"Easy now, Dave. I'm no threat. I'm your best friend."

"Be damn sure it stays that way."

Anxious to change the subject, Harold asked, "When you go, you going alone?"

"I'm taking one other guy. Except he doesn't know it yet."

"Who's that?"

"Arvin Lacey."

"Thought he was in jail."

"He is. Out in California. San Quentin."

"What's he in for?"

"His momma tells me he was riding with a bunch of motorcycle trash, mostly Irish guys, when they pulled an armed robbery. He went down with them. Be in until July of 1962. I'm going to take a ride out there and pay him a visit. Offer him some substantial cash to help me. Tell him I'll meet him the day he gets out and explain the job. Don't want him blabbing about it to his friends while he's inside."

"He's not Klan."

"Next best thing. Belongs to this gang his biker friends formed in San Quentin. Call themselves the Diamond Tooth Gang. Turns out a lot of these guys have pieces of glass embedded in their teeth. Don't ask me why. His momma showed me a picture she took of him when she went out to see him. When the flash hit all that glass, his mouth lit up like a movie marquee."

"What's that got to do with the Klan?"

"That's the best part. The gang is all white. It was formed to keep white men from being attacked by mud people in jail. The Diamond Tooth Gang hates mud people. Believe in the superiority of the Aryan race."

Harold was silent for a moment.

"I recall Arvin. Crazy-wild when he was a kid. Now he has glass stuck in his teeth? Sounds nuts."

Deputy Dave Scuttler smiled for the first time since arriving.

"Doesn't he just, though?"

Deep Desert Deception

CHAPTER 22

September 1959 Smoke Tree, California

A week after Labor Day, Horse was finally able to pry enough time from his busy schedule to pay a courtesy call on his local counterpart, Police Chief Oscar Rettenmeir of the Smoke Tree Police Department. Horse had been putting in sixteen-hour days ever since returning to Smoke Tree from Ron Nelson's funeral. At first those days were consumed by dealing with the aftermath of the flash flood. After that, most of his time was devoted to familiarizing himself with his new duties as substation commander.

Before he was finished with the second task, Labor Day weekend arrived. That meant an influx of boaters, water skiers and sunbathers on his section of the Colorado River, a section stretching from the San Bernardino County line north of Blythe to the Nevada State border just below Davis Dam. The smell of beer, barbeque and two-stroke oil would be floating up and down the river from dawn to dusk. A lot of visitors on that big stretch of the Colorado. Most of them were well-behaved families out for the last weekend of summer, but some were rowdy drunks, and some of those were insanely reckless.

When Horse was a teenager, there had been few boats on the river. Mostly aluminum fishing boats with outboard motors. Then, when he returned home from the Korean War and went to work for the Sheriff's Department, the first of the waterskiing boats showed up. They were aluminum too, and then fiberglass came along. Boats got shorter. Flatter. Outboard motors got bigger. Speeds went up. And noise. And the number of people coming to the river from Los Angeles and its suburbs.

In the late fifties, hot rodding enthusiasts began adapting car engines for use in drag boats. And then in ski boats. More horsepower. More speed. More boats on the river. More people on the river. More drunks on the river. And more noise. Lots more noise. On hot summer days, Horse and Esperanza could hear inboard ski boats from their place, and they lived four miles from the river.

The noise started before sunrise. The river was

glassy smooth at dawn before the wind came up: the best time for serious water skiers. The noise didn't end until after sundown.

Fisherman got irritated because some of the drivers of the big inboards liked to see how close they could come to a fishing boat. Ruined the fishing. Scared hell out of the fishermen. A fisherman or two had been known to throw cans of beer at the inboards. One even pulled a gun. Bad feelings all around.

On Labor Day weekend, hydroplane boats with outboard motors racing on the river opposite Sunset Beach were added to the mix. Small, light boats, wood and fiberglass, usually not much over a hundred pounds. Big engines, usually Mercuries. Brave drivers. Some a little too brave. Skillset: go fast, turn left. Try not to hit the guy next to you or flip over. Get a trophy. Yippee! Maybe get a sponsorship. Double yippee!

Combine all of this activity with families on beaches up and down the river. Swimmers and sunbathers. Some of the swimmers not understanding how dangerous the current and whirlpools could be. Some of the families not paying close enough attention to their small children.

Toss in what happens when an eighteen-foot fiberglass ski boat travelling over fifty miles an hour hits a sandbar submerged just under the water. Add what happens to the skier being towed behind the boat.

The local motels and restaurants and boat dock owners loved the boaters. The Chamber of Commerce did too. For his part, Horse longed for the old aluminum boats with their twenty-five horsepower Johnson and Evinrude and Scott Atwater engines droning up and down the river with a fishing rod hanging over the stern.

When a water skier is badly injured on the river that forms the boundary between Arizona and California, or a tourist swimming in the river is hit and killed by a ski boat, who investigates? If it's near Parker, the Yuma County Sheriff's Department substation responds. If it happens above Parker Dam on Lake Havasu or points north all the way to Davis Dam, guess who catches the investigation? Not Mohave County. Their office is in Kingman, miles away. They act like they don't know half of the river is in their county. Not the Smoke Tree Police Department. Everybody leaves the river to the Smoke Tree Substation of the San Bernardino County

Sheriff's Department.

By the fourteenth of September, the long Labor Day weekend was one week in the past, and the conflicts and tragedies had all been reported and sorted when Horse walked into Chief Oscar Rettenmeir's office. The Chief got up and extended his hand.

"Congratulations on your promotion, Lieutenant Caballo."

"Thank you, Chief Rettenmeir. I only wish it had happened under less tragic circumstances. And please, call me Horse. Everyone else does."

The Chief indicated a chair in front of his desk and settled back onto his swivel rocker as Horse sat down.

"All right, Horse. I'm glad you came by. There's a couple of things I want to talk to you about. First, apparently a lot of Smoke Tree people are calling you. The number of calls to this office from the east side have dropped way off since you took over."

"Well, Chief..."

"Please. It's Oscar."

Horse nodded.

"Oscar, these people have known me all my life. I

grew up east of the tracks. I'm a known quantity."

"So, when there's an emergency, they call your office."

Horse smiled.

"They don't just call my office. They call my office and want to talk to me and only to me. They knew my dad. They know my mom. She still lives over there in the house where I grew up. They feel better if they can talk to someone who speaks Spanish."

"There are people over there who don't speak English?"

"No, they all speak English. It's just that some of the old ones are more comfortable with Spanish."

"I see."

"If it's not an urgent matter, we try to direct them to your office. But if it's an emergency, we're not going to tell them to hang up and call the STPD. We roll a unit."

"Well, I guess I can see that.

But you know, Horse, I hear you're getting calls from people in other parts of town. Even from some of the businesses."

Horse shrugged.

"Known quantity, again, I guess. I went to high school here, Oscar. Quarterbacked the football team. Forward on the basketball team. Pitcher in baseball season. You, they don't know very well yet."

"I've been here five years."

Horse smiled.

"That's five minutes in Smoke Tree time.

You retired from the LAPD, right?"

"That's right. Retired as a patrol sergeant."

"And you took this job out here because you like Smoke Tree?"

The Chief shook his head.

"Took this job to augment my pension. I knew I wasn't going to get a job in a bigger city. I never rose above sergeant. Wasn't good at department politics. Wasn't even a detective.

The only two, small-town chief's jobs open when I retired were Smoke Tree and Brawley. You ever been to Brawley?"

Horse smiled.

"Played a baseball game there one March. The wind was blowing in, and I hit a shot right on the screws that would have been a home run anywhere else. By the time the wind got done with it, the infield fly rule applied."

"That's Brawley. Plus, no river there, and I like to fish."

"There you go. Perfect match."

"Look, Horse, to be truthful, I don't mind your office handling those east side calls. Might be better for all concerned. I don't have a single officer who speaks Spanish. I sure as heck don't. But I'd appreciate it if you'd encourage the businesspeople to call here. Keep the Mayor and Council happy, and all that."

"I'd be glad to try."

"Trying's good.

Now, I have something else for you."

Horse listened attentively while the Chief related the call he had received from a sheriff's deputy in Caddo County, Oklahoma in early August. He explained he had intended to relay the information to Ron Nelson, but the flood hit before the Chief bumped into him.

"That's a strange story."

"Gets stranger.

Same guy called me back a few days after the flood. Claimed a civilian from his county, a man named Purvis Davis, was going to be in Smoke Tree on the seventeenth of August and intended to go out and talk to Burke about the case as a favor to the Caddo County Sheriff's department."

"He sent a civilian to interview a witness in a capital crime case?"

"There's more. This deputy, Dave Scuttler is his name, told me Purvis Davis never came home. I asked him if he had heard about our flood that day. Said he had. Asked him if he thought Davis had been lost in the flood. He said, no. Said his truck was found abandoned in the parking lot of the Dunes Casino in Vegas"

"Doesn't sound like it has anything to do with us, then."

"That's what I told him. Told him he should be dealing with Las Vegas law enforcement.

I also told him something I should have mentioned the first time. About Burke's place being out of my jurisdiction. I gave him your name if he wants more information."

"I see."

Horse sat and thought for a moment.

"I agree there are some pieces of this story that don't fit together. For example, this deputy was calling about something that happened in nineteen forty-two? I mean, wouldn't the statute on an attempted murder have run a long time ago?"

"I'm not sure. It would have in California, but some states treat attempted murder the same as murder, and there is no statute of limitations on that."

"Yeah. Maybe it's different in Oklahoma. But it still sounds like it's all coming out of left field. Any idea what he's really after?"

"I don't know. And I apologize for passing him on to you. I'm telling you about the calls so you'll have some background if he contacts your office. But I gave him quite an earful about the lack of professionalism. I don't think I'll hear from him again, but he might call you."

The chief paused for a moment, struggling with how to put what he was going to say next.

"There's something else you should know. When I told the deputy your name, he asked me what kind of name it was. I told him it was a Mexican name."

The Chief hesitated again.

"Yes?"

The next sentence came out in a rush.

"He said he couldn't believe a Mexican was in charge of white deputies."

"I see."

"Just thought you should know."

"Thanks for passing that on. I'll keep it in mind if he ever calls. And I'll cross Caddo County, Oklahoma off my vacation list."

Horse got to his feet and the Chief rose with him. The two men shook hands again.

"Thanks, Oscar, for your time."

"Congratulations again on the promotion, Horse. I hope our departments can work closely together in the future."

"I hope so, too."

After Horse left, Chief Rettenmeir sat thinking about what the deputy in Oklahoma had said about a Mexican being put in charge of white deputies.

He realized he didn't disagree with the man all

that much.

CHAPTER 23

September 1959

The blast furnace heat of August and early September slowly gave way to almost bearable temperatures. No new interlopers appeared at Piute Creek, but Burke still spent his nights outside on the ground beneath the cottonwoods lining Piute Creek and his days glassing the Old Mojave Road from his vantage point in the Piutes.

He still drove to Boulder City for his groceries and kept his scoped .308 in the rifle rack mounted above the back seat in his flatbed whenever he left Piute Creek. And on the way to Highway 95, he stopped every mile or so and used an entrenching tool to make a narrow, diagonal slash across the road that would reveal any fresh tire marks if a vehicle crossed the rarely-used road while he was gone. When he took Pepper out for a run, he carried the .308 in a scabbard. To keep in practice, he often stopped after running a particularly demanding section and pulled out the rifle and dropped into a prone position with the sling of the rifle wrapped tightly around his forearm. Working hard to control his breathing while his heartbeat was still elevated, he would shoot a few rounds at a rock on a distant hillside, timing the squeeze of the trigger with a long exhalation.

An additional purpose of the shooting was to familiarize Pepper with the sound of the .308 sending rounds downrange. After all, it wouldn't do to have the horse carrying his supplies run off and leave him on the open desert if he had to open fire on a hostile party.

Once two months had passed from the time he left the truck with Oklahoma plates in Las Vegas, he began to believe he was not in imminent danger of being attacked. He drove to Smoke Tree and picked up a fistful of messages from Brenda at Sunset Beach and made the callbacks that put him back in the farrier business. Once he returned to work, he felt like his life was returning to normal. Almost. But there was a sense of wariness that never left him. Whether awake or sleeping, the wariness became an endless background hum: part of the unconscious, continuous conversation he had in his own mind about his survival.

CHAPTER 24

October 1959 Smoke Tree, California

Contacting Burke Henry about the conversation with Chief Rettenmeir had been relegated to Horse's 'to-do' list. It had never left his mind, but it was early October before he had time to follow up on it. At eleven o'clock one Saturday morning, he put in a call to Brenda Rangel at Sunset Beach.

"Sunset Beach Saloon."

"Good morning Brenda. Horse calling."

"Do I have to call you Lieutenant now?"

"You know about that?"

"This is Smoke Tree. Of course, I know about it."

"Sorry. I should have known. But it's still Horse. Don't really think of myself as Lieutenant Caballo. Doubt anyone else does either.

Anyway, got a minute?"

"Got quite a few now that Labor Day is long gone."

"Must have been good for business."

"Oh, it was. Too good. Sold a lot of beer and burgers, but the noise from those boat races about drove me crazy."

"Reason I called, I was wondering if you've talked to Burke lately."

"He's been busy. I didn't see him for a long time. When he finally showed up, he had a lot of business stacked up here. He's playing catch up."

"I guess the flood stranded him for a while. I can only imagine what it did to the road to his place. When do you think you might see him again?"

"Usually drops by on a Sunday to check for messages."

"If he comes in, could you tell him I want to talk to him?"

"Sure."

"Tell him I'll drive out his way next Wednesday around noon if that's okay with him."

"Will do."

Horse was working the next day when the weekend

dispatcher buzzed him.

"Lieutenant? Burke Henry for you on line one."

"Got it.

Hello, Burke. Are you in town?"

"At Sunset. Brenda said you were going to drive out and visit me on Wednesday. Not a good idea. I can get my dual wheel truck over that road, but I'm not sure you could make it. Since I'm in town, I took a chance you might be in the office.

What do you want to talk to me about?"

"Couple of things. Nothing urgent, but I'd like to get together soon."

"I'll come out to the station."

"That sounds too official. I'm just about to head home. Why don't you come by the house? Esperanza will be glad to see you."

"Don't want to intrude on your time off. You're supposed to be the boss now. What are you doing working on a Sunday afternoon, anyway?"

"Apparently, it goes with the job. And you wouldn't be intruding. You know you're our favorite guest."

"Okay. Be over."

A half hour later Horse, Esperanza and Burke were sitting on the front veranda. It was a pleasant afternoon. They were sharing a huge plate of nachos and a pitcher of lemonade as Horse told Burke about his promotion after the funeral in San Bernardino.

"That Sheriff of yours must be a smart man. Knows nobody's better for the job out here than you."

"That's exactly what I told him," said Esperanza.

"I appreciate the kind words, Burke."

"Just stating a fact. You're a cut above any lawman I've ever known."

"Okay, enough. You two are going to make me blush.

Changing the subject to you, Brenda tells me you've been very busy lately too."

"Woman keeps track of me, doesn't she? Don't begrudge her the nosiness though. She takes my messages and talks me up when someone new calls. Hasn't let me pay for a burger since that Sunday you and I met over two years ago."

"Woman thinks the world of you, Burke."

Burke smiled.

"I believe she does. I still manage to slip a ten under the register now and then when she's not looking, though."

There was some more small talk before Horse got down to business.

"Now that I'm the substation commander, I'd like to have you give our deputies the appropriate force training you and I talked about back in '57."

"There's no way I have time to do with them what I did with you."

"I'm not asking you to take it to that level. What I'm asking for is more along the lines of what you mentioned the first time we ever talked about this idea. How to use the nightstick as something more than a club. Maybe toss in a few arm bars and submission holds. That kind of thing.

I've already talked to the Sheriff about it. He likes the idea. Says that since you're a member of the mounted posse you've already been through the same background check as a reserve officer. Says he can find money in the budget to pay you for the training.

I'm sure I can talk the school district into letting us use the high school gym for the sessions. They've got those big mats they use for the tumbling classes."

"Okay, I think I can find time for it."

"Thank you. I'll start making the arrangements. Give me a call when you've got time to start.

There's something else I wanted to talk to you about. This is kind of a head's up. Something you should know about."

Horse related everything Oscar Rettenmeir had told him about the two phone calls from Caddo County, Oklahoma. He included the information that the caller had initially asked about Kyle Sommers, but then shifted gears when the Chief told him Burke was the owner of the truck with Smoke Tree Farrier on the door. Horse didn't mention the name of the deputy who had made the calls.

When Horse had finished, he asked, "Any of that make any sense to you?"

"He said the missing guy's name was Purvis Davis?"

"That's right."

"I don't know him. I haven't been in Caddo County since I left to join the Army in January of nineteen forty-two, and I haven't talked to anyone in Caddo County since then."

"Maybe this will shed some light on the situation. When you lived there, did you ever hear of a deputy named Dave Scuttler?"

There was a flicker of something in Burke Henry's eyes. Something suddenly intense and hostile.

"Why, is he missing too?"

"No, he's the deputy that called Chief Rettenmeir."

Burke sat thinking for a moment before he replied.

"I don't remember Purvis, but I sure remember Deputy Scuttler. Evil man. Rather shoot someone than take him to jail. It's like he was mad about something all the time."

"Any idea what he's fishing for with these calls?"

"With Scuttler, there's no way of knowing. Crooked as a dog's hind leg. Liar and a bully. Especially hated Indians. Or maybe it was just that Indians were poor and powerless, and he could do anything he wanted to them because he had a badge."

Horse could tell Burke's thoughts had gone to a time and place far away.

"Anything at all," Burke said, his voice nearly a whisper.

Then, he seemed to be back.

"I can tell you there were rumors that Scuttler was a member of the Ku Klux Klan."

Horse realized what Burke had just told him squared with the remark Scuttler had made to the Chief about a Mexican being in charge of white deputies.

"What about this first guy Scuttler was looking for. This Kyle Sommers. Scuttler said you and this Kyle Sommers are cousins."

Burke hesitated for so long Horse didn't think he was going to answer. Then he realized Burke was trying to frame his answer in exactly the right way. That meant he was holding something back. Horse didn't think Burke would lie to him, but he wasn't going to get the whole story.

"Kyle Summers was a guy who righted a wrong. A big wrong. And now that you bring up Scuttler's name, I'm thinking the deputy might have been part of that wrong.

Does that answer your question?"

Horse noticed Burke referred to Kyle Sommers in the past tense.

"Sort of. But Burke, sometimes different people see 'wrong' a different way."

"I can guarantee you, Horse, the only people who wouldn't see what was done as a 'wrong' are the evil men who committed it."

"And you think I would see it the same way this Kyle Sommers did?"

"There's not a doubt in my mind you would."

Burke turned his head and stared directly into Horse's eyes.

"Kyle Sommers was not a bad guy."

"That's good enough for me. This is a conversation between friends, Burke, not an investigation. I mostly wanted you to know about these calls. From what this Scuttler told Chief Rettenmeir, the man seemed to be hinting you had something to do with that truck they found in Las Vegas."

"Not into truck rustling."

"Never thought you were. I'm just trying to figure out whether this guy's going to be a problem for you down the road."

They sat on the veranda for a while longer, but the late-afternoon mood had shifted. Horse could tell

Burke's mind was elsewhere. It wasn't long before he made his excuses and got up to leave.

Horse and Esperanza walked out to the driveway with him. Burke climbed on his motorcycle and started it up. Horse had an uneasy, disquieted feeling as he watched Burke drive away, the rays of the setting sun painting his back with reddish orange light.

Horse questioned people all the time as part of his job, and sometimes it was hard for him to leave it at the office. He hadn't been trying to trap Burke or get him to admit to anything, but it was obvious Burke had avoided direct answers to his question about the phone calls and his relationship to Kyle Sommers.

And there had been something more than recognition in Burke's eyes when Horse mentioned Deputy Scuttler. Some dots had been connected. He was sure of that. There had been that momentary flash of anger. More than anger. Hatred. He would not like to be on the receiving end of that kind of hatred from a man as dangerous as Burke Henry.

That worried him. Didn't worry him *about* Burke. Worried him *for* Burke, a man he thought of as a friend. Maybe his best friend.

For his part, Burke was lost in thought as he rode back to Piute Creek in the dying light of day. He was thinking about Dave Scuttler, the deputy his sister had recognized. And now Burke knew that Harold Nevins, the man he had thought for all these years that he had killed, was still alive! The fact that he was confined to a wheelchair was good enough. Nevins had suffered for his sin and would continue to suffer.

Apparently, Purvis Davis a known member of Lawton Klavern of the Ku Klux Klan, had been the other rapist. Since that had been the name on the registration in the glove compartment of the green Dodge, the man with the tobacco-stained beard had probably been the driver of the pickup. He had looked older than the others and seemed to be in charge.

Burke didn't know the names of either of Purvis's companions who now lay buried with him beneath tons of rocks and sand somewhere in the desert. Nor did he care to know. Men who kept bad company deserved to come to bad ends.

Scuttler, now the only one of the original three who was any threat to him, was getting nervous. But the deputy wasn't stupid. He had been clever enough not to mention the other two missing men when he called Chief Rettenmeir the second time.

While Burke was not inclined to go to Oklahoma and hunt down a man with a badge in his own backyard, he thought he would probably see Scuttler someday. All in all, it would be better to let Scuttler come to him. On his home ground. In conditions that would be under his control. Where he would have space enough and time to dispose of his body.

Burke didn't think Scuttler would be sending others a second time. It was going to be hard to find volunteers when the last three who left for Piute Creek hadn't come home. But he didn't think Scuttler would come on his own. Like a lot of bullies, Scuttler was a coward. Would he be able to convince another Klan member or two to come with him? Burke didn't really care. In fact, he was looking forward to the visit.

Come on ahead, deputy, he thought. I'm dying to see you.

CHAPTER 25

Autumn 1959 to Spring 1961

On an evening in October, the deputies of the Smoke Tree Substation were gathered in a semi-circle facing Burke Henry in the high school gym. The gym smelled of sweat and floor wax and the rubber mats stacked against the wall behind the deputies. The deputies, as ordered, were wearing sweat pants, sweat shirts and tennis shoes.

As Burke outlined how the training in the application of gradually increasing force would proceed, they began to shift from foot to foot. He pushed it as far as he could without losing them completely. He talked about readiness stances. About projecting confidence and always appearing friendly but professional. About take-down and come-along techniques if attitude and confidence failed to control the situation.

Certain in the knowledge that they always had a gun on their hip, the deputies weren't convinced of the value of the training Burke was describing. They were getting bored. Burke had known they would. Just when their eyes were starting to glaze over, he stopped abruptly in the middle of a sentence.

"Lieutenant Caballo, could you join me out here?"

Horse, dressed in his working uniform but without his gun belt, walked out and faced him.

Burke promptly picked Horse up and threw him over his shoulder, slamming him hard to the floor. The deputies gasped. There was a loud boom as Horse slapped his palms and forearms against the floor to break his fall. He rolled into an offensive stance and swept Burke's legs out from under him. Burke recovered and delivered a side kick to Horse's abdomen, pulling the kick at the last instant. Horse spun around the leg and hit Burke on the side of the head with an elbow. Burke countered with a two-knuckle punch to the heart. Horse shot out a left jab that snapped Burke's head back, but Burke captured the hand and locked Horse into an arm bar and took him to the floor.

The two men rose to their feet and bowed to each other before turning to the deputies. The deputies who were suddenly eager to learn what Burke Henry had promised to teach them.

The one thing missing in Burke's life was a lady friend. It was a lack he was used to. He had never had a deep and meaningful relationship with a woman, or with a girl either, for that matter.

Growing up half-breed in Caddo County, Oklahoma, he had been viewed with equal suspicion by both Indian girls and white. His years in the service, almost all of them in combat zones, had not afforded many opportunities to forge lasting bonds. The closest had been the woman in Saigon. But even there, Burke had been under no illusions about the situation. He had always known that the day he stopped paying her rent and buying her food and clothing would be the day she said *Tạm biệt.*

When he got to know Carlos and Esperanza, he became aware of what he was missing. He began to dream of something as complete and compelling as the love that united his friends. Realistically, he doubted he would be that lucky.

In November of 1960, Burke met Caroline McCollum. It began with a phone call about some farrier work. He made his weekly stop to pick up his messages from

Brenda at Sunset Beach. As usual, he drove to the pay phone next to the Greyhound Bus Station and stacked his nickels, dimes and quarters on the metal tray inside the booth to make his callbacks. Although Brenda had offered many times to let him use her phone, he resisted. He did not want to impose on Brenda. She was already doing him a huge favor by letting him use her phone number as his business phone contact. In a sense, she was his office. Also, he knew that anything overheard by one Smoke Tree resident could be in the breeze before sundown.

In the stuffy phone booth that Sunday, he dialed what he recognized as an Arizona number. The person who answered had a pleasant and friendly voice.

"Sunnyside Ranch, Caroline McCollum speaking."

"Mrs. McCollum, this is Burke Henry, Smoke Tree Farrier."

"Thank you so much for calling. You come highly recommended, so I know you must be very busy. And, by the way, it's 'Miss', not 'Mrs.'"

"Who recommended me?"

"Jim Durning."

"The owner of the pretty little ranch in the foothills

of the Hualapais."

"That's Jim."

"Where is Sunnyside Ranch?"

"Outside of Seligman."

"Yavapai County?"

"That's right."

"That's a little farther east than I usually work."

"I'm hoping you'll make an exception, Mr. Henry. The need here is great. It will be a lot of work for you, well worth the drive."

"Is Sunnyside a dude ranch or a working ranch?"

"Working. Hard working. We just finished fall roundup, and I've got so many horses with foot problems that we almost didn't have enough to finish the job."

"I like a working ranch, Miss McCollum. I like cow ponies. I'll take the work."

"Good!"

"What seems to be the problem with the horses?"

"I'm not sure. A few of them went lame during the roundup, and an awful lot of them just don't act comfortable. I'm worried."

"If I leave Smoke Tree right away, I can be at your place before noon to take a look. I won't start work today, but I want to get an idea what I'm up against, if that's all right with you."

"That will be fine. Let me tell you how to get to the place."

The sun was almost directly overhead when Burke turned his motorcycle onto a ranch road that wound into the hills north of Seligman. The road led him to a long driveway lined on both sides with massive cottonwoods, their turning leaves flashing like gold pieces beneath the autumn sun. The driveway led to a handsome, two-story ranch house made of volcanic rock. He came to a stop next to an expansive lawn of Bermuda grass that was in the early stages of going dormant for the coming winter. As soon as he stopped, he was surrounded by a swirling mass of barking and snarling ranch dogs. They encircled him but did not seem inclined to come close enough to bite. He kept his engine running while he waited for someone to come out of the house.

After a few minutes, the screen door banged shut behind a woman with bright red hair. She put two fingers in her mouth and produced a shrill whistle.

"You dogs! Under the porch!"

The pack moved as one and slunk away while whining and looking back at the stranger and his noisy machine. As the woman came down the steps and walked toward him, Burke estimated her age at late thirties to mid-forties. She was dressed in Levi's and had on a sweater to ward off the autumn chill. The Levi's were tucked into unadorned cowboy boots that looked like they had a few miles on them.

Burke hit the kill switch on his bike and took off the goggles that pinned his Army field cap to his head. He hooked the goggles over the clutch handle and the hat over the accelerator and ran his hands through his blonde hair, longer now than it had been since his teenage years.

"Fancy motorcycle," the woman said as she stopped beside him.

Now that she was closer, he saw she had green eyes and a splash of freckles across her face.

"Yes, ma'am, it is."

"You're Burke Henry?"

"I am."

He climbed off his bike and leaned it onto the

kickstand.

"I'm Caroline McCollum. Welcome to the Sunnyside Ranch, Mr. Henry, and thanks for coming so soon."

She extended her hand, and he shook it. She had a firm grip and the callouses of a person used to hard work.

"Where are the horses you want me to look at?"

She smiled. "You get right to it, don't you?"

"Yes ma'am. I want to plan my work."

Caroline McCollum talked as she led him to the corral.

"This is a bit of a downtime for us. On Thursday, we finished rounding up over fifteen hundred head and loading them onto cattle cars on the Santa Fe siding outside Seligman. That's why it's so quiet here today. I gave the hands three days off. Everybody will be back to work tomorrow."

"You must have a pretty big operation here."

"The ranch itself is over two thousand acres. The grazing allotments surrounding the ranch are many times that acreage. They've been in the family for generations."

They walked past the barn. It was a huge, two story wood building built of what looked like hand-hewn, unpeeled logs of ponderosa pine. The large, sliding front door was rolled to the side. Burke could see farming equipment in front and horse stalls and sacks of grain in the rear. A smell of hay and green alfalfa drifted down from the second story.

The big corral was to the east of the barn. It was of sturdy construction and in excellent repair. As Burke and Mrs. McCollum approached the gate, a number of horses moved toward them. It was obvious they were used to getting treats when she came out to visit.

"See one good thing already."

"What's that?"

"You're on clay out here on this hillside. Horses would stamp it into mud when it rains. Someone had the foresight to dig out the inside of the corral with a dozer and replace the clay with sand"

"That was my father's idea."

"Is he around today?"

Caroline McCollum turned away and stared at the distant mountains for a moment. When she turned back, her eyes were damp.

"No, he passed away a little over six months ago."

"I'm sorry to hear that."

Burke turned back to the corral.

"He sure enough knew horses. The sand is easy on the horses' legs and good for their feet. Keeps them from getting thrush when the winter rains come."

He turned to face her again.

"Miss McCollum, has the ranch ever had the kind of problem you've been having with your horses before?"

"No. The former ranch foreman was very good at taking care of them."

"You said 'was.' He's no longer with you?"

"Unfortunately. Juan Delgado was foreman even before Daddy took over from my grandfather. When Daddy died, Juan said his heart just wasn't in the work anymore. He's getting old, and like a lot of men who have spent their lives working with cattle and horses, he's busted up and suffering from rheumatism. He went back to the town in Mexico his mother and father came from. Said his savings would last a lot longer there."

"I see. Well, if it's all right with you, I'm going to go inside your corral and spend some time with your horses. Once they get used to me, I'll start checking their feet."

"That will be fine. There are ropes in the barn. There's a post in the middle of the corral where you can tie whichever horse you want to examine."

"I don't tie a horse to work on it."

"That's a little unusual."

Burke shrugged.

"I've learned if I cooperate with a horse, it will cooperate with me. I can usually get one to trust me pretty quick. If you tie a horse, there's a lot you can't learn about it."

"Why is that?"

"People express themselves by talking and waving their hands and their expressions. Horses show how they feel by their posture and by the way they move their feet. If you tie them, especially if you snub them close to the post, you can't see how they move. Also, they can get anxious and uncooperative. It's better to leave a horse untied and work with it until it calms. That can take a while, but when the horse stops and settles, I can start my work."

"How do you know when a horse has settled?"

"Any horse in a corral has a favorite spot. I just walk around beside the horse for a while until it feels comfortable enough with me to stop in its favorite spot."

"That's a different way of doing things than I'm used to seeing, but Jim says you know your stuff. How long do you think this will take?"

"Probably until sundown. Horses won't be hurried."

Burke walked over and opened the gate and went inside. When he had latched it behind himself, he walked toward the horses. Unsure of this stranger and his intentions, the horses began to mill. Burke stopped moving until the horses stopped. When they did, he walked slowly toward them. Again, they began to mill. Burke stopped and turned toward Caroline McCollum.

"This is going to take a while. It always does. If you've got something else to do, you might want to go ahead and do it."

"Okay, I'll leave you to it."

She turned away from the corral and walked back to the house. When she got there, she climbed the steps to the veranda that encircled the house. She stopped before going in the back door and turned and looked toward the corral.

Burke Henry had not moved. He was still standing in the middle of the corral. Her horses were all bunched in one corner, their heads turned toward him as if they expected him to do a trick or speak in a way they could understand.

She went in the house and walked through the kitchen. It smelled of the bread she had baking in the old porcelain stove. She walked into the hallway beyond and climbed the stairway, the heavy oak bannister with its smell of furniture polish worn and familiar beneath her hand. At the second story landing, she turned and walked along the railing that surrounded the entire floor. She followed the railing to her office at the back of the house and stepped inside.

Caroline sat down at her desk and looked out at the corral. Burke Henry was walking slowly toward the horses. They continued to move away from him, but more slowly now. She looked beyond the corral out over the broad expanse of Chino Wash and the mountains on the horizon to the northwest. It was a view she had been seeing since childhood, but one she never tired of. She daydreamed for a while about her youthful days when her mother was alive and her father ran the ranch with Juan Delgado at his side. There was so little to worry about back then.

She shook her head to come out of her reverie. She opened the bottom right desk drawer and got out the ledgers for the ranch and went to work. As she labored through the financial condition of Sunnyside Ranch and established realistic projections for the coming year, she occasionally glanced out at the corral. The third time she looked, Burke was walking in circles among the horses. A half hour later when she raised her head again, he had isolated one of the horses and was standing beside it. The horse was looking away from Burke, but it did not seem agitated.

She returned to her figures.

A while later she looked up to see Burke next to another horse. As she watched, he leaned against the horse's shoulder. The horse moved away from the pressure but did not seem alarmed. Burke followed the horse and leaned against it again. Once again, the horse moved away. Fascinated, she put down her pencil and watched as Burke and the horse reprised their roles over and over until finally, the horse stopped moving away. Burke remained leaning against it. He seemed to be talking. Then, he slowly bent over and picked up the horse's leg by the pastern and bent its knee. The horse adjusted its weight to allow what Burke was doing. Cradling the pastern, the farrier examined the horse's hoof and foot.

Caroline McCollum smiled and went back to work. Later, when she stood up to stretch her back, she looked out at the corral again. The gate was still closed, but Burke was nowhere to be seen. She was sure she hadn't heard his motorcycle leave. She went out of the room and walked around the railing to one of the front bedrooms that had a view of the lawn and driveway and the plains sloping off to the south. Burke was at his motorcycle. He removed some tools from his panniers and walked back toward the corral. She returned to her office and got lost in her calculations until she heard the timer on the oven buzz.

She went downstairs and turned off the oven. She opened the door and took out the bread pans and set them on racks to cool. When she was done, she went outside. It was colder than before. Reaching back inside, she got her lined Levi jacket off the peg before crossing the yard to the corral.

As she approached, Burke was removing the left front shoe from one of the horses. She realized there were stacks of shoes piled just outside the fence all around the corral. Burke finished removing the shoe and carried it and three others to the gate. The sun was tilting toward the Black Mountains outside Kingman as he unlatched the gate and put the shoes on the ground before closing and re-latching it.

"That's the last one."

"You've taken the shoes off all the horses?"

"I have."

"Why?"

"You've got some horses with serious foot problems. They all need hoof trimming before I put the shoes back on. In fact, they'll need a number of trimmings to adjust their feet before they get comfortable again."

"And will you know which shoes should be on which horse?"

"Of course."

"What happens next?"

"Let the horses walk unshod in this soft sand until

I come back tomorrow to start trimming and re-shoeing. Only three of them need new shoes. The rest just need a preliminary trim to get their feet in good enough shape to put the existing shoes back on. But, like I said, all these horses will need a series of trims to get their feet right. It can't all be done at once. They're a mess."

"Mr. Henry, I just took some bread out of the oven. Would you like a slice or two?"

"That would be fine."

"And how about some coffee?"

"You're speaking my language."

They crossed the yard and went into the kitchen. Caroline got the coffee pot going and sliced fresh bread while Burke washed his hands in the small bathroom just off the kitchen.

As they ate hot bread dripping with butter and drank coffee at the kitchen table, Burke explained what needed to be done to the horses and why.

"Whatever went wrong with your horses must have happened within the last few months. If this had been going on for much longer, a lot more of your horses would have come up lame. If you don't mind my asking, who's been doing your farrier work?"

"When Juan retired, Larson Michaels, one of the hands, took it on."

"And he's been doing it ever since?"

"No."

"If he's not doing it anymore, who is?"

"Randy Jenkins."

"Another hand?"

Color rose in Caroline's face.

"No, he's a real estate agent."

Burke waited for her to say more.

"When Dad died, the ranch passed to me. Randy showed up out here and asked me if I wanted to sell. He wanted to handle the sale. But I had no intention of selling.

Anyway, Randy seems to know a lot about horses. He certainly rides well."

"And he convinced you he should be doing your farrier work instead of this Michaels fellow."

"That's right."

"What's he charge you?"

Caroline blushed again.

"He doesn't charge me anything. I guess you could say he's been courting me. We've been out on a date or two."

"What's your old farrier say about what this Jenkins has been doing?"

"Larry's not very forceful."

"He's never commented on the work at all?"

"Oh, no. Larry would never do that. You have to drag words out of him. He never volunteers any."

"I'm beginning to understand how this happened."

"What's wrong?"

"It looks like Mr. Jenkins is more concerned with appearance than function. That tells me he doesn't know his stuff."

"Explain."

"He's trimming the hooves flat. Flat looks good to us. Satisfies our human need to have things nice and neat. But this is not a fashion show. For most horses, a flat hoof means a painful foot.

A good farrier understands the way the bones in a horse's leg align. The hoof has to be trimmed so the weight moves toward the front of the hoof. This allows the tendons inside the leg to cradle the bones so the horse will be comfortable on its feet. Does this make sense?"

"Sort of."

"Let me put it another way. Imagine you had to run a long way with a pebble in your shoe. A pebble you can't stop and get out. Pretty soon, your foot hurts every time you take a step. You begin to alter your gait to try to take the pressure off the foot that's contending with the pebble. Because of this, both your feet begin to hit the ground a different way than before.

If you ran that new way for weeks and weeks, you'd begin to have trouble upstream. First with the muscles and tendons and ligaments in your legs. Eventually, all the way to your hips."

"I see."

"If you could get the pebble out of your shoe at that point and stay off your feet and get some rest, you might have some trouble with the hamstring of the most severely affected leg for a while, but you'd recover. But if you weren't able to remove the pebble, and you continued to run, eventually the problem would extend into your lower back. When that happened, you'd be in serious trouble.

A horse with its feet badly trimmed does what you'd do if you had to run with the pebble. It tries to compensate. Tries to find a less panful way to move. It begins to move unnaturally. That leads to problems that are much worse than sore feet. If it goes on long enough, it can end the animal's life as a working horse.

Some of your horses are nearing that tipping point."

"This is new to me. How do you fix it?"

"By achieving balance and protecting the sole and frog of the foot. I'll work with a rasp to give the frog proper ground clearance so it doesn't distort the weight of the horse. I'll rasp the heel at an angle so the hoof gets slightly higher near the center of the foot. This leaves a small gap between the ground and the hoof wall at the heels. That way, the frog can bear more of the horse's weight, and it doesn't crush the heel."

Burke paused.

"Stop me if I'm boring you."

"Please, go on."

"The same thing applies at the toe. There has to be a space between the hoof and the ground at the front of the toe. Right now, all your horses are too long in the toe. When they move, the toes are landing first, and that's not right. They should land more toward their heels.

If the feet and hooves are trimmed right, the bones, tendons, frogs, soles, and hoof walls all work together to allow the foot to settle back under the weight of the horse. When that happens, you have a horse with happy feet.

Happy feet: comfortable horse. No more injuries."

Outside the kitchen window, the day was descending into twilight.

"Didn't' your father or Mr. Delgado teach you any of this?"

"Mr. Henry, I heard talk of cattle and horses all my life. But it was directed past me, not at me. Dad didn't seem to think I needed to know it. What I'm saying is, I heard a lot and absorbed some of it almost by accident, but no one ever sat me down and taught me this stuff. Not just the horses, but the whole operation.

I guess Dad always thought there'd be time for all of that stuff later. But then one day, he was in one of the fields way out by Chino wash. He was using the tractor's power take-off to run a piece of equipment. The belt got hold of his flannel shirt somehow. It just ate him up. It was hours before anyone found him."

"So, all of a sudden you were the boss."

"I was. I am."

"You must have thought about selling from time to time in the last six months."

"No. I love this land. Love these hills. Love this life. I'm here for the long haul."

Caroline got up and refilled their coffee cups from the blue enamel pot on the stove.

Burke took a sip.

"I guess we should discuss prices. Do you have pen and paper handy?"

Caroline pushed back her chair and went to the kitchen counter and opened a drawer. She came back to the table with a steno pad and a pen.

Burke wrote on the pad for a few minutes and then signed it before pushing it across the table to her.

"This is my price for the work it will take to correct

the problems these horses have. The work is described on the paper. The price is at the bottom above my signature. The bill will not be due until all the work is done. If you accept the price, sign your name below mine. If you don't, there's no charge for what I did today. I'll come out tomorrow and put the shoes back on all the horses. Again, at no charge."

Caroline took a moment to read what was on the pad before she looked up.

"It says here you're going to do the first session tomorrow and then come back two more times, three weeks apart."

"That's right."

"Then there's only one thing wrong with your price. It's not enough."

Burke smiled.

"You get the working ranch discount, Miss McCollum. The price is enough for my purposes."

She signed her name under Burke's and stood up.

"We have a deal."

Burke rose with her and they shook hands.

"I'll take care of the least-troubled ones first, so your hands can use them for work between my visits.

But some of them should not be ridden until after the last time I come."

"That shouldn't be a problem. Fall round up is over, and we've already had first cutting on the alfalfa we planted in September. Right now, we've got lots of work in the hay fields. No horseback work is required there. We'll work around your schedule."

"I'll be back to start work tomorrow."

When Burke returned early the following morning, he drove his truck directly to the corral. When he rolled down the window, he smelled smoke from a pinyon wood fire. The ranch dogs followed him, kicking up a ruckus, but when he stepped out they recognized his scent and contented themselves with barking at him. After a few minutes, they lost interest and returned to the house. He was laying out his tools on the flatbed when he heard someone walk up behind him. By the heaviness of the tread, he knew it wasn't Caroline McCollum.

He turned to face a florid-faced, scowling man dressed in brown gabardine slacks, an elaborately decorated western shirt with mother-of-pearl snap buttons, a bolo tie with a thick chunk of turquoise, and heavily-tooled, highly-polished cowboy boots that had picked up a patina of Colorado Plateau dust. The ensemble was topped off by a spotless white Stetson.

"So, you're the fancy farrier dude."

Burke stared at him, amused. Then he smiled.

"Mister, I don't think I'd be calling anybody a dude if I was wearing a drugstore cowboy outfit like yours. Who are you?"

"I'm Randy Jenkins. Caroline told me what you said about my work."

He waved his hand toward the corral.

"And?"

"I want you to take it back!"

"Excuse me?"

"I want you to tell her you were wrong, and then I want you to pack up your tools and get off our property."

Burke noticed the pronoun.

"Counting your chickens a bit early, aren't you?"

"What's that supposed to mean?"

"It means you haven't married the lady in question just yet, even though she tells me you're sparking her."

"That's none of your beeswax, whatever your name is."

"The name is Henry. Burke Henry. But you can call me Mr. Henry."

He heard the screen door slam and saw Caroline McCollum starting toward them.

"Now, I've got work to do. If you'll just mosey along there, cowboy, I'll get to it."

Randy Jenkins stepped closer, so close Burke could smell the aftershave on his beefy face. He also thought he picked up a faint odor of bourbon.

"I told you to clear off."

He reached out and grabbed Burke's denim shirt and yanked it. Burke went with the energy and allowed himself to be pulled forward. He closed on the bigger man. The move surprised Jenkins. He stumbled slightly. As he did, Burke seized the hand holding his shirt at the thumb joint and twisted it down and to the side.

Burke stared into Jenkins' startled eyes and spoke in a low voice.

"This is not some schoolyard."

He increased the pressure on the joint and read the pain in the other man's face.

"I'm going to turn loose of your hand and step away now. Then I'm going to talk with Miss. McCollum. Unless you want to look bad in front of your lady friend, you'll act like nothing happened."

He released the hand and stepped to the side to speak to the approaching woman.

He touched his hand to the bill of his Army field cap.

"Good morning, Miss McCollum. Mr. Jenkins here was just introducing himself to me."

"I told this yahoo to clear off. I was just trying to help him to his truck when he did some kind of sneaky, trick thing with my hand. If you hadn't walked up, I'd have bashed him into the ground."

"You're not bashing anybody, Randy.

And let me tell you something: I will decide who comes and goes on this property, not you."

"Ah heck, honey. I was just trying to protect your interests."

"I'm capable of protecting them myself."

Randy's face turned the color of a ripe plum.

"I'm not going to stand for this. I'm telling you right here and right now, either he goes or I do."

"Is that an ultimatum?"

"It is."

"Then you've made the choice for me. Get in your car and go. Don't come back until you can act like a grownup."

"I can't believe you! You're choosing a guy you barely know over me. Well, let me tell you something, sister." He pointed toward the front of the house. "If I go down that driveway, I'm never coming back."

"Okay."

"Okay what?"

"Okay, don't come back. It's entirely up to you."

Randy turned on Burke and jabbed a beefy finger at him.

"This is your fault. You're coming between me and my girl."

"Miss McCollum is not a girl. As for coming between the two of you, it looks like there's enough space there right now to drive a tractor through."

"You haven't heard the last of this."

"You talk so much, I'm sure I haven't."

Randy dropped his hand to his side and balled it into a fist. He stood for a moment, looking back and forth between Burke and Caroline. Then, something in Burke's eyes gave him pause. Without another word, he turned and walked toward the house.

Burke stood and watched as he stalked away and got into a maroon Oldsmobile. A moment later, the sedan spun its wheels at it fishtailed and headed for the driveway, leaving a billowing cloud of dust hanging in the autumn air.

Burke turned to Caroline and touched the brim of his cap again.

"I'd best get started."

"Mr. Henry, I'd like to apologize for Randy."

"You don't have to. He put on that display all by himself.

Now, I better get to work. Got a lot to do."

In between her tasks, Caroline stopped by the corral to watch Burke work. A few of the hands drifted by from time to time for the same reason.

At eleven, she came out of the ranch house and

walked to the dining hall next to the bunkhouse where she rang the triangle several times. Ranch hands began to appear and wash up at the pump outside before entering the building.

Burke continued to work.

After a few minutes, he heard Caroline's voice from the gate.

"Mr. Henry, dinner is served. You better get in there before the boys eat it all."

Burke walked to the gate.

"I didn't know meals were included. I brought something to eat."

"Whatever it is, it isn't as good as the platter of chicken-fried steak our cook has put on the dining hall table. There's biscuits and gravy and potato salad, too.

And yes, meals are included in your employment. Breakfast, dinner and supper, if you want them."

"Thank you, Miss McCollum. I appreciate your hospitality. I'll be right there."

Caroline returned to the dining hall. A few minutes later, Burke walked in the door. He was carrying his cap, and his blonde hair was damp. The room fell silent as the hands turned to look at the newcomer.

Burke smiled.

"Don't stop chewing on my account. Food will get cold."

"Men," said Caroline, "This is Burke Henry. He's going to be doing a lot of work on the horses."

As he crossed the room, Burke nodded, and the hands nodded back. Everybody on one side of the long table scooted down so he could find room at the end of the bench. The platter of steaks and the steaming bowl of gravy started his direction, as did the potato salad and the biscuits. In a few minutes, Burke had melded into the group, and everyone was eating again.

As Burke ate, he fielded questions about the work he was doing. There were knowing nods at his responses from some of the more experienced men. After dinner, he filed outside with the other hands and headed back to the corral. He worked steadily there until almost four o'clock when the triangle rang again. He joined the others for supper and then went straight back to work.

He continued until the light was completely gone from the sky. When he walked toward the gate, he realized Caroline was there.

"Mr. Henry, you don't have to do it all in one day."

"Believe me, I didn't. I've got the shoes back on the ones that I think your hands can use for work tomorrow, but I want to watch them move around the corral in the morning before I'm sure. Then I'll start on the ones that have the worst problems."

"Are you going back to Smoke Tree, or were you planning on staying overnight out here."

"I planned on staying. If I get an early start, some of your hands can be on horseback by lunch."

"You're welcome to stay in the bunkhouse. Plenty of room in there."

"Thanks, but I'll just toss my bedroll on the bed of the truck. I like to hear the horses in the corral when I'm going to sleep."

"See you at breakfast then. We serve a half hour before sunrise."

"Good night, ma'am."

"Goodnight, Mr. Henry."

When Caroline looked out her office window in the gray, ambient light that preceded the sunrise the next morning, Burke was already at work. When she rang the triangle for breakfast, he didn't come to the dining hall to eat. When she rang it for dinner, she walked over to the corral again.

Burke was standing outside the gate. He showed her the horses that could be used for work immediately and pointed out the ones that should be rested.

"The ones that should be rested are shod, too. Ask your hands to take them out on a lead for a run now and then, but don't let them be ridden. I'll be back in three weeks for their next trim. I'll trim them once more after that. By then, they should be ready to work.

I'm going to go to work now on the ones that have come up lame."

"Come and join us for dinner."

"Thank you. I got so busy I missed breakfast."

He worked all afternoon on the remaining horses, but didn't stay for supper. When he climbed in his truck and drove away, she walked to the front of the house and watched until he disappeared down the long driveway.

After he completed his work on the second visit,

Caroline invited him into the house for coffee again. As on that first day, she had fresh bread on the table, and this time there was a big jar of blackberry preserves. He stayed for quite a while, going over the status of each of the horses with her. The second group of problem horses, the ones that had been led out for exercise on leads, were now ready to be ridden.

"The ones that were lame are ready for exercise now. In two weeks, they can be saddled and ridden slowly, but only in the sand inside the corral, and only for a circuit or two."

"I've been watching those four. They're moving better."

Burke nodded.

"They're no longer landing toe first. That's a good thing. They're going to have better circulation in their feet, and hoof growth will speed up because the frogs in their feet will get wider and shorter. By the time I come back, each of these horses should have a wider base at the back of the foot. When I trim them and re-shoe them one more time, they'll be ready to be ridden outside the corral."

"I'm very pleased with their progress."

"I am, too. That palomino especially. I wasn't sure

I could save him as a working horse."

Burke stood up.

"Many thanks for the coffee and bread and jam, Miss McCollum."

"Thank you. I put up that jam myself last summer."

She got up and walked to the door with him. She stood in the open doorway and watched as he went down the steps. He turned at the bottom and looked up at her.

"I noticed the ranch dogs didn't bark at me when I got here this morning."

Caroline smiled.

"Smart dogs. They know who's a friend and who's not. You know, as often as he came here, they never stopped barking at Randy."

"Don't mean to be nosy, ma'am, but has Mr. Jenkins been back?"

"Only once. The next time he showed up, I told him he was no longer welcome here. I could have called his office and saved him a trip, but I wanted to tell him in person. To tell you the truth, I think he was just after the ranch."

Burke smiled.

"I'm not at all sure about that, Miss McCollum. You're a handsome woman. I can see how he would be attracted to you."

Caroline could feel color rising to her face.

"Thank you, Mr. Burke, for the compliment."

As he walked toward his truck, the dogs came out from under the porch and walked beside him. Before he climbed in, he petted each of them in turn.

By the time Burke returned for the final trim on the last Sunday before Christmas, it was very cold on the Colorado Plateau. The cottonwoods were dropping their leaves. There was a dusting of snow on the distant Hualapais.

When he had finished with the last of the horses, Caroline invited him into the kitchen. She had baked an apple pie, and she served him a big slice covered with cheddar cheese along with coffee. She sat down across from him at the kitchen table and wrote a check for the work.

She pushed it across the table to him.

"I want to thank you for a job well done."

He folded the check and put it in his shirt pocket without looking at it.

"The check is thanks enough."

"I still don't think you charged enough for what you did."

"Like I said when I started, 'working ranch discount'."

They sat silently for a moment, drinking coffee in the warm kitchen.

Caroline broke the silence.

"I have to admit, Mr. Henry, I'm going to miss seeing you every few weeks."

Burke smiled.

"Miss McCollum, if you're going to miss me, you should call me Burke. And anyway, I'll be out about every five or six weeks or so if you'd like me to keep seeing to your horses."

It was Caroline's turn to smile.

"I would. And since you're going to be Burke from now on, I'll be Caroline. And every five weeks isn't often enough."

"Why not?"

"Do I have to hit you between the eyes before you get it? I'm not talking about taking care of my horses."

"I see."

Like a lot of farm and ranch women, Caroline McCollum was very matter of fact and completely unembarrassed about sex.

"It's about time! Now, it's a Sunday, and none of the hands will be coming to the house today. I've got a big feather bed upstairs that could use a good workout. So, would you like to stay a while, Burke Henry?"

"I would, Caroline McCollum."

He drank the last of his coffee before he got up from the table. They climbed the stairs together, Caroline in the lead and Burke enjoying the view her tight Levi's afforded.

When they got to the landing, Burke said, "I should wash up, Caroline. I smell of horses."

"I love the smell of horses, Burke. Always have. Let's not keep that bed waiting."

And thus began an arrangement that worked for both of them. Burke was glad to be with Caroline when they were together. He enjoyed her company and took great pleasure from their time in bed together.

He wasn't sure about Caroline's take on the matter, but he was pretty sure he was not much more than a passing diversion to her. She was rarely affectionate with him unless they were in bed. And while she was very forthcoming about herself and talked endlessly about her past and the ranch, she never asked him about himself. From some of the remarks she made, it was obvious to Burke she had been conditioned by her father to believe that anyone who showed an interest in her was probably trying to get a piece of the ranch.

He saw those remarks as a warning not to get too serious about her. But outsiders were not aware of the limitations of their situation, and Burke and Caroline quickly became in item on the Colorado Plateau.

Burke often went out to her place when he was between jobs, but he always called ahead to be sure he would be welcome. When he arrived, he would saddle up Sugarfoot for Caroline and one of the cow ponies for himself, and they would ride out over the ranch. While they rode, Caroline liked to talk about the pioneers who had settled the area and the history of ranching on the plateau. A lot of the history involved her family.

Burke was very aware she never mentioned the Hualapai Indians who had been living in the area for centuries before the pioneers showed up and pushed them aside. It was clear to him that from her point of view they were just incidentals on the landscape, like the pronghorn antelope, mule deer and rattlesnakes.

He did not comment on the gap in her histories.

Sometimes, they drove into Kingman for a restaurant meal. When they did, Burke was partial to the Ichiban. He liked Japanese food and was obviously familiar with every item on the menu. Caroline never showed the slightest interest in why that was so.

As winter came down across the high country, temperatures dropped so low that riding was no longer enjoyable. When that happened, Caroline began to trailer Sugarfoot down to Hugh Stanton's station at Arrowhead Junction on the weekends. Burke and Pepper would be waiting for her. They would leave the horse trailer there and ride across the desert to Burke's place, a place she referred to as "primitive, but charming."

When they weren't in his bed, or in front of a fire,

they rode the desert trails that branched off the old road and fanned out through the Piutes and into the Lanfair Valley and the Castle Peaks. Sometimes, they would ride east instead and follow the pass between the Newberry and Dead Mountains down to the Colorado River.

Burke thought things were going well between them. He even allowed himself to think they might have a future together. But that was before the romance came to a crashing conclusion.

Easter fell on April second in 1961. It was blustery and cold on the high desert, as Easter often can be on the Mojave. Caroline and Burke climbed out of his warm bed on Sunday morning before first light and rekindled a fire from the previous evening's coals in the wood-burning stove. After breakfast and coffee, Burke saddled Pepper and Sugarfoot, and he and Caroline headed east on the Old Mojave Road. The wind was blowing in from the north, but a bright sun shone from a cloudless sky as they rode.

A little before noon, they stopped and watered the horses at Government Holes. They were riding on toward Round Valley when Caroline saw the big, white-washed-adobe hacienda with its red tile roof on the side of Pinto Mountain.

"Who owns that beautiful house?"

"John Stonebridge. It was built by his father, a transplanted English Lord. He died a few years ago, and his son, John, inherited the place."

"This John Stonebridge, he lives there with his family?"

"As I understand it, John has never been married."

"Do you know him?"

"Done some work for him, time to time. Good man. Knows his stuff. Keeps his wits about him."

"How big an outfit does he run?"

"Big. Not as big as yours, but pretty big. It's a different operation than any of the other ranches in the area."

"How so?"

"The others all run steers. The Box S is cow and calf."

"I'd like to learn more about it. Do you think he'd mind if we stopped by?"

"Only one way to find out."

They turned their mounts northeast and crossed Cedar Canyon road at the point where it met the two-track that ran north to the Box S. When the road began to climb Pinto Mountain, Burke reined Pepper to a halt and climbed down.

"This is a steep road, even with the cutbacks. I'm going to lead Pepper to the top. He's had enough exercise for a while, and I need some."

"You can spoil your horse if you want to, cowboy, but cowgirls always ride."

When they reached the top of the hill and rode past the corral, John's horses turned as one to watch them pass.

Before they reached the big house, a tall, slender, rangy man with reddish blonde hair came out and walked across the veranda to meet them.

"Burke Henry. Didn't expect to see you out here today."

"I apologize for dropping by unannounced, John.

The pretty lady on the pretty horse is Caroline McCollum. She owns the Sunnyside ranch over by Seligman."

"Pleased to meet you, Miss McCollum. My father greatly admired your ranch. He visited it when he was searching this country for a place to put down roots.

Please, come inside. I've got coffee on the stove and a nice fire in the great room."

Caroline swung down from her horse.

"Thank you. Hot coffee and a fire sounds inviting. A bit brisk today."

"I'm sure it's not nearly as cold as out your way."

"I'll see to the horses and join you in a few minutes," said Burke.

Leading Pepper and Sugarfoot to the corral, he unsaddled them and hoisted the saddles onto the pipe that formed the top rail. He hitched the to the middle pipe and went into the feed room. He brought each of them two scoops of grain. He hobbled them and removed their bridles so they could enjoy their grain without contending with a bit. The horses in the corral watched with great interest as he took care of Pepper and Sugarfoot. They were especially interested in the scoops of grain. By the time Burke turned toward the house, they had moved closer to the horses hobbled outside.

When Burke went into the great room, he saw that John had lowered the huge chandelier and lit the oil lamps before hoisting it back into position. There were three leather chairs in front of the blaze in the huge fireplace and mugs of coffee on the low table in front of the chairs. Caroline was oohing and aahing about the furniture and fixtures in the ornate room while John explained how his father brought the furniture home after an extended trip to Europe.

It wasn't long before he and Caroline were involved in a discussion about how ranching on the Colorado Plateau compared to ranching in the East Mojave.

Burke paid scant attention. While he would talk horses with anyone, cattle did not interest him. In fact, he felt sorry for steers and cows and calves. He noticed that while ranchers held horses in high regard and had only contempt for anyone who would mistreat one, they seemed casually and callously abusive of the cattle they ran. As if they failed to understand that the cattle they treated so poorly made their financial success possible.

After listening to the ranching talk for as long as he could stand it, he excused himself and went back out to the corral. He spent over an hour in the cold wind checking the condition of the horses and making mental notes for future trimming and shoeing.

When Burke returned to the house, Caroline and John were getting to their feet. Caroline and Burke thanked John for his hospitality as they walked to the door.

"Come anytime. Always glad to talk ranching."

Outside, John accompanied Burke and Caroline to the corral. He and Caroline stood some distance away and watched as Burke bridled and saddled the horses

"I've never seen a man who was more comfortable with horses," said Caroline. "And I've never seen a man who made horses feel more comfortable. He has this amazing rapport with them."

"I know what you mean about horses. Maybe he was born to it."

"Born to it how?"

"Burke grew up on the KCA Indian reservation in Oklahoma. He was probably riding before he could walk."

"I didn't know that. Was his father with the

Bureau of Indian Affairs?"

John suddenly realized he may have put his foot in his mouth. He looked embarrassed.

"I'm sorry. I thought Burke had told you. His father was white, and his mother was Indian."

A swarm of emotions moved across Caroline's face. She opened her mouth to say something, but at first nothing came out. When she finally managed to speak, it was to say, "Excuse me."

She left a chagrined John Stonebridge standing alone in his driveway as she walked to where Burke was cinching Surgarfoot's saddle.

"Let's get out of here," she hissed.

Burke picked up the urgency in her voice.

"What's the matter?"

"I'll tell you later. Let's just go. Please!"

"Okay."

Burke helped her onto her saddle and walked over to say goodbye to John. Pepper trailed behind. Caroline turned and started down the road as the two men shook hands.

Burke looked after her.

"Don't know what's got into her."

"Maybe with all the ranching talk, she thought of something she has to do back at her place."

Burke shook his head.

"Maybe. I'd better catch her up. Thanks again for inviting us in on no notice at all."

When Burke caught up with Caroline, she did not turn to look at him. Her mouth was set in a straight line and her face was red. Burke couldn't tell whether she was mad or had been crying.

"What was that all about?"

"All what?"

"You were very rude back there. Didn't even say goodbye. Just rode away and left John and me standing there."

She didn't reply.

They rode on silently until they reached Cedar Canyon Road and cut south across it. When they were on the Old Mojave Road, Caroline spoke without looking at him.

"You never told me you were an Indian."

She spat out the word 'Indian' as if it were a curse.

"You never asked. Just like I never asked you if you were white. You are, aren't you?"

"Of course!"

"Well, I have to admit I suspected. I forgive you, though."

"You forgive me?"

"Sure. Why not?"

"Who else knows."

"That you're white?"

"Stop it. Stop trying to turn this into a joke."

She turned and looked at him, her eyes wide in anger. When she did, she saw something cold in his eyes. She turned away.

"I mean, who else knows you're an Indian?"

"A lot of people. My mother knew, I'm pretty sure."

She felt her face flare hot again.

"I mean in Smoke Tree."

"Quite a few, I suppose. I've never made a secret of it."

"Oh, God, I'm ruined! The Santa Fe crews from Smoke Tree spend their rest periods in Seligman waiting for a westbound job. If people in Smoke Tree know you're Indian, it's just a matter of time before the word gets around Seligman that Caroline McCollum, a woman from one of the most respected families on the high plains, is sleeping with an Indian."

"I wouldn't call it sleeping, Caroline, even though we do that from time to time."

"You should have told me, Burke. Told me before this all got started."

"Like I said, you never asked. You do almost all the talking in this outfit. I rarely get a word in edgewise."

She turned her face toward him again, her green eyes flashing.

"I never suspected, you idiot. You have blonde hair and blue eyes, for God's sake."

Burke laughed, but there was no humor in the sound and no smile in his eyes.

"Haven't you ever seen the blue-eyed Indian on the Navajo Freight Line trucks that roll through on 66?"

"Just what the hell kind of Indian are you, anyway?"

"I'm Kiowa Apache."

Caroline let out a shriek.

"An Apache."

"Yep."

"This has got to stop."

"Being an Apache?"

"No, damnit! Whatever we've been doing. It has to stop."

"If you say so."

"That's all you can say? 'If you say so?'"

"Seems to me, Caroline, if two people have been screwing, and all of a sudden one of them doesn't want to anymore, then they're done. Whatever they had is finished. What else is there to say about it?"

"Is that all this was to you, Burke? Just screwing?"

"I've thought for some time now it might be turning into something more. Now that I hear the way you talk, I know it was never going to."

They reached the steep hillside that led down into Watson's Wash and started down, the horses stepping cautiously. They crossed the wash and climbed into the Joshua Tree forest beyond the crest of the steep hill.

The sun was angling toward the western horizon. The temperature was dropping fast. They rode all the way back to Piute Creek without speaking another word. When they reached Fort Piute, Caroline brought Sugarfoot to a halt.

"I'm going home."

"Okay, I'll ride to your horse trailer with you and help you get Sugarfoot inside."

"I don't need your help, Burke."

"No, I'm sure you don't. You're quite the cowgirl, Miss McCollum. Quite the cowgirl. In more ways than one."

He watched Caroline ride away. She never looked back before she disappeared from view.

Burke rode home and unsaddled Pepper and turned him into the corral. He walked to the house and sat at the kitchen table for a long time. He wondered how much Caroline's decision had to do with him being Apache and how much to meeting the interesting, wealthy and single son of an English Lord.

If she makes a run at John, he thought, she may

be in for a surprise. Because while he had been in the corral with the horses, he had caught a glimpse of a petite, Asian woman over near the barn. Someone who probably thought Burke was inside. Someone who clearly did not want to be seen. Someone John had not mentioned to his guests.

Burke stayed at the table for a long time. Darkness had fallen before he got up and lit an oil lamp. He knew he might not be able to forget Caroline, but he was determined not to miss her.

CHAPTER 26

Christmas 1961 Smoke Tree, California

Burke spent his sixth Christmas in Smoke Tree with Horse and Esperanza. He had gratefully accepted their kind invitation to come to their home for dinner on Christmas afternoon, and it was a delightful occasion. The day was warm, sunny, and filled with friendship. Horse's mother, Consuela, was there. She and Burke hit it off immediately. She was full of questions about his life at Piute Creek, and Burke was more than willing to answer them, as long as they did not stray into his life before he arrived in Smoke Tree. When they did, he became very vague, and she was quick to realize it would be best if she confined her questions to the recent past and the present.

At two o'clock, they gathered around the dining room table for a wonderful meal of pork, chicken and beef tamales and enchiladas with Christmas Tree chili sauce. They had a dessert of *pastel de tres leches* and coffee in the living room next to the tree.

The only somber note of the day was struck when Esperanza excused herself from the table to call her mother in Santa Fe. She made the call from the phone in the kitchen. It was a conversation that began with "*Feliz Navidad*" followed by a long silence and then the words, "*Si, por supuesto,*" and then "*Adios, Madre.*"

When she returned to the table, they could tell she had been crying.

"Are you all right, Esperanza?"

"Yes, Carlos. She just makes me so angry. She tells me all about her life in Santa Fe. 'A real Spanish community' she calls it. She talks so fast I can't get in a single word. And then she asks the same question she asks every time I call. '*Están todavía casados a eso Mestizo*'?"

"When I say, '*si, supuesto,*' she hangs up before I can even say '*adios.*'"

Consuela spoke up.

"*No ser demasiado duro en su madre. Ella es una persona muy orgullosa que creció en un tiempo cuando ser mexicano en árbol de humo debía ser irrespetado.*

Aprendió a protegerse por ser cien por cien español."

Esperanza wiped her eyes and turned to Burke.

"I'm sorry. We shouldn't be speaking Spanish. It's rude to our guest. Let me translate what we said."

"No es necesario, Señora Caballo. Hablar en Español."

"You never told me you spoke Spanish."

Burke shrugged.

"There was never a need to. But it's been a long time since my days in the Philippines. How about we all speak Spanish for the rest of the day so I can get in some practice?"

And they did. Right up until the time there was a knock on the door.

Horse stood up.

"That'll be two of the deputies. You'll know them, Burke."

He smiled.

"You've bounced them off the mats in the gym."

He opened the door and invited the deputies inside. They followed him to the dining room table.

"Mom, this is Stuart Atkins, and Andy Chesney.

These are the guys who got me into this bow shooting stuff."

Stuart and Andy nodded.

"And you both know Burke."

"Sure do," said Stuart. "I ache every time I think about him."

"Mom, I'd better explain that. Burke has been conducting some escalation of force training for the deputies. Sometimes, that means he throws them around a little."

Andy laughed.

"'A little' hardly describes it."

"A couple of the guys from the mounted posse will be along too. We've set up some hay bales up the road in the hills. We're going to practice a little archery. We were hoping you'd come along. I just got a new bow, and you're welcome to share it with me."

Burke smiled.

"Sure, if I can still walk after that wonderful meal. I haven't shot in years, but I'd like to give it a try."

By three thirty in the afternoon, the sun was tilting

toward the western horizon as the group, now augmented by three men from the sheriff's mounted posse, walked toward the hillside course.

"You say Stuart and Andy got you into this?"

"Andy, mostly. He started the group. Stuart was the first to join."

"What got you interested, Andy?"

"When I was a kid growing up in Fontana, my dad worked for Kaiser Steel. There was an archery range for the employees, and my dad had an old bow. We started shooting there on the weekends. It wasn't long before Dad and I were pretty good. We got better bows, and one of the other shooters told us about the National Field Archery Association course in the hills just east of Redlands. As soon as we started shooting up there, I was really hooked. It was so much more interesting than shooting at the same target at the same distance time after time.

That's why we laid out this course. All the bales are at different distances from the shooting spot. Some are uphill shots, some down. Only this first one is level.

"Who owns this property?"

"It belongs to the Bureau of Land Management. Which means it belongs to all of us," said Horse.

The group was soon gathered thirty yards from the first bale. There was a colored bullseye target on the bale. A balloon was pinned in the center.

"I was out here earlier this morning and pinned balloons to every bale. Thought it might be fun to try to pop them. For our competition today, we'll make a circuit of all eleven bales on the course and shoot for points. Ten for a bullseye, seven for the yellow ring, five for the blue and two for the white. Ten-point bonus if you pop the balloon."

"Great day for it," said Stuart.

"No wind. Warm sun."

"Better enjoy it," said Horse. "It's due to change. Be cold and windy in a couple of days.

Since Burke here hasn't drawn a bow in a few years, I'm going to let him take a few practice shots. Then we'll start around. Everyone gets two arrows for each bale."

He handed Burke his bow. It was a fifty pound, twenty-eight-inch draw, Black Widow recurve.

"That sight is set for me. If you want to change it

after you shoot, that's fine. I know my setting."

"Don't use a sight."

The gathered men exchanged glances and knowing smiles.

Burke strapped on Horse's arm guard and borrowed his shooting glove to protect his fingers.

He knocked an aluminum arrow and pulled the heavy recurve as casually as a child would pull a toy bow with suction cup arrows. He held it at full draw for a moment. There was no tremor in his arm while he got the feel for the powerful bow before slowly returning it to its undrawn position.

He stood with the bow at his side and stared at the target for a moment before pulling the bow to full draw and quickly releasing the arrow.

It hit the white ring.

The second arrow, pulled and released just as quickly, popped the balloon.

"Beginner's luck," laughed one of the men from the posse.

But it wasn't. Burke easily bested everyone in the group, even the two men with elaborate stabilizers and sophisticated sights on their bows. Because the scoring system rewarded the high-point scorer on the last bale with the first shot at the next one, Burke hit the balloon on nine of the eleven bales before anyone else had a chance to shoot.

Horse and the others had never seen anything like it. From the time Burke knocked an arrow until the time he let it fly was a matter of seconds. He didn't seem to actually aim: it was more like he was doing some complex geometric and spatial conception calculation at lightning speed before the quick release.

"How do you do that?" Horse asked his friend.

Burke smiled.

"Apache Zen."

As they walked the course, Burke questioned Horse about his bow. He noticed the phrase, "Custom made for Carlos Caballo, Nixa, Missouri" on the face of the lower limb of the recurve and wanted to know how long it took to get one made.

Back home that night, Burke thought about the fall his Ukrainian father decided to abandon the family. The fall he was ten years old. He remembered hunting rabbits with the small bow hand-crafted for him by a kind neighbor. He brought home rabbit after rabbit as his hunting skills improved. His mother cut them into pieces and sealed them in quart jars with chicken broth and spices before she cooked them in the pressure canner. The rabbits helped the family survive the long Oklahoma winter.

But that winter took a toll on his mother. She never recovered from being left to raise him and his sister on her own in his father's absence. By the following autumn, she had turned to prostitution. By winter, the mental anguish of prostitution had driven her to alcoholism.

She was soon forever lost to him and his little sister.

Burke also thought back to his experience with Zen archery in postwar Japan. There, he discovered a kind of shooting that grounded him in the effortless accuracy of a physical activity that made complex and difficult movements without conscious control: The Seven Coordinations that balanced the energy of mind, body, and bow.

He had taken much solace from that practice. It aided his mental recovery from the years of combat in the Pacific.

Within in a week, Burke had ordered his own bow from Black Widow. When it arrived, he set out a course of his own around Piute Mountain. It soon became part of his weekly routine to practice and find peace there. And although he sometimes shot on the course north of Horse's place with the other archers, he never invited anyone but Horse to shoot with him at Piute Creek.

And so, Burke returned to his solitary life. His contact with others was limited to working with their horses, training the Smoke Tree Substation deputies, and visiting with Horse and Esperanza from time to time.

It was a lonely life, but one he found satisfactory.

And always, in the back of his mind, was the expectation that someone from Caddo County, most probably Deputy Scuttler, would show up to extract revenge for the disappearance of the three incompetent Klan members who had been swept away in Piute Gorge.

Expectation probably wasn't quite the right word. Anticipation was probably more like it. Eager anticipation.

Come on ahead, Deputy, he thought. What's

taking you so long?

Deep Desert Deception

CHAPTER 27

July 12, 1962 San Quentin, California

Recently retired Caddo County Deputy Dave Scuttler met Arvin Lacey outside the gates of San Quentin Prison the morning of his release. Clouds were scudding across the sky, and salt-water-tinged wind was blowing across the parking lot.

"Thanks for coming, Dave," said Lacey as he climbed in the pickup.

Scuttler gave him the briefest of cold glances.

"It's not a favor. It's a job."

They drove away from the prison and were soon on the San Rafael-Richmond Bridge.

"Dave? This is the wrong bridge! You've got to get on the Golden Gate to get to San Francisco."

"Why would I want to go to San Francisco?"

"Because I've been dreaming about The City for twelve years."

"Yeah? Well, dream about it some more. This is

not a vacation. You're being paid three thousand dollars to do a job. We're on our way to do it."

They rode in silence across the broad waterway that stretched out beneath the massive bridge. A half hour out of prison and Arvin Lacey was already in a bad mood. But at least he didn't have to report to some parole officer. That was the benefit of going out max-time-served.

He decided to try to get along with the former lawman.

"You know, I watched them build this thing. Watched from the prison yard."

"Good for you."

"But I never wanted to ride on it. Like I said, I dreamed of going to The City."

"Why would you want to go to a place full of faggots, mud people, beatniks and other Commies?"

"Are you kidding, Dave? Frisco's where it's at."

"When we finish this job, you can go there. Or anywhere else you want. With three thousand dollars, you can buy a new car and have plenty of money left over."

"Speaking of that, what are we doing, exactly? You

never told me."

"Too many ears in the visiting room of a prison."

"You could have written it down and slipped it to me."

"You're full of dumb ideas, aren't you? What if some guard had got hold of it? What if you talked about it to someone in the slammer and it got out?"

"I wouldn't have told anyone but my brothers in the Diamond Tooth Gang."

"Yeah, and they're all great thinkers. That's why they're in prison."

"Hey, I was in..."

"That's right, Lacey, you were."

Lacey fell silent for a while. He was trying to decide if he had been insulted. If he had, he would have to take some action. In prison, you don't let insults go unchallenged. You either act or get a reputation for being weak. And once cons think you're weak, you're a target.

After thinking it over, he decided he was going to have to get used to living in the world outside the walls where different rules applied. He tamped down his anger.

"So, do you have my money with you?"

"Not your money yet, sonny."

"I know, but I mean for after."

"I'll explain that later."

"I want to know now, Dave!"

"Hold your horses a minute."

After they got off the bridge, Scuttler pulled to the side of the highway. He shut off the engine and turned toward Lacey.

"You ask too many questions."

Lacey looked at Scuttler. Really looked at him. The man had to be at least fifty years old, if not older. There were streaks of gray in his hair, lines all over his face.

Lacey decided to set him straight.

"Listen to me, old man..."

Which was as far as he got before Scuttler's hand shot out and clamped onto his neck. Scuttler's thumb and fingers dug into nerves that Lacey didn't even know existed. His left arm immediately went numb. He reached up with his right and tried to pull Scuttler's hand off his neck.

He might just as well have tried to pry open a pair of vice grips with a toothpick. The man's grip was like a steel claw. The more Lacey struggled, the tighter the claw squeezed.

He screamed in pain and tried to twist away.

It didn't work. More pressure. More pain.

"All right! All right!"

"All right, what?"

"All right whatever you want, man!"

The pain decreased from unbearable to merely excruciating.

"That's better. Back there in that prison, you probably strutted around the yard and thought you were tough because you were part of a gang. But there's no gang in this truck with you today. There's just you and me. There's men in the ground all over Oklahoma who thought they were tougher than Deputy Dave Scuttler. Believe me, boy, you don't want to get crossways with me. If you do, you might never get over it. You got that?"

"Yes."

The pain ramped up again.

"Yes, what?"

"Yes, sir."

The pain eased but did not go away completely.

"Now, ask your question."

"What is the job?"

"We're going to kill a man."

"Why?"

Scuttler glared at him and Lacey braced for more pain. But Scuttler relented.

"He killed three members of the Lawton Ku Klux Klan and put another in a wheelchair."

"This is a white man?"

"A stinking Apache."

"A mud person."

"That's right."

"I hate mud people. That's why we started the Diamond Tooth Gang in prison: to protect white men from them. To let mud people know this is a white man's country.

But this one you're going after killed three guys from the Klan. I can see why you're going to need my help."

Scuttler's eyes flared, and Lacey was afraid the

terrible pain was about to increase.

"There's a little more to it than just killing. We're going to cut him up and bury him where no one will ever find him. You're going to help me with that. When we're done, you get your three thousand."

"Where is this man?"

"Out on the Mojave Desert."

"A town out there?"

"A long way from any town."

"Don't sound too hard."

"We'll just see, won't we?"

"Can I ask another question?"

"Go ahead."

"It's the same one I asked before. Do you have the money with you?"

The thumb and fingers bore down again. The pain shot up to unbearable.

"Ow, ow, Goddamnit."

"That's the same question that got you in trouble before. Do I look stupid to you?"

"Oh no! No sir. Not at all," Lacey practically screamed.

The pain lessened.

"Then here's all you need to know.

This place we're going to is close to the Nevada border. Once we do the job, we drive to Las Vegas to a bank there. I have your money in that bank. We go in the bank together and you get your pay. Then I go away and leave you there. In Las Vegas. With three thousand cash dollars. In a place full of casinos and cheap booze and beautiful women."

"That sounds good!"

The hand fell away.

Arvin Lacey was massaging the muscles on the left side of his neck as Scuttler started the truck and pulled back onto the highway.

"One more question."

Scuttler glared at him.

Arvin Lacey held up his hands.

"Not a bad one.

I just want to know where we're going now?"

"Stockton. We'll pick up Highway 99 there and take it to Bakersfield. Outside Bakersfield, we'll get on Highway 58 and go up over Tehachapi pass and drive to Barstow. Should be there not long after sundown.

We'll stay in Barstow overnight. Early tomorrow morning, we'll get on 66 and head for a town called Smoke Tree. Just before we get there, we'll turn onto a different highway and drive to a service station where we'll talk to an old man who knows how to get to this man's place in the desert. We'll drive out that way and take a little scout around. Then, we'll drive to Smoke Tree and get a motel and go to bed early. Before daylight on Friday morning, we'll be on our way to take care of our business."

"Why do you want to...?"

Scuttler held up his hand.

Lacey immediately clamped his mouth shut.

"One more thing. Stop calling me 'Dave'. It's either 'sir' or 'Mr. Scuttler' from now on. Got it?"

"Yes, Mr. Scuttler."

"Good. Now, like I said, you know everything you have to know. I don't want you to ask another question or even say another goddamned word before we stop for something to eat in Stockton. Got it?"

"Yessir."

And he didn't.

When they arrived in Barstow, night had fallen.

CHAPTER 28

July 13, 1962 Arrowhead Junction, California

Acts of kindness sometimes pay 'unexpected dividends. It may be that they pay the most when they are performed without any expectation of either benefit or reciprocity. Ever since completing his house on Piute Creek, Burke had made it a habit to stop by Hugh Stanton's Arrowhead Junction service station once or twice a week to make sure the Chickasaw Indian was all right. After all, the man was eighty-six years old and living alone, and Burke was very fond of him.

In the warm and hot months, they sat under the service station overhang, Mr. Stanton in his rocking chair and Burke beside him on the cement steps that led to the office. In the winter, Mr. Stanton moved his rocker south of the overhang to pick up what warmth he could from the weak, winter sun. During those months, Burke was close beside him in the effortless squat he had acquired from years and years of martial arts stretching, his elbows across his knees, his head resting on his forearms and angled toward the old Chickasaw.

Mr. Stanton was grateful for the company. Very few travelers ever stopped by the old station and even fewer visitors. In the fall months of 1959, two young men from Smoke Tree, Aeden Snow and Johnny Quentin, had sometimes stopped by on weekends on their return from hunting trips in the Providence or New York Mountains. In the fall of 1960, Johnny stopped coming, but Aeden continued his weekly visits. Then, in 1961, "young Master Snow" as Mr. Stanton called him, went off to college on California's central coast, and Burke's visits became ever more important.

The most common topic of conversation when Burke stopped by was Oklahoma. Mr. Stanton had lived on a farm there until he was in his fifties, save for a stint in the Army in Belgium and France during World War One. He was very familiar with the area around Oklahoma City, including Caddo and Comanche Counties. He sometimes told Burke stories about the people who had farmed in that area, and some of those families had still been in Caddo County when Burke was growing up.

For the most part, Burke was content to listen, although he sometimes prompted Mr. Stanton with question about the old man's life as a wheat farmer in the years before drought and short-sighted farming practices had turned the area into the Dust Bowl of the 1930s. Mr. Stanton had come west in 1934 and he often talked to Burke about the difficulty of the journey he had made down the Mother Road with his brother and his brother's wife.

At noon on a blistering hot day in July of 1962, Burke was returning from an appointment in Las Vegas. Since he had been doing a preliminary assessment on the work to be done for a doctor who owned a number of horses, he was riding his motorcycle: no need to spend a lot of money on gas for his truck when he didn't have to carry tools.

Driving the Royal Enfield south on 95 through Searchlight and the series of dips beyond was like riding a pogo stick into the mouth of a blast furnace. The scorching heat sucked moisture from his skin, cracked his lips, and scorched the tips of his ears. He wanted nothing more than to get home to Piute Creek and have a cold drink on his back porch, but he had not visited Hugh Stanton in a few days. The old man was getting increasingly forgetful, and Burke worried about him.

He continued on past his turn-off and drove to Arrowhead Junction. He was glad to see Mr. Stanton in his rocking chair. Pulling his motorcycle into the shade, he walked over and took a seat next to him on the cement steps under the overhang. As they talked, mostly about the weather, Mr. Stanton reached in his pocket and pulled out a slip of paper.

"Got something to tell you, Burke. Wrote a note to myself so as not to forget. Getting terrible forgetful as the years pass me by."

He paused while he unfolded the scrap.

"Wrote it down because it reminded me of something that happened back in the summer of the big flood.

I was outside having my coffee at sunrise this morning when two men come by the station in a pickup truck. Wanted to know how to get to Fort Piute. It called to the mind the year the flood killed them poor railroad workers on down toward Smoke Tree."

Burke was suddenly very interested, but he did not interrupt. He knew Mr. Stanton would fill in the details in his own time.

"Let me tell you about that time in the flood year first.

They was three of them in a pickup. Three big men. The one who was driving had real mean eyes and did most of the talking. Said they was from Chicago. Said they was big fans of western lore. Said they studied it all the time and went on trips to find the trails the pioneers had used on the way west. They mentioned the Chisolm and the Santa Fe, as I recall.

Parts of their story didn't hold up. The truck they was a-drivin' had Oklahoma plates. The driver give me some cock 'n bull story about starting out from Chicago in a car, but said it broke down in Oklahoma City. Overheated, I believe he said, Froze up the engine solid. So, he says, they bought a truck there and come on ahead. Dodge pickup it was. '56 C-Series. Had the V8 engine and so forth, you see?

Well, the story rung hollow. Sure as God made little green apples, them boys was Okies, ever one. Why they wanted me to believe otherwise is beyond me, but I know a Oklahoma accent when I hear one.

Another thing. Said they had studied western lore about the pioneers and all. Knowed all about the Old Mojave Road. But if they had, they'd a knowed it was never a pioneer road a'tall. It was a freight and mail and army road, pure and simple. That's why some folks out this way still call it Government Road."

He paused for a long time. Burke waited patiently.

"Where was I? Oh, yeah, I told them how to find the road. Give them some free advice about desert travel too. Mostly advised them not to go down that road in August. Told them to come back in winter and try her then. Whether they did or not, I don't know. I never saw them again."

Mr. Stanton stopped again and became very still. If his eyes hadn't been open, Burke would have thought he had fallen asleep. These kinds of interludes had been happening more and more frequently in the last few months.

When Mr. Stanton spoke again, it was to ask Burke if he had seen Horse lately. He knew Burke and the Lieutenant were good friends. As soon as he put the question, he seemed to notice the piece of paper he still held in his hand. He took off his long-billed green cap and mopped his brow with the back of his hand.

"Almost forgot, same as I forgot back in the flood year. That's why I wrote it down on this here paper.

So's I wouldn't forget to tell you again, you see?"

He paused again, this time to collect his thoughts.

"Like I said when I started, they was two of them this very morning. Lookin' for the fort, I mean.

I told them the same as I told them other boys all those years back about how to find the Mojave Road and take it to Fort Piute. I started to tell them about needing to be prepared before they drove out there in the heat of summer too, but the one who was driving said they didn't want to go that way. Said they wanted to hike a bit. Wanted to know exactly where they could park along Old 66 to strike off and come at the fort from the south. Said they was used to desert hiking and had plenty of water with them. Knowed there was water at Piute Creek they could fill up on for the hike back. Said they had driven a long ways to get here and were too tired to do her today, but said they'd come back early tomorrow morning and give her a go.

So, I told them about where the railroad trestle next to old 66 goes over the big wash. Told them they could park off the road there and walk under the trestle and head off to Fort Piute. Give them real good directions all the way to the fort.

They thanked me and drove away. But I have to

tell you, Burke, when I thought about it later, it seemed a story with a big hole in it, just like that story all those years ago."

"Why's that, Mr. Stanton?"

"Well sir, the driver looked like a man who could walk any number of miles. Real fit looking. Had the face and arms of a man who had spent a considerable part of his life out in the sun. Hard lookin' feller. Smiled at me the whole time he talked, but his eyes told a different tale entire.

But the other one? Quite a bit younger, but didn't look like no desert hiker no ways. Kind of a pasty complexion, you see? Like a man who hadn't spent no time a'tall in the sun for a long, long time. And wild lookin' eyes. Eyes just kept jumpin' all over, like he couldn't hardly keep a-lookin' at just one thing at a time.

And somethin' else. That one didn't say much. Mr. Hard Man did most of the talking.

But the times Mr. Crazy Eyes did say somethin', they was something sparkly in his mouth. Like pieces of quartz or something. Made me think he'd been chewin' rocks. Darndest thing I ever saw."

Again, Mr. Stanton fell silent and sat staring out

at the Dead Mountains across the highway. The heat of the day was so intense the shimmering waves of hot air made the range appear to be floating in the air.

Again, he seemed to rouse himself like a man waking from a trance. He turned to look at Burke.

"Dagnabbit, they was one more thing I was a-goin' to tell you about them boys. Something important."

"Maybe you wrote it on that piece of paper," Burke gently prodded.

Mr. Stanton looked down.

"Why, I surely did. Thank you, Burke!

What I was a-goin' to tell you was that when them boys drove off, I noticed their truck had Oklahoma plates, same as that truck come by the summer of the flood. It was gone afore I could write down the number, but they was Oklahoma plates, sure enough."

Deep Desert Deception

CHAPTER 29

July 13, 1962 Piute Creek

Burke left Mr. Stanton in the shade of the overhang and drove his motorcycle up Old 66. He didn't think Scuttler and his unknown accomplice would come for him in the bright light of day, but it was best to be sure he was not driving into an ambush by going home.

He rode past the place where Mr. Stanton had told the men to park if they wanted to hike to Fort Piute from the south. There was no vehicle there. He drove a few more miles up the road to be sure they hadn't parked farther away and then come back. He drove back to the trestle. He left his bike beside the road and went in on foot. It didn't take him long to find the tracks of a vehicle that had driven off the road and gone a short distance into the desert before stopping.

He found four sets of footprints. Two sets leading away from where the truck had stopped. The same two sets returning. Adults, probably male by the size of the tracks. One in a pair of good boots, the other wearing something cheap. Smooth on the bottom. He followed them under the railroad trestle and a few hundred yards farther up the wash before he turned and headed back.

So, the men had been here. Had walked into the desert and made their reconnaissance and then returned to the vehicle and driven somewhere. Smoke Tree, most likely, or perhaps Searchlight or even Las Vegas. Somewhere they could hole up and avoid the heat of the desert afternoon. But they would be back. Perhaps that night beneath the light of the gibbous, nearly-full moon, but more likely in the light of pre-dawn tomorrow morning.

He started his motorcycle and headed home. As he drove, he thought about the two men. He knew from Mr. Stanton's description that one was Dave Scuttler. He had no idea who the other one might be. Scuttler wasn't stupid like the Klan boys who had shown up in 1959. Burke now knew they would be coming in on foot from the south, although he doubted they would show up hungover and unprepared after noon like the first bunch.

Back at his place, he forked hay into Pepper's

corral. He added a scoop of oats from the steel barrel in the tack room. He went up to the house. Although he had left all the windows open that morning, it was like walking into an oven. He got a Nehi grape soda from his propane refrigerator and went out to his back porch for a think.

He felt no fear. No anxiety. Instead, he felt a low hum of excitement. A kind of exhilaration. The time had come at last. The third of the evil trio who had assaulted Alicia was close by. As he sat sipping his grape drink, he thought about the man who hated Indians. The man who had probably killed more than one in Caddo County without being called to account. Because he carried a badge. A license to hunt Indians.

You like to hunt Indians, you mean sonofabitch, he thought. I'll give you an Indian to hunt.

He finished his drink and took the empty to the kitchen. He went to his bedroom and took off his chukka boots and traded his Levi's for an old pair of fatigue pants. He dug around in his closet for his Corcoran jump boots and then exchanged his white t-shirt for one of olive drab.

He crossed the room and sat down at a little table in front of the mirror he had hung on the wall for

Caroline in a time long past. He picked up the tube of bright red lipstick she had left behind and drew two long, wide streaks from beneath his eyes to his jawline. Then he drew another from his hairline to the tip of his nose.

In the kitchen, he opened the firebox of the wood-burning stove. Reaching inside, he coated both hands with charcoal. Back in the bedroom, he sat in front of the mirror again and spread the charcoal all over his face and neck, careful not to smear the three red streaks

Satisfied, he picked up his Army field cap and smeared the remaining charcoal all over it before clamping in on his head.

He took his bow down from above the fireplace and took it to the bench in his workshop. He unclipped the aluminum arrows from the attached quiver and unscrewed all the field points. He replaced them with razor-sharp, serrated-edge broadheads and snapped them back into the quiver. When he was done, he stood up and flexed the bow across his calf and strung it before going back to the living room and putting it on the couch.

Returning to the kitchen, he filled a desert bag

with water from the pump in the sink. He took a plastic bag filled with roasted, unsalted almonds out of the refrigerator.

Down at the tack room, he wrestled one of the sheets of half inch plywood that was leaning against the outside wall onto the sawhorses. Collecting a saw from the tack room, he cut the sheet in half.

He carried one of the four by four pieces to the house and put it on his work bench. From his box of wood-working tools, he selected the Miller's Falls 2A hand drill and inserted a bit into the chuck. He drilled holes in the top two corners of the plywood. In the bedroom, he pulled the rawhide lace out of an old hunting boot and carried it back to the bench. He threaded the lace through the holes and tied knots on each end to keep it from sliding free.

He slipped the lace over his head and let the board hang down his back. It slipped too far down, and the rawhide lace cut into his throat. He took the board off and moved the knots. He got a bandana from the dresser in the bedroom. He twisted the bandana around the lace and put the contraption back over his head. The board hung just about the right distance down his back. The bandana-wrapped rawhide cord no longer bit into his neck.

In the kitchen, he picked up the desert bag and slung it over his shoulder. It was heavy and damp against his thigh. He opened the refrigerator and got a handful of carrots. He picked his bow up off the couch and went out the door without locking it.

At the corral, he snapped the carrots into pieces and fed them to Pepper off his palm. He listened to the satisfying crunch as the big gelding chomped the treats. It made him smile When the carrots were gone, Burke stroked the horse's head.

He went into the tack room and emerged with a pack saddle, three coils of rope and a rope halter. He hung them over the top rail of the corral.

"I have to start on a chore. If I survive first part, I'll be back for you, and you can help me with the second part. Wish me luck."

He turned away from his horse and picked up the spade leaning against the corral. He struck off southward with the spade in one hand and his bow in the other. The water bag was banging off his thigh. The four by four piece of plywood hung down his back.

From the rear, he looked for all the world like a

man carrying a sandwich board advertising nothing at all.

He was headed for a packrat midden. The big one in the wash just north of the railroad bridge that was itself just north of Old Highway 66. When he got there, he was going to build a hunting blind.

The humble desert wood rat, called the pack rat by most, is an aggressive and inventive little mammal with skills that allow it to survive and thrive in the hostile environment of the Mojave Desert. Since there is no surface water where it lives, and it cannot metabolize water from seeds like the kangaroo rat, it relies on the pads of prickly pear and beavertail cactus for liquid.

The pack rat brings things home. It builds its middens from them. Big ones. Mounds over a foot high made of chunks of teddy bear cholla, pads of beavertail cactus, sticks, small stones, and bits of animal dung. The packrat urinates on the growing debris pile as it builds. The urine crystalizes and turns into an amber-like material that binds the disparate materials into a more secure matrix. The most common predator on the desert, the clever coyote, would love to get into the midden for a packrat snack, but the fiendishly barbed cholla segments make that almost impossible. Some middens are many hundreds of years old.

Some are built against rock crevices where boulders jut out of the sand on the edge of a desert wash. But those are not the best locations. Rock crevices, while solid and secure against four footed predators like the coyote and the bobcat, often harbor a more insidious enemy: the rattlesnake. Should a rattler get inside the tunnels and dens beneath the midden, chaos and death are sure to follow, which is why many of the rock crevice middens are eventually emptied of packrats and abandoned.

The most successful middens are built in washes, some at the base of a Mojave Yucca, and some within the branches of a large creosote bush. Over many years, as generations of packrats are born and live and pass away, the midden grows, often to a radius of a yard or more. The growing home also expands underground, sometimes increasing to as many as eight chambers at varying depths and six or more entrances.

Coming down into Sacramento Wash, Burke again

came across the footprints of the two men he had tracked earlier.

So, he thought, they walked all the way out here this morning right after leaving Mr. Stanton's place. Following his directions. Trying to get the lay of the land in the light of day. He thought about tracking them back to see how much farther they had gone before they turned around, but he had somewhere to go and something to do.

Burke arrived at the big midden. It was sited beneath a Mojave Yucca on the east side of the wash just north of the railroad bridge. The outbound and returning tracks of the two men had passed very close to the midden.

Perfect.

He put down the spade and his bow and lifted off the piece of plywood hanging down his back. He pulled the damp desert bag off his hip and took a long drink before laying it on top of the plywood.

If the men came back in the dark of night, simply hiding in some creosote might be sufficient for his purposes. But if they waited for first light and came armed with rifles, he could not chance being seen.

Which is why he was planning to be ready regardless of what time they came.

He got up and surveyed the midden.

Three feet from its northwest edge, he began to dig on an angle toward the complicated structure with its cactus defenses and underground chambers. The ground was hard and the digging was difficult. He was soon sweating heavily. But the hard ground was a good thing. It meant the shaft he was digging would be less likely to collapse around him as he angled beneath the surface.

Because he carried each shovelful of dirt a few yards north of the excavation and scattered it, the digging progressed very slowly. But eventually, he was crouched on his knees in the rough opening and beginning to tilt it eastward. When he reached the area below the midden itself, the work went faster. By then he was lying face down in the shaft, the bandana that had been wrapped around the rawhide lace now covering his mouth. As he pushed the spade farther forward, the underground chambers began to collapse in layers upon themselves, leaving behind a hollow that would accommodate his legs.

But this was the critical moment. If the ground

above the chambers did not hold, the midden would fall into the area where the chambers had been dug. As he inserted the spade ever deeper, he listened closely as he rotated and twisted it, ready to scramble backward so he wouldn't be buried in the event of a cave-in.

The midden held. He inched forward and dug some more. The structure still held.

Although it was too dark and dusty inside the narrow tunnel to see, he was sure the packrats were long gone. After all, a man with a spade is an even more formidable digging machine than a marauding badger.

My apologies, clever and resourceful creatures, he thought, but I will make it up to you if I survive. The bag of raw almonds in my pocket will be yours if I last beyond tomorrow's sunrise. You're going to have to spend the night away from home, though. Beware the owl! Do not run when it calls. If you stay hidden, it will not find you. But if you lose courage and break cover and run when it hoots, things will not go well for you.

When he had hollowed out enough room below the midden for his legs and hips, he backed out of the angled shaft, emerging feet first. He pulled the bandana off his mouth and took off his field cap and shook the dust out. It cost him a coughing fit. He got to his feet and walked to where the desert bag lay atop the plywood. He took a long drink. And then another.

The work had taken a long time. The rays of the setting sun, streaks of orange, vermillion, burgundy and a strange sort of greenish gold, were forking through the western sky. Bats from distant caves in the Piutes were flicking and flaring overhead on their way to the Colorado River for a long night of hunting insects. Tarantula hawks, huge wasps that avoid the extreme heat of the desert during the daylight hours, were visible here and there, actively hunting. None of the bats were foolish enough to attempt to eat one. Two inches long, with blue-black or yellow-orange wings, it has the most painful sting of any insect in North America.

When he had drunk his fill, he slung the bag over his shoulder and carried the four by four piece of plywood to the opening of the slanted shaft. He situated it above where his head and shoulders would be and looked at the configuration. Dropping the water bag on top of the plywood, he walked far north into the wash and chopped some blackbush out of the ground with the spade, selecting those that were two to three feet high. One by one, he carried five of them back to the midden and arranged them in front of where the plywood covered the hole.

He put the desert bag over his shoulder and pushed the wood aside and crawled feet first into the hole. When his feet were in the chamber beneath the midden, there was enough room on his left side for his bow and on his right for the spade. By twisting and pulling, he could get the desert bag up to his mouth for a drink.

He peered out over the edge of his place of concealment. In the rays from the setting sun, he could see through the blackbush screening to the south and to the west across the wash. He reached over his head and slid the plywood completely over the opening. It was immediately pitch black and claustrophobic in the shaft, but he could tolerate it. He pushed slowly against the plywood with his head and raised it enough to see the edge of the world outside.

He lowered his head. The plywood settled back into place.

He pushed it away again and climbed out. Moving into the wash, he turned and looked back. The midden could be seen above the blackbush. His blind could not be seen at all.

He walked back to his position, removing any traces of his passing as he went. He picked up his bow and carried it to the shaft. He removed three arrows from the quiver and slid feet first into the hole, taking the bow and the three arrows with him.

As the light began to go out of the sky around him, he tried rotating his bow from its position at his side far enough toward the opening above him to allow him to nock one of the arrows in his hand onto the string. He was very careful not to touch the razor-sharp broadheads in the process.

He quickly discovered it could not be done. He set the bow outside the hole while he considered various solutions to the problem. Reaching into his pocket for his knife, he opened the blade and began to dig into the dirt next to where his hand would be holding the bow. It was not long before he had a narrow, horizontal opening deep enough to permit the insertion of an arrow to a depth of about twenty inches.

He retrieved the bow and the three arrows. Holding the bow and arrows in his left hand, he grasped the nock of one of the arrows and rotated it ninety degrees and inserted it into the narrow opening. That made it possible to nock the arrow onto the string. He removed the arrow from the string and began to work out a sequence. Rotate one of the arrows. Push it into the narrow opening he had created until he had room to nock it. Draw the bow far enough that the broadhead cleared the opening. Bend his knees to gain purchase and leverage. Rise until his head was above the ground. Slowly stand and emerge from the hole with the Black Widow at full draw.

He thought of an improvement. He climbed out the hole and set the bow aside. Wriggling head first back into the hole, he used his knife to dig out indentations into which his knees could fit and help him begin his push out of the shaft.

Backing out of the hole, he turned around and slid back in, feet first. Once inside, he found that pushing his knees into the indentations gave him more leverage. Also, once he had completed the first part of the movement, he could place one foot and then the other into the kneehole indentations and rise close enough to a standing position that he would be able to release an arrow without climbing all the way out of the angled shaft.

He got back in the hole and practiced. He found he could accomplish the nocking of the arrow much faster if he only had to deal with one. He placed the other two outside the hole and to the right of where he would be when the first arrow was on its way. Rehearsing that part of the sequence over and over again, he eventually had the arrows in such a position that when he dropped his hand to the ground, he found the fletching of the next arrow. He left the broadheads pointed off to the north so there would be no chance of cutting his fingers by touching one of the devilishly sharp, serrated edges.

If his calculations were correct, three arrows would be all he would need.

Once he had the routine down perfectly without the cover, he practiced it repeatedly with the cover over his hiding place. Rotate the arrow and nock it, draw the bow, push with his head against the cover and slowly apply pressure as he got to his knees and then into a half crouch with his feet where his knees had been, cover pushed away, bow fully drawn and arrow pointed to where the expected his adversaries to be.

Once he was satisfied with the procedure, he

climbed out again and set the bow to the left side of the opening. The sunset had given way to twilight while he had practiced and prepared. Now even the purple twilight had faded from the sky. Night had fallen.

He put the cover over the hole and sat on the ground, legs crossed in front of him, hands on his knees. I have a spider hole, he thought. And remembered Vietnam. And thought about the tragedy he was afraid awaited the United States Military in that strange place.

Spider holes.

The Viet Minh had used them in their fight against the South Vietnamese government when he had been in that poverty-stricken country with Colonel Lansdale. Now the Viet Minh were the Viet Cong.

Whenever he was in Las Vegas, he went to the newsstand on Fremont Street and bought the New York Times or the Washington Post. They were the only papers paying any attention to what was happening in the Far East. He knew that the number of advisors in Vietnam, totaling only a few hundred before he had DEROSed, had increased to over twelve thousand.

We'll be in it soon, he thought. And it won't go well for us. Because of spider holes.

To a Viet Cong, a spider hole was a place to lie in ambush for as long as necessary to kill a member of the Army of the Republic of Viet Nam or an American soldier.

A VC would dig a spider hole and climb in and stay there, living on almost nothing and drinking only the water he had carried in with him. He would stay in that fetid, black, damp place. As long as necessary. He would live in his own filth. When an enemy patrol came by, he would pop out of the ground, firing whatever miserable remnant weapon that had been cockroached from the French Army or taken from a dead French soldier. He would take out as many of the startled enemy as he could before they recovered enough to kill him.

And that is why, he thought, we should not be there.

Put a typical G.I. in the same hole in the same conditions, and he would last an hour: maybe less, maybe more. But not much more. Before long, he would be out of the hole, having a smoke and pawing through his C-rats for a piece of chocolate.

But Burke Henry was not a typical G.I. He was an Apache warrior. He would sit in the hole for as long as it took.

The waxing, gibbous moon, which had risen like a pale, lonely and desiccated wafer in the eastern sky just after four thirty that afternoon, was climbing and giving the smoke trees in the wash an eerie, ghostly appearance. The nearly-full moon was so bright it was casting soft shadows on the west side of the pale trees. It would set close to four in the morning.

Burke decided to rest for a while.

Remaining in his seated position, his wrists on his knees, he closed his eyes and began to slow his breathing and his heart rate, recalling for equanimity the peacefulness of his aikido dojo in Japan: the place he had learned to channel his *chi*. Soon he was at peace, drifting away from the chaotic world of wakefulness and worry to a comforting place of acceptance of whatever was to come.

Anyone watching would have thought he was asleep.

He was not. Although he was in a state of deep relaxation, he was preternaturally aware of the world around him. He remained that way for over an hour before allowing his breathing to slowly return to normal.

He rose to his feet and walked to his spider hole. He situated the spade in the right side of the hole so he could retrieve it when needed. He put the bow in position on the left side and checked the location of the second and third arrows one last time. With the desert bag over his shoulder and the first arrow in his left hand, broadhead pointed toward the star-strewn sky, he lowered himself into position. With his right hand, he pulled the plywood over his head. His world went completely black.

He settled down to wait, refreshed from his relaxation. With every sense vibrantly, vigorously alive and alert, he thought about his enemy.

If you boys come at night, it will be under a nearly-full moon. You may think you'll see everything, but you won't. But I will see you, and unless you're a lot better than I think you are, I'm going to hear you before I see you. You have guns, and you think you're going to kill me. But you'll be wrong. Dead wrong.

In fact, you were dead the instant you set foot on my desert. You just haven't fallen down yet.

CHAPTER 30

July 14, 1962 Smoke Tree, California

Dave Scuttler's travel alarm went off a half hour after midnight inside the tiny bungalow at the Desert Vista Motor Court on the south side of Smoke Tree. He was already wide awake. The window-mounted air conditioner was clattering and groaning in an attempt to keep the room cold enough to allow a good night's sleep. As far as Scuttler was concerned, it had failed. He climbed out of bed and gave Lacey a hard shake.

Scuttler hadn't slept much, but then he never did. Lacey, on the other hand, had been snorting and snoring ever since his head hit the pillow at eight o'clock the previous evening.

He had slept the same way the night before in Barstow: like a man completely oblivious of what lay ahead of him. Scuttler supposed after uncomfortable prison bunks and the unrelenting noise of cell block life, a lumpy mattress in a cheap motel is a luxury. He had grumbled when Scuttler prodded him awake at three thirty yesterday morning so they could get across the Eastern Mojave before the sun rose.

While Lacey showered himself awake, Scuttler checked the two .30-30 Model 94 Winchesters. Not that he hadn't checked them when he first brought them in from the truck the evening before and again when he woke up at midnight. They were both fully loaded: one round in the chamber under the half-cocked hammer and eight in the-tubular magazine under the barrel.

Still, it never hurt to check once more.

The only time he had ever been injured in his law-enforcement career was when he had responded to a robbery in progress at a Piggly-Wiggly in Caddo County and pulled a service revolver he had forgotten to reload after a session on the gun range.

Maybe if he had just pointed it at the robber, everything would have turned out all right. The man, armed only with a knife, probably would have surrendered. But Scuttler had wanted to shoot the guy: some Comanche off the KCA res. Wanted to shoot him just because Scuttler was a sheriff's deputy, and he could, and he had never yet had the occasion to shoot anyone but was itching to. So, Scuttler had pulled the trigger and got nothing in response but the sound of the hammer falling on an empty chamber.

When the Comanche heard the 'snap,' he knew the deputy had tried to kill him. Adjusting his grip on the knife he had been waving at a store employee to an underhand hold, he lunged at Scuttler and stabbed him in the stomach. Twice. And ran out the door, leaving a bleeding Deputy Scuttler sitting on the floor staring at the blood seeping into his uniform shirt. He still had the two white scars where the knife had pierced his abdominal muscles.

Hurt like hell. Cost him two weeks in the hospital after he nearly died of sepsis. Just like a dirty Indian to carry a dirty knife.

When he was released, he had to endure the snickers of his fellow deputies at his rookie mistake. Few of them laughed at him ever again. It wasn't worth a busted jaw or a bloody nose just to have a giggle.

The Comanche who stabbed him had wisely left the area, never to be seen again, but Scuttler never stopped looking for him. Was looking for him still, even though he was retired.

Satisfied that the rifles were loaded to capacity and in working order, he shoved them back into their hand-tooled leather scabbards just as Lacey emerged from the shower.

"How the hell can a place this hot have only cold water," he asked?

Scuttler did not answer.

"Get dressed. Let's get out of this shit hole."

When they went outside, it was not much cooler than it had been at sundown. It's not right, thought Scuttler, for a place to be this hot this close to midnight.

At one in the morning, they were the only two customers in the all-night diner next to the Shell station. There was a different waitress on duty than the one who had served them the previous afternoon. Lacey tried flirting with her, just as he had tried to flirt with the one who had waited on them the first time. The result was the same: disinterest bordering on revulsion.

Scuttler didn't understand how women could fail to be attracted to a guy with pieces of glass stuck in his teeth. And wild eyes that darted around the room like a water bug before alighting on some part of a woman's anatomy and staring at it for minutes on end. The night shift waitress was tired and irritable.

She took offense at being so openly ogled.

"Take a picture," she sneered. "It'll last longer."

Lacey smiled. He thought he was making progress.

By 1:30, they were westbound on 66 and looking for the turn-off to 95.

The day before, after talking to the old man at the dilapidated service station just after sunrise, they had crossed the railroad tracks and turned north onto Old 66. A few miles up the road, they arrived at the place he had described to them. It was not hard to identify. The road, which had proceeded in a nearly straight line that paralleled the railroad tracks on an embankment high above them, suddenly dropped into a wash filled with smoke trees and jogged north before angling west again.

Scuttler pulled off the road just before it turned west. Straight in front of them was the railroad bridge the old man had told them about. Scuttler drove the truck forward as far as he could go without sinking into the sand. He and Lacey got out. They took their rifles. There was almost zero chance they would encounter Sommers on this reconnaissance, but why not be prepared?

They walked through the smoke trees and desert willow to the bridge. They went under it, smelling the creosote from the coated timbers, and emerged into the wider wash beyond.

They had a long walk up the wash as it trended northwest. When the wash began to angle westward, they began to look for the trail the old man had said would meander off northeast through the hills. When they found it, it led them to an intersection with a well-maintained dirt road. They stayed on that road, but only for a short distance, until they found the old wagon road.

The road was a remnant of the eighteen-hundreds, but the tracks the heavily-loaded freight wagons had carved were still etched into Piute Hill. But while the marks could still be seen, the track was so rough it could not have been driven by any kind of vehicle without metal treads.

The road took them east. They followed it until it turned north toward Piute Creek and Fort Piute.

"Local feller lives there," the old man had said. "Leave him be. He don't much care for being bothered."

They had walked far enough on the wagon road to

get their bearings. It was clear to Scuttler that they could easily follow the trail beneath the moon that would be high in the sky when they came back. They could have gone farther, but there was no reason to chance sky-lighting themselves at the top of the hill and being seen from Piute Creek. He didn't want to give Sommers the slightest warning.

Besides, the incredible heat had taken a toll on both he and Lacey. They were exhausted and almost out of water. Lacey had been bitching nonstop for over an hour now about the sun, the heat, his cheap shoes, the cactus, the funny bushes that snagged their clothing and the hot water in their big canteens. The water that did not seem to satisfy their thirst, no matter how much they drank.

"What kind of place is this, anyway?"

"It's a desert."

"I know that, Mr. Scuttler, but I don't know why anyone would live out here."

"Maybe, Lacey, because he doesn't want to be found."

"Found by who?"

"By me, Arvin. By me."

"If this is where he has to live to keep away from you, we'll be doing the bastard a favor by killing him.

Anyway, tell me what happens after we do him in."

"I already told you."

"I know, but say it again. It cheers me up to think about what comes next."

"We cut him up into eleven pieces and bury him in eleven separate holes. The Klan calls this the eleven-piece solution."

"See, that's something new. You didn't tell me that before. Why eleven pieces?"

Scuttler ticked them off on his fingers, making a slash with his hand with each description.

"Arms, in half. Legs, in half. Torso, in half."

That was all ten fingers.

He made a fist with his right hand and shot it into the air.

"One head with no teeth."

"Why no teeth?"

"We knock them out so the skull can't be identified with dental records if it's ever found. Take them with us and throw them out the window one at a time as we drive to Vegas."

"Tell me about that part again. The Vegas part. About how we go to that Bank in Las Vegas."

"Nevada Southern."

"And I get my money."

"That's right. And then you never have to see me again."

"Can I say something here and not have you go nuts on me?"

Scuttler smiled. It was an ugly smile.

"Go ahead."

"I think you didn't carry the cash with you because you thought I might try to rob you."

"That was one of my considerations."

"But Mr. Scuttler, I'm not some stranger. I'm Arvin Lacey. You know me. Hell, you know my momma!"

Scuttler smiled again.

"I do, Arvin, I do. And I don't trust her either."

Arvin Lacey looked offended for a moment. But then, he burst out laughing."

"Neither do I, Mr. Scuttler."

You dumb smack, thought Scuttler as they turned back the way they had come, there's no money in any bank in Las Vegas. I've never been in Nevada in my life. The spade you'll be carrying tomorrow will dig the hole I'm going to bury you in after we bury Sommers.

You're just lucky I'm not going to make you dig that one, too.

CHAPTER 31

July 14, 1962 The Open Desert

Before Burke heard the two men coming to kill him, he heard many other things during his long hours in the stifling-hot, pitch-black hole.

Two long freight trains strained westbound up the grade toward Goffs, diesels thundering and thrumming as they hauled a heavy load. Around ten o'clock, the Super Chief roared by at full throttle, screaming down the tracks toward Smoke Tree. Interspersed with the trains, a few big rigs, seeking to avoid the steeper climb over South Pass west of Smoke Tree, chose the Old 66 cut off with its less-demanding grade.

Every time the sound of a train or a semi reached his ears, Burke lifted the plywood enough to peer out through the blackbush shielding his hiding place into the moonlit wash. He was concerned his adversaries might pass his position without his knowledge, the sound of their passage masked beneath the sounds of the mechanical world of man.

After the Super Chief hurtled past, there was no more activity, either on the road or the rails. In contrast, the world not made by man never fell completely silent. Coyotes barked in the distance. Occasionally, there was an odd roaring sound as a nighthawk pulled out of a dive during the pursuit of some insect beneath the bright glow of a ninety-percent moon.

Owls hooted, and Burke thought of the packrats he had turned out of their home. He hoped they stayed safe long enough to have their almonds if he survived the danger the coming hours were sure to bring. And yet, he thought, the owls had to eat.

Throughout the entire period, Burke stayed in his hole. On full alert in the tightly confined space.

After a long time, during which only the sounds of the natural world reached his ears, a door slammed. Possibly a truck door. A truck that had come up Old 66 so slowly he had heard neither the sound of its engine nor of its tires. It had to be his would-be killers. Nobody else would be pulling off the highway out here this time of night.

Only one door had slammed. Which meant one man had come alone. Or that two men had come, and one of them was stupid enough to bang metal door against metal frame after stepping down from the truck.

Burke slid the plywood cover above his head a few inches to the side, the better to hear his adversaries. With his right hand, he carefully lifted the cord hooked to the desert bag over his head. He took one last drink and eased the bag away from his body and let it slide down by his feet.

The railroad bridge north of where the vehicle had stopped was over a half mile away, but the sound of the door had carried that far in the deep stillness of the desert night. For a long time, Burke heard nothing else.

But then, he began to hear the sounds of two men moving up the wash. One of them was fairly quiet, but the other was hopelessly clumsy, or careless, or both.

One man stepped down hard.

One man kicked rocks that clattered off other rocks.

One man stumbled from time to time.

Once, Burke heard a curse. He assumed the clumsy man had veered into a cactus and picked up a puncture for his stupidity. Burke hoped it had been a cholla with its barbed thorns.

He thought the quiet one was probably Scuttler; the clumsy one the pale man with the wild eyes. Burke hoped Scuttler was getting irritated at his companion. Irritation and anger worked in Burke's favor. They took concentration away from the task at hand. That could lead to mistakes in judgement.

Burke marked the progress of the two men as they came closer. When he estimated they were less than fifty yards from his position, he carefully moved the plywood above his head so it once again completely covered the hole. The men were now close enough that he could hear them with the cover in place.

He mentally rehearsed the actions to come. The moves he had practiced over and over in the late afternoon and early evening of the previous day.

Take the most dangerous one first, he thought. The most dangerous one will be on the right, closest to me. The dominant walker is usually on the right. If he is right handed, he will be carrying his rifle in his right hand, or perhaps at port arms, so it will be easier to move it quickly to his shoulder without bumping his clumsy companion.

The companion will be close to the more dangerous man. Too close. Tactically speaking, the two should be a good distance apart, but the companion, unlike Scuttler, is afraid of the desert night: afraid of the unknown in general. A mean man, just like Scuttler, but not competent.

The steps came closer.

And closer.

Finally, they were parallel to him.

Then, slightly northwest of him.

He grasped the arrow at the nock with his right hand and rotated it so he could push the broadhead into the hole. He nocked the arrow onto the bowstring. As he began to draw the bow, he simultaneously leaned forward slightly until his knees found the indentations in front of him.

He began to push upward, slowly applying pressure to the underside of the plywood. As it rose, he could see two men backlit by the moonlight. Their soft shadows were tilted slightly to the east.

The man on the right was the bigger of the two. He was carrying a rifle in his right hand. The other man had some kind of pack on his back. He was carrying a rifle in one hand and a spade in the other. Both men were hatless.

Burke rose up completely with his bow at full draw.

The man on the right heard the soft, sibilant sound as the plywood slid away. He reached for the barrel of his rifle with his left hand as he turned to locate the source of the noise.

It placed his torso at a slightly oblique angle to Burke.

Burke released the arrow. The Easton aluminum with its broadhead tip sang off the string and hurtled through the windless night air at one hundred and sixty feet per second. As it flew, Burke was already reaching down and to the right for the second arrow. He had not taken his eyes off the second man.

The first arrow reached its intended target in less than four tenths of a second. The serrated, razor-sharp broadhead entered just behind Scuttler's right deltoid at a slightly downward angle. It ripped through his body, pierced his upper left lung, and severed the cartilage between two ribs on the left side of his torso before stopping with four inches of the shaft and the broadhead itself sticking through the skin.

Scuttler grunted and dropped his rifle. He reached for the protruding arrow with his right hand.

The second man turned toward the wounded man in the moonlight. He was now facing directly toward where Burke had already nocked the second arrow and drawn the bow.

The shaft he released took the second man to the left of the sternum. It pierced his chest wall and tore into his heart, ripping through the pericardium and left ventricle before continuing all the way through his torso and striking something metallic in the pack on his back.

He collapsed like a marionette with the strings cut, still clutching the rifle and the spade.

Burke was already moving toward them with the third arrow nocked.

As he covered the twenty yards to his targets, he paid no attention to the second man. He was certain that man would be dead in seconds. So Scuttler, who by now had toppled to the ground, was his focus.

As soon as he arrived, his bow fully drawn and pointed at Scuttler's heart, he knew the man was no longer a threat. He had rolled away from the excruciating pain of the arrow projecting from his side and was lying on his back. His right hand was covered with dark blood from grasping the broadhead in a futile attempt to remove it.

His rifle lay where he had dropped it. Burke kicked it away. He eased the tension on his bow and set it aside, simultaneously lowering himself to the ground and kneeling next to the grievously injured man.

Scuttler had no gun belt.

Burke patted down his lower legs to be sure he did not have a pistol in an ankle holster.

Burke squatted back onto his heels. The three men made a strange, moonlit tableau beneath the owl that winged silently northwest above them. Three motionless men on the floor of a sandy desert wash: one of them dead, one of them dying, and the uninjured third watching the life flow from the badly wounded man who was still breathing. Above the owl, the moon. Beyond the moon, the darkness of space. A darkness so vast it rendered the three men on the desert floor of a tiny planet orbiting a minor star in the far-off corner of a minor galaxy completely inconsequential.

The dying man opened his eyes.

By the light of the moon, he saw above him a black face streaked with red.

"Sommers?"

"Who else?"

Scuttler released a breath held against the pain in a long, shuddering sigh. Blood was dribbling from the lower left corner of his mouth.

"Is Harold Nevins still alive?"

Scuttler said nothing. He continued to breath in shallow, strangling gulps.

"It's too bad you're dying so fast. I'd like you to suffer like Alicia did."

"Who...Alicia?"

"My sister."

Scuttler struggled to say something more. Nothing came out. He grimaced and died. His final breath rattled from his throat, accompanied by a gout of black blood from deep inside his mutilated lung.

His eyes stared vacantly into the moonlit sky, already losing their shine.

Burke did not close the eyes. He simply sat and stared at Scuttler for a time before searching his pockets for the truck keys. He stood up and looked at the broadhead protruding from his side.

"That was for you, Alicia. Sorry it was twenty years too late."

He picked up the bow and the remaining arrow and returned to his spider hole. He set them aside. He reached deep into the hole and pulled out the desert bag. The surface, damp with evaporation, was coated with dirt. He uncapped the bag and took a long drink before setting it on the plywood square.

He reached into the hole again and retrieved the spade and put it on the ground.

Returning to the bodies splayed in the sandy wash, he rolled Scuttler's companion onto his stomach. He opened the pack strapped to the man's back. Inside, he saw two cleavers and two meat saws. The broadhead that had exited the man's back had been stopped by one of the cleavers.

It took Burke an hour to haul both bodies, their heels digging grooves in the sand, to the slanted shaft. He jammed them inside as far as he could. When he was finished, he went back into the wash and got the rifles and the spade and put them in the hole alongside the bodies.

He picked up his spade and covered the men with dirt.

When he was done, he piled the blackbrush on the mound he had created.

Do for now, he thought. Hope the coyotes don't chew them up too bad before I get back.

He moved a few yards from the hole and got the bag of almonds out of his pocket. He broadcast handfuls of the nuts in an arc around where he stood.

"Thanks for your help, little fellows," he shouted in his booming voice.

His own voice sounded alien to him. As if he had been someone else, but was that person no longer.

He returned to the hole and picked up the desert bag and put it over his shoulder. Carrying his bow and the spade, he set off down the desert wash, weaving his way through the smoke trees, creosote, catclaw and cactus toward the truck he knew he would find near the highway to the south.

Forty-five minutes later, he pulled up in front of his house in Scuttler's truck. When he got out, carrying the desert bag and his bow, Pepper nickered from his corral.

"Hello, horse," he called.

With the canvas desert bag over his shoulder, he carried the bow into the house and set it down inside the door. He lit the oil lamp on a small table and carried it to the drainboard at the sink. He rinsed the sand off the canvas bag and refilled it and set it aside. Pumping some water into the washbasin in the sink, he scrubbed the charcoal and lipstick from his face as best he could with laundry detergent. When he was finished, he dumped the black liquid down the drain. He filled the basin with water again and washed his field cap. He put the cap on. The evaporating water cooled his head.

Lifting the desert bag back onto his shoulder, he picked up the oil lamp and carried it into his workshop. He pulled a hacksaw off the tool rack.

The moon was angling toward the west but still lighting the night sky when he came out of the house. He extinguished the oil lamp and left it outside the door. His pale shadow tilted to the east as he walked to the corral. He opened the gate and went inside. He put the hacksaw on the ground and pulled the packsaddle off the top rail of the corral and put it on

Pepper, talking softly to him the entire time. He attached the coils of rope to the packsaddle, as well as the hacksaw and the desert bag. He picked up the bucket next to the water trough and hung it by the bail from the packsaddle.

He gently lowered the rope halter over Pepper's head and led him out of the corral. In the moonlight, they went down into the creek bed and crossed it the old road that rose up the side of Piute Hill. They walked in the ruts that the iron-capped, wood-spoked wheels of the freight wagons had carved into the red rock many years before. The arid desert air had already sucked all the moisture from Burke's field cap.

By two thirty in the morning, he was jogging up the hill. Pepper trailed behind him at an easy trot. Burke was trying hard not to trip on any of the stones lying loose in the track, but he occasionally stumbled. Very unlike him. He realized the adrenalin that had surged into his system earlier had washed away, leaving him a little shaky.

Doesn't matter, he thought. The dangerous work is done. Scuttler is dead. I'm still alive. Everything else is just details.

When he reached Sacramento Wash, he had to

slow to a brisk walk. The footing was uncertain beneath the slanting moon. He moved south until he arrived at the place he had killed Scuttler and the other man. He tied Pepper to a nearby smoke tree.

He removed the bucket and the desert bag from the pack frame. He filled the bucket and held it up so Pepper could drink his fill. He listened to the satisfying sound of the water gurgling down the horse's throat.

"You're not going to like this, old friend. We're going to haul two dead men away. I hope it won't spook you too bad."

He moved to where he had stuffed the two men and their weapons and gear into the shaft angling under the midden. Coyotes had already partially uncovered them. Scuttler's accomplice was the uppermost body. The coyotes had eaten away part of his face and chewed off a chunk of his arm.

Must have run off when they heard me and Pepper, he thought. Probably just as well they didn't reach Scuttler. Bastard was probably too tough to chew.

A giggle at his own weak joke escaped his lips.

Going soft in your old age, he thought. Get a grip. Master Sergeant Burke Henry would have taken this in stride.

He picked up the spade and finished uncovering the bodies. Rigor mortis was present but minimal. The bodies were still flexible. He dragged the younger man close to where Pepper was tied. The horse snorted and tossed his head. Burke let go of his burden and walked to Pepper and leaned against him.

"I know you don't like this, but it's got to be done."

Returning for Scuttler's body, he dragged him close to where the other man lay in the wash. He went back to the midden and pulled out the rifles. He took off his t-shirt and wiped them both down. He crawled down into the shaft head first and pushed each of the rifles as far as he could into the dirt. The collapsed underground dens made it easy. He shoved the spade Scuttler's accomplice had carried in next to the rifles. Backing out of the hole, he brushed himself off. He put his t-shirt back on. Sand stuck to where it had been splotched with oil from the rifles. He picked up his spade and filled the hole with dirt.

When he was done, he stamped the blackbrush he had used to screen his position into pieces. He scattered the pieces and threw more dirt on them. Then, he smoothed out the entire work area.

It was now very unlikely anyone would be able to figure out what had happened in that place. Picking up the plywood, he unknotted the rawhide lace and put it in his pocket. He took the spade and the board out into the wash and skimmed the piece of plywood off into the distance.

He carried the spade back to where Pepper stood stamping nervously at the smell of blood.

With the hacksaw from the pack saddle, he sawed the broadhead off the part of the arrow protruding from Scuttler's side. Grasping the shaft, he pulled the arrow all the way through the body. It emerged covered in gore. He put it on the ground beside the broadhead.

Turning the other body face down, he sawed through the shaft jutting from its back. He pushed the canvas pack aside and tried to pull the arrow all the way through the body. The fletching snagged. He put his foot on the dead man's back and tugged hard before it came all the way out. He set it aside. Opening the pack, he extracted the small piece of arrow with the broadhead attached, careful not to cut his fingers.

Scooping up the broadheads with the spade, he carried them and the bloody arrows out into the middle of the wash and buried them in four separate holes. Each of the holes was a good distance from the others.

He returned to his horse. Lowering himself onto all fours, he pulled Scuttler's upper body to a vertical position. The body was stiffening but still malleable. Burke wrapped his arms around the corpse in a hideous embrace and got to his feet. He loosened his grip and stooped toward the ground. The body tilted over his right shoulder. Staggering slightly, he pushed himself erect.

He walked to Pepper and tried to shift the body onto the pack saddle. Pepper shied and stamped his feet and moved away. Burke stood with his awkwardly shouldered burden and talked to the horse patiently until it calmed. On the second try, Pepper rolled his eyes and shook his head but stood still long enough that Burke was able to lever the body face down over the horse's back. Some force was required to make it bend sufficiently at the waist.

That done, he removed one of the coils of rope and used it to link the dead man's hands and feet beneath Pepper's body. When he was finished, he walked to the gelding's shoulder and talked to him. Pepper shied again at the smell of blood on Burke's hands.

Burke picked up the second body and repeated the process. Both bodies were now secured over the pack saddle, the second slightly overlapping the first. Burke picked up the spade and smoothed thee grooves the mens' heels had made when he dragged them earlier that morning. He smoothed the area where he had just worked Then he attached the spade and the hacksaw to the pack frame.

By the time he had finished all that had to be done, the moon had long since set in the west, followed by the remaining stars that had twisted away from view beyond the horizon.

Untying the halter from the smoke tree, he led Pepper up the wash.

The horse was not happy, but he followed Burke without bucking or stamping.

The faint purple of pre-dawn twilight had begun to tint the morning sky. That strange light that seems to come from nowhere and everywhere dimly lit their way as they moved northwest with their gruesome cargo.

The sun was well up in the sky by the time they reached Piute Creek. With the sunrise, vultures had

432

begun to appear high in the sky overhead. More and more were soon added to the spiraling crowd. Burke led Pepper past Scuttler's pickup truck and relieved him of his burden one body at a time. The bodies were stiffer. They landed in comma-shaped positions when he cut them free. He removed the spade from the packsaddle and left it beside the bodies.

He led Pepper into the corral and removed the equipment and the halter and the packsaddle before turning him loose. The horse dropped to the ground and began to roll from side to side in the sandy corral. Glad to be home. Glad to no longer be carrying dead men.

Burke went to the house and got two apples from the refrigerator. He cut them in quarters and put the pieces in his pocket. When he came back outside, he stood looking at the bodies. He was briefly tempted to remove the identification from the second man's wallet and find out who he had killed. Deciding he really didn't care, he crossed to the corral instead, more concerned about his horse than the dead man.

He put a piece of apple on his palm. Pepper trotted over and ate it. Burke fed him the rest of the first apple before going into the tack room. He came back out with a curry brush and a curry mitt. He brushed Pepper down and then worked him with the mitt. The horse leaned into him as he worked, ears turned out to the side.

When he was finished, he fed Pepper the pieces of the second apple.

While Burke had curried Pepper, the vultures had circled lower and lower. The huge carrion eaters are very cautious birds, but a few had now landed on the ground. They formed a circle around the bodies. One or two edged closer as Burke watched. He walked toward them, clapping his hands and shouting in his deep voice. They lumbered, complaining and croaking, into the air.

Burke went into the house and came out with a skinning knife and a pair of rubber gloves. He walked to the dead men. Unbuttoning their shirts, he unhooked their belts and partially pulled down their pants before he cut them both from sternum to groin. Fluids gushed out. Reaching inside the bodies, he pulled out the intestines and offal and slung them away.

The stink was terrible, but the job had to be done. Otherwise, the bodies would bloat. One at a time, he dragged them to the pickup. He pulled down the tail gate and hoisted each body. He left them partially on the tailgate and partially in the bed while he went to the tack room and got two tarpaulins. By the time he came back, the vultures had landed again. They reluctantly moved away when he approached the truck, but they did not rise into the air.

Tossing the tarps onto the bed of the truck, he climbed over the bumper and the bodies and spread one tarp out on the bed. He jumped down and returned to the tack room and came back with a bag of the slaked lime he used for the outhouse. He shoveled a layer of the lime onto the tarp. Setting the shovel aside, he partially lifted and partially dragged each of the bodies onto the lime-covered tarp. He shoveled the rest of the lime over the dead men and their gaping wounds. They soon looked like mummies unearthed by archeologists as evidence of some ancient, unspeakable ritual.

He spread the second tarp over the lime-shrouded bodies. Tossing the spade to the ground, he stepped onto the bumper and down from the truck. The vultures were now covering what Burke had discarded. Fully engrossed in their meal and their arguments with each other over the prized parts, they paid no attention to Burke as he carried rocks to the truck and weighed down the tarps. When he was finished, he stripped off the rubber gloves and threw them aside. He got into the truck and drove to the corral.

The noise made the vultures, their beaks smeared with gore, reluctantly take to the air again.

At the corral, he hoisted bales of hay onto the truck. He jumped into the bed and arranged the bales so they covered the tarps. The pickup now looked like just another rancher with a load of hay.

He stepped off the truck and closed the tailgate.

When he walked back toward the house, the vultures were again squabbling over the steadily diminishing feast. In the kitchen, he removed the metal washtub from its hook on the wall. He filled bucket after bucket of water from the pump and poured them into the tub until it was nearly full. He stripped off his bloody and lime-dusted clothing and piled it on the floor. Setting his field cap on the sideboard, he picked up a bar of soap and stepped into the tub.

The water was very cold. It was difficult to get the soap to lather.

It took a long time to wash his body and his hair. When he was finally clean and free of the stink of death, he climbed out of the washtub and stood naked on the floor. In spite of the cold water in which he had bathed, he felt like he had a fever, so he didn't dry off. He let the evaporating water cool his body even more.

When he was completely dry, he picked up his field cap and put it on. He dragged the tub out the back door and dumped it off the porch. When it was empty, he took in inside and returned it to its place on the wall.

He took an old towel and wrapped it around the clothing he had stripped off and left on the kitchen floor. He jammed his sockless feet into his Corcoran jump boots. Dressed in only his field cap and boots, he carried the clothing, the towel, and a box of matches outside to a place north of the house. Putting everything on the ground, he went to his truck and removed the five-gallon can of gasoline from the flatbed. He carried it to the other items.

He retrieved the rubber gloves and added them, his field cap and his jump boots to the pile. Soaking everything with half the gasoline, he scratched a lucifer match against the box and tossed it. The fire ignited immediately. Smoke rose, black and noxious, and twisted into the pure blue desert sky. The stink from the burning rubber was very strong. When the blaze died down, he poked the remains with a stick. He poured on the remainder of the gasoline and set everything aflame again.

When he was finished, he used the stick to pick up his belt buckle. When it had cooled enough to be handled, he side-armed it as far as he could.

He picked his way back to the house in his bare feet and went in and lay down on his back beside his bed on the Mexican floor tiles he had so carefully set in 1956. He could hear the vultures still squabbling outside.

In spite of the incredible heat, he fell asleep immediately. He dreamed of the South Pacific. Of the Philippines. Of Korea. Of Vietnam.

In each of those places, he was lifting faceless bodies off of piles and stuffing them into holes. Holes that could not be filled.

Outside, as Burke slept on, the sun rose higher in the cloudless sky. Having consumed everything Burke had cast aside, the vultures lifted, one by one, into the air, their pinions creaking as they flapped their leathery wings. Soon, they were nothing more than tiny, dihedral specks against the blue vault of the sky.

Pepper moved into the shady corner of his corral.

Deep Desert Deception

CHAPTER 32

July 14, 1962 Piute Creek, Highway 66, &-Points East

Burke came awake just before sunset. In spite of lying uncovered and naked on a tile floor, he was covered with sweat. He rolled onto his side and stood up and stretched. His lower back complained. Probably from levering the bodies onto the pack saddle, he thought.

And with that, the events of the early morning hours pushed to the forefront of his consciousness. He thought about the killings. He did not think of them as murders. He thought of them as self-defense. As justified. As necessary and right.

He thought about Scuttler dying in the moonlight. The dark blood that had come out of his mouth. The intensity of the hatred in his evil eyes before the light fled from them forever. Burke had no regrets. He was glad the man was dead.

As to the other man, he had been defined by the

company he kept. A bad man following a worse man. Like a lemming hurtling off a moral cliff into a sea of despair.

Burke moved into the kitchen and leaned into the sink and pumped water over his head. It was very cold. A huge contrast to the temperature in his house. He padded out the door in his bare feet and onto the porch. Still naked, he went down the steps and onto the series of large, more-or-less flat stones he had embedded in the hard ground years before. Following the primitive, curving walkway to where it came to an end in front of a honey mesquite, he relieved himself.

World's largest outdoor restroom, he thought.

When he was finished, he returned to his house. In the kitchen, he got a bottle of Dad's Old Fashioned Root Beer and carried it out to the porch. He sat down on the old cane chair and studied a sky tinted crimson and gold while he sipped his soda and made his plans.

When he was sure about what he was going to do and the order in which it would be done, he got up and went inside and rinsed the empty bottle. He put it in the wooden Pepsi Cola crate under the sink before going into the bedroom.

Dressing in a pair of Levi's and a white t-shirt, he

picked up an old straw cowboy hat and put it on. At the corral, Pepper trotted over to meet him. A double scoop of oats from the steel barrel in the tack room went into his feeding trough. As Pepper ate, Burke forked hay into the corral.

He opened the gate and went to the water trough and checked the float that allowed the line from the windmill to keep it full. It was working. There would be plenty of water for Pepper while he was gone.

He walked over to where Pepper was finishing his oats. He leaned against the horse's shoulder and scratched his ears.

"You did good this morning. Man could not ask for a better horse.

Now listen, I'm going to be gone for a few days. There's no way around it. What I'm going to do has to be done, just like what you helped me do this morning. You've got plenty of hay and plenty of water. Be sure to shade up in the midday heat, and you'll be fine."

Horses, he suddenly realized, had been what he had missed the most during his years in the army. He put his cheek against the side of Pepper's head, his heart filled with love for the animal. He gave it a final pat and walked out and latched the gate behind him.

He walked to the green, Ford F-150 pickup and stood beside it. He could detect no odor of decay through the slaked lime, the covering tarp, the rocks and the bales of hay.

Better get moving, he thought, and keep moving until you reach your destination.

In the house, he picked his bow up off the floor and returned it to its place above the mantle. At the sink, he filled the desert bag with water. He got a dish towel, a bottle of vinegar and a bottle of rubbing alcohol from his cleaning supplies and took everything outside. He did not bother to lock the door.

He was soon headed east on the Old Mojave Road, the sunset dying a violent, magenta death in his rearview mirror.

Turning south on 95, he drove to eastbound 66. In Smoke Tree, he turned off the highway and crossed the railroad tracks north of the Santa Fe Depot. He followed the potholed asphalt road until it turned to dirt and ran parallel the Colorado River. The dike road took him to the wooden Bureau of Reclamation bridge. He crossed into Arizona and drove to Oatman. The route would allow him to avoid the Arizona Agricultural Inspection Station on Highway 66.

Beyond Oatman, he got back on 66 and drove through Valentine, Hackberry and Peach Springs and then on to Seligman. He stopped for gas. As he filled up, he thought of Caroline McCollum, but he didn't think of her much. He was a different person now. She might be too, but he doubted it.

Early morning of the following day found him in Holbrook. He remembered exploring the town on his motorcycle in 1956. Remembered the abused buildings and the Wigwam Motel and the nosy cop. He stopped for gas and coffee and drove on.

In Albuquerque, gas, more coffee, and a donut.

He continued across New Mexico, leaving the state just beyond Tucumcari and entering the Texas Panhandle at Glenrio. He gassed up again in Jericho. Another donut shop. Another extra-large coffee. He was determined not to stop again until he reached his destination.

When he pulled into Oklahoma City at ten o'clock that night, he had been on the road for more than twenty-four hours. He was tired and jittery and over-caffeinated. It seemed like only a few hours before that he had patted Pepper on the head and walked out of the corral. It made him realize he had actually seen very little of the highway for the last five hundred miles or so.

Hope I didn't run anybody over, he thought.

He turned off 66 and drove to Reno Street. At the truck stop, he pulled the pickup into the far corner of the lot. No one seemed to pay any attention to him. Just another pickup truck with a load of hay. When he shut off the engine, he felt like he was still moving.

When the feeling went away, he wet his towel with vinegar and wiped down everything he thought he had touched inside the cab. He poured rubbing alcohol onto the towel and repeated the procedure. He exited the cab with the towel and the two bottles and the keys to the truck.

He thought he detected the sickly-sweet smell of death rising from the bed of the truck. Looking around to be sure no one was watching, he quickly wiped down the door and door handles and then the sides of the truck and the tailgate. When he was finished, he walked away and threw the towel and bottles into a trash can near the pump islands.

Setting off down Reno Street for the bus station in his straw hat, he was just one more ambling cowboy in a cow town. As he walked, he pulled each key off

Scuttler's key ring and threw it into a storm drain. When they were all gone, he threw away the ring itself.

In a diner near the bus station, he put his straw hat on the seat beside him and scanned the menu for something he thought he might eat. He felt sick from all the coffee, but he knew he should get some food in his stomach. He ordered a bowl of tomato soup and a vanilla milkshake and managed to get most of it down. It seemed like it was going to stay there.

At the bus depot, he used the restroom and washed up. He went to the ticket window and bought a one-way ticket on the Greyhound to Los Angeles. No reason for anyone to ever remember that a man bought a ticket to a little town like Smoke Tree, California, at a bus depot not far from where a pickup truck with two dead bodies had been found.

A half hour later, he was westbound on 66. The bus smelled of unwashed bodies and bologna sandwiches. He had an entire row to himself. He watched the country roll by outside the window for a while, but he couldn't keep his eyes open. Pushing his wallet deep into his front pocket, he tilted his straw hat down over his eyes and went to sleep.

Twenty-two hours later, the Greyhound drove into Smoke Tree. It was nearly midnight. The service station that served as the bus depot was open, and the driver slowed to see if there were any passengers to pick up. There were none. He was about to pull away when Burke tapped him on the shoulder.

"I'll get out here."

"Your ticket's good to L.A."

"I'll get out here."

"Suit yourself, cowboy."

"I intend to."

Burke climbed down from the bus. He cut across the park in front of the Santa Fe Depot. The waiting room was open, but the ticket window was closed. He walked through the waiting room and out onto the platform. Moving north on the platform, he stepped off onto the right-of-way beside the tracks. He continued north until he came to the substandard city street that crossed the tracks. Turning onto it, he kept going until he reached the recreation center and Little League field. There was no one around.

He walked out onto the field and stepped down into a dugout. Lying down on the bench, he put his straw hat over his face and went to sleep.

He woke up, as was usual with him, to the ambient, gray light that told of the coming of new day. Swinging his legs off the bench, he stood up and walked back downtown where he went into the Bluebird Café.

"Good morning, Burke," said the waitress as he walked in the door and moved toward the counter.

"Good morning, Robyn. The usual."

"Denver omelet, hash browns, wheat toast, right?"

"As always. And coffee, of course."

She put his order on the wheel and brought his coffee. When his food came, he realized his appetite was back.

He finished his breakfast and had a bear claw for desert. Leaving a generous tip, he walked to the market where he bought a gallon of distilled water. Outside, he set off in the searing head of a July morning heat for the bus station, the bottle of water dangling from his hand.

"Trailways bus to Vegas gone through yet."

"Oh, hello Burke. No, not yet. Be along shortly though, if it's on schedule."

"I want to take it to Arrowhead Junction."

"Can't sell you a ticket to there. Searchlight okay?"

"Just fine."

Twenty minutes later, he was seated behind the driver. Halfway between Arrowhead Junction and Searchlight, he stood up.

"This will do me fine."

The driver looked in his rearview mirror to see if there were any vehicles coming up behind him. There weren't. He slowed, but did not stop."

He caught Burke's eyes in the mirror above the driver's seat.

"You sure? There's nothing out here."

"I'm sure."

"Where are you going?"

"Going home."

The driver pulled onto the shoulder and stopped. He looked at the gallon of water Burke was carrying and surveyed the sun-blasted desert again.

"You're going to need that."

"Why I bought it."

Burke stepped down and watched the bus until it

dropped into the first big dip. He waited for the stink of diesel exhaust to be borne away on the prevailing breeze. When it had been, he crossed the highway and set off through the desert beneath a blazing sun in a cloudless sky.

It felt good to be home.

Deep Desert Deception

CHAPTER 33

June 8, 1964

Carlos Caballo and Corporal Andy Chesney were headed for Piute Creek in the Sheriff's Department Search and Rescue pickup. Just beyond the Smoke Tree city limits, the traffic ahead of them suddenly slowed but did not stop. In a few moments, they saw the problem.

Under a fierce, white-hot sun in one hundred-and-twelve-degree heat, a bearded man was dragging a huge cross down the shoulder of eastbound 66. He was wearing a white robe. Both the cross and his sandaled feet were kicking up dust as he struggled forward beneath his burden.

"There's something you don't see every day," said Andy.

"Yeah, and something tells me we're going to be seeing more of that guy. That will give us three things to contend with. Operation Desert Strike, the carnival coming to Smoke Tree, and a crazy man coming into town dragging a cross."

They turned off 66 at onto 95 and drove past Arrowhead Junction. Horse honked and waved at Hugh Stanton who was sitting outside in his rocker in his usual spot under the station overhang.

A few miles later, they turned onto the Old Mojave Road and headed west.

"Andy, I haven't had a chance to ask you. How did the visit go in Pennsylvania?"

"Real good, Captain. Christine's family made me feel very welcome. Nice people. Her mom fed me so many apple pies, I think I gained five pounds."

"What did you think of Brush Valley?"

"It's so small, it makes Smoke Tree look like a city. Pretty countryside there. Nice and green. But too humid for me."

"You're turning into a desert rat."

They caromed off another big rock in the road.

"I can't believe Burke has to drive this road to get home."

"It's the way he likes it. Cuts down on visitors."

"Seems to me it would cut it down to zero."

"Just about.

You've never been to his place, have you?"

"Never been invited. I don't think he ever invites anyone but you."

"And Esperanza and the twins. The twins call him 'Uncle Burke'."

"Is he a good uncle?"

"The best. Burke never says much, but I can tell he loves Alejandro and Elena. They adore him."

As they passed the ruins of Fort Piute, Burke's place came into view below.

"Nice setting."

"It is.

It looks like Pepper's not in the corral."

"Is that unusual?"

"Considering that Burke asked me to come out, it is. I hope he's around. His truck and his motorcycle are here. Maybe he took Pepper out for a run and isn't back yet."

"I wouldn't think you'd want to run your horse in this heat."

Horse laughed.

"When I say Burke runs Pepper, I mean Burke runs *with* Pepper."

"He doesn't ride?"

"Says he doesn't like Pepper to have to carry him. Besides, he says, he needs to exercise too."

"So, who gets tired first? Burke or the horse?"

"Probably Pepper. I think Burke could run forever."

Horse parked the pickup next to the old Ford flatbed.

"Burke told me where he keeps the key. Said to go in and have a cold soda pop if he wasn't around when we got here."

"That's nice of him."

"Yes, it is. But it's also a bit odd."

"How so?"

"I've never known Burke to lock his place up."

Horse found the key and opened the door. He and Andy went inside.

The house had the stuffy feel of a place that had been closed up for quite a while. Horse started to get a bad feeling, but he shook it off.

"Let's take him up on that soda pop."

He went to the small refrigerator and pulled the door open. On the bottom shelf, next to the bottles of Nehi Grape, there were two envelopes. Leaning closer, he saw that one of them said, "Carlos Caballo. Read this one first." The printing on the other one read, "Carlos Caballo. Number two". He picked them up and turned them over. They were sealed.

Putting them under his arm, he got two bottles of pop. He opened them with the Pepsi-Cola opener attached to the kitchen table and took them back to the living room.

Andy was standing in front of the fireplace.

"I like his place."

Horse handed Andy one of the bottles of pop.

"Built it himself without power tools. Made a good job of it.

Let's take these drinks out on the back porch. It's too hot in here."

They went outside.

Horse sat down on one of the cane chairs. Andy stepped off the porch and wandered off toward the creek with his cold Nehi.

Horse took a long drink of his own and set the sweating bottle on the porch beside him.

He opened the first envelope. Inside was a fifty-dollar bill and a multiple-page letter. He unfolded it. When he read the first few sentences, he was glad he was sitting down.

Carlos,

Do not show this letter to anyone but Esperanza. You can tell others about some of what it says, but there are some things that are for you and Esperanza only. As you read on, you will understand why that is so.

As I write this, I am dying. By the time you read it, I will have been dead for a few days. You will find my body in a small limestone cave just north of the Foshay Pass powerline road. Very few people know the cave is there, and very few who stumble across it ever find it again. Chemehuevi Joe can take you there.

The powerline road is in good shape. The department pickup will handle it with no problem. The guys in the mounted posse should be able to tow a horse trailer a pretty good distance up the road. With a little work, they can figure out how to use an aluminum stretcher as a travois. They can pretend they're plains

Indians when they drag my body bag to the pickup.

Carlos, my friend, I know this will be gruesome work. And believe me, I would rather die in the open and be carried off by coyotes and buzzards, but you will need my body to have me declared dead so you can probate my will. A notarized copy of my will is in the other envelope. The original is in my safe deposit box at the Bank of America. The key to the box is buried under an interesting rock that you and I often talked about when we walked the archery course. Nobody but you will know which rock that is.

I have pancreatic cancer. I began to notice something was wrong about two years ago. A year ago this month, I was doing some farrier work for a regular customer, a doctor in Las Vegas. He said he noticed I had lost weight and was looking a bit run down. When I went back six weeks later to do some follow-up work, he said he could see more changes in my health that he found worrisome. He tried to get me to come to his clinic for some tests.

I refused, but a few months ago, I could no longer ignore what was happening. I had lost so much weight, I kept punching new holes in my belt. I had no appetite at all. I went in for the tests.

The news wasn't good. The cancer was stage three at the time. It is worse now.

The doctor told me the cancer was incurable. I refused to go to the hospital for treatment. The best outcome I could have hoped for was a little more time. Miserable time. A time with tubes stuck in me.

I will not die in a hospital bed. I am going to kill this cancer before it kills me. I am its host. It dies when I die.

Three weeks ago, the same day I called you, I took Pepper to the Box S and asked John Stonebridge to board him for me. The fifty-dollar bill is for his expenses.

Two weeks ago, after I finished writing this letter and put the envelopes where you found them, I set off on foot for the place I intend to die. One last trip on foot across the desert. I am very weak now. It will take me almost a week to get to the place where you will find me.

I have a little food with me, but I don't know how much I'll be able to eat. Nothing tastes good anymore.

I know where all the springs are along my route. I will have plenty of water.

I will travel at night and hole up during the days.

When I get to the cave, I will drink no more water. I suspect I will last three or four days at the most after that, and then it will be over.

I have to admit I am curious to learn what happens after death.

In the Kiowa Apache language, the same word means spirit, soul, and owl. The spirit or soul is like the owl, able to see in the darkness and soar in the night, but unable to escape the bonds of the earth.

My aikido sensei told me the Buddha once said the spirit of life passing on can be compared to lighting candles where each new candle is lit by the dying flame of the candle that preceded it. Each flame is connected because each dying flame is the source of the next. But each flame is unique unto itself. It is not the same flame as the one that came before it, even though it owes its existence to that flame.

My flame has gone out by now, but a flame somewhere else has been lit. It will not remember the flame that was mine. That is as it should be.

Please, have my remains cremated. As I understand the law, if you scatter my ashes quietly on federal land, away from well-used trails and waters, there will be no repercussions. Leave them on top of the New York Mountains so the owl that is my spirit can soar above the Mojave Desert that will now forever be my home.

Enough philosophy.

Now, to practical matters.

When you open the safety deposit box, you find the name of the lawyer in Barstow who prepared my will. The name, address and phone number is on the folder that holds the will.

You are named as the executor of the estate. I have already paid the lawyer for his costs in helping you handle the probate. The receipt for the payment is in the folder with the will. Carlos, I apologize for putting this burden on you, but I need someone I can trust to take care of all these details. You are the most trustworthy person I have ever known.

Here is a summary of what is in the will.

Give my motorcycle to Mr. Stanton. He always wanted one, and even though he is probably too old to ride it, I think it will please him to own it.

Give my truck back to Ellis McCready. I think he regretted parting with it the moment he sold it to me.

The pink slip is in the safe deposit box. It is signed over to him.

The Black Widow bow above the fireplace is for Andy Chesney. He has admired it for a long time.

The house and its contents and the land itself now belong to Joe Medrano. The quit claim deed I have signed over to him is in the safe deposit box. I know he has his own place in the Chemehuevi Mountains, but I also know Piute Creek is sacred to the Chemehuevi. Tell Joe I said he now has two places. He can live at Piute Creek part of the year and go south for the winter if it gets too cold.

That may make him smile. If Joe Medrano ever smiles.

There are trust accounts for Alejandro and Elena in the amount of twenty-five thousand dollars each at the Nevada Southern Bank in Las Vegas. The accounts are drawing interest. The passbooks are in the box. The money is for their college education. If they choose not to go, whatever money is in the account becomes their personal property when they turn twenty-five.

Pepper now belongs to the twins. They love to ride him. I am sure they will take good care of him.

What follows is not in the will. This is why I don't

want anyone but you and Esperanza to see this letter.

In my safe deposit box, you will find a map. It is in an envelope labeled, "Carlos Caballo only." The map will lead you to a metal box I buried out in the desert a month ago. Inside, you will find over four hundred and twenty-five thousand dollars.

Do not concern yourself with the source of the money. I assure you, no one is looking for it. No one ever will. It is not the proceeds of a crime.

The money is for the orphanage in Mexico where you adopted the twins. You have told me many times how great the need is there and how inadequate their funds are. I would suggest providing the money in increments. Perhaps fifty thousand dollars at a time. See if they use it well and if the money is really being used to benefit the children. If you suspect it is not, give whatever remains to the Salvation Army. They helped me in Los Angeles when I was very young. They asked nothing in return. They help a lot of people that way.

Of course, if at any time you and Esperanza have an emergency and need money, feel free to take as much as you want. I have complete faith in both of you to always do what is right.

One last thing. Put two hundred dollars in an

envelope and mail it anonymously to Anadarko High School in Anadarko Oklahoma. Put a note inside explaining the money is to be given to the high school library. The night I left Anadarko, I was carrying a canvas bag with two things in it, a change of clothes and a book from that library, The Complete Works of William Shakespeare. I don't know why I took it along. It was in my room, and I stuck it in the bag. I carried it all through my time in the army and continued to read it after I got out. It has brought me great joy. The money should cover the replacement of the book and pay the accrued fines.

Thank you, Carlos Caballo, for your friendship across these years. You are the best friend I have ever had. You and Esperanza are the best people I have ever known. I wish both of you long life and great happiness.

Burke

When he finished reading, Horse realized he had been crying for some time. He put the letter back in the envelope and stuffed it in his pocket.

Deep Desert Deception

Epilogue

October, 1964 Oklahoma

In the fall of 1964, Horse drove to Fort Sill, Oklahoma to pick up a prisoner. A former Master Sergeant, now a private, he had been court martialed and was going to be spending quite a few years in an Army stockade. But first, he had to be tried in San Bernardino County for a felony committed in off-duty hours against a civilian during Operation Desert Strike. It was unusual for a substation commander to personally transport an out-of-state prisoner, but Horse had other business in Oklahoma.

He picked up his charge at Fort Sill and drove to Anadarko. Pulling into the parking lot at the Sheriff's station, he got his handcuffed prisoner out of the back of his unit and led him inside.

The station smelled like dust, grime, fear, desperation and floor wax. The smell of law enforcement stations everywhere.

The desk sergeant looked up to see a dark-complexioned man in the uniform of the San Bernardino County Sheriff's Department escorting a handcuffed man. He had a sidearm in a holster on his hip and captain's bars on his collar.

"Help you with something, Captain?"

"Is the Sheriff around?"

"No sir. Unfortunately, he's not."

"Then I'd like to speak with the deputy in the building who has the most time in the department."

"That can be arranged."

He pointed at the thigh level gate in the railing that separated the waiting area from the interior of the office.

"Come on through and go down that hallway to the break room on the right. Sergeant Mitchell will join you there in a moment."

"Thank you.

I'm taking this prisoner back to California. Could you put him in a holding cell until I'm ready to leave?"

"Be glad to."

The Sergeant opened a drawer and got a ring of keys. He came through the gate and took custody of the prisoner. Horse followed him through the gate and went down the hallway and into the empty break room.

He had only been in the room long enough to pour himself a cup of coffee and drop a quarter into the coffee kitty before a trim, older man wearing sergeant's stripes came through the open door.

"Sergeant Mitchell, thanks for taking the time to see me."

The two men shook hands.

Horse followed him to a table. They sat down across from each other.

"What brings you all the way from California to Anadarko, Captain?"

"Picked up a prisoner at Fort Sill for a trial. I came to Anadarko to clear up a mystery about something that happened here a long time ago."

"Be glad to help, if I can. How long ago?"

"Were you on the force here in nineteen forty-two."

"I was."

"Was a deputy named Dave Scuttler working here then?"

"He was."

"Does he still work for Caddo County?"

"No sir. He retired in '62. Why do you ask?"

"In nineteen fifty-nine, he called Smoke Tree, California, the place where I work. He was looking for a man named Kyle Sommers. Then, a little over a week later, he called again. This time he was looking for a man named Purvis Davis."

"I remember hearing about Davis. He and a couple of other guys went out to Nevada and never came back."

"When this Deputy Scuttler called the first time, the time when he asked about Kyle Sommers, do you know if he was he investigating a crime on behalf of this office?"

"Not that I'm aware of, but something about the name Sommers rings a bell.

The sergeant sat silently for a few minutes while Horse finished his coffee.

"Sorry. Something familiar there, but I can't call it to mind. Maybe it'll come to me."

"What about anything involving the name Burke Henry?"

"That name I know. But it was a death, not a crime."

"What happened?"

"I was a new deputy then, and I took the call. Solo auto accident. Burke Henry was a young Kiowa Apache from the KCA. His truck went off the highway at high speed and hit a telephone pole. No rain, good visibility, no skid marks. If another car was involved, we didn't find any evidence of it."

"Alcohol involved?"

"That was my first thought, but we found no evidence of it at the scene.

I have to tell you, Captain, it looked a lot like a suicide to me."

He snapped his fingers.

"The Sommers thing just came to me. Another suicide."

Horse leaned forward.

"Early nineteen forty-two. Not long after Pearl Harbor. Young girl, last name Sommers, first name Alice or something. Hung herself from a tree in her back yard."

"Was there any doubt it was a suicide?"

"No sir. None at all."

"Do you remember if she was related to this 'Kyle'?"

"Might have been. I don't recall."

"What about the girl's mother. She still around?"

"No sir, she died not too long after that. Found her frozen to death in an alley. Woman had a few arrests for prostitution and a big problem with alcohol. But then, a lot of them do."

"By 'them' you mean...?"

"Indians. Off the KCA. Both women, the daughter and her mom, were Kiowa Apache."

"This retired deputy, Dave Scuttler, do you mind giving me your impressions of him?"

Sergeant Mitchell stared at Horse for a long time without speaking. He seemed to reach some kind of decision. Getting to his feet, he walked over and stuck his head out the break room door and looked down the hall before closing it. He came back and sat down and leaned toward Horse and spoke in a low voice."

"Mean bastard. And scary. Always lots of rumors about him. Lots of complaints. Shooting deaths. Badly injured prisoners. Women complaining they'd been violated. That kind of thing."

"Any charges ever brought against him?"

Mitchell's voice dropped even lower.

"Never. Rumor was he had friends in high places."

"Did you believe that?"

"No, Captain. I think he had dirt on people in high places. Everyone in politics was afraid of the guy."

"I'd like to talk to him. Does he still live around here?"

"No sir. He's dead. Strange story. He was found in the bed of his truck in a parking lot in Oklahoma City. Him and Arvin Lacey, a local who had just got out of San Quentin."

"I assume the Oklahoma City police investigated."

"They did. Forwarded us a copy of the report since Scuttler had spent his career in this department. Bodies were lying on top of a tarp. Covered in lime. Another tarp on top of them, weighted down with rocks. Bales of hay on top of everything. Both men had their wallets. There was money in the wallets. Truck keys were gone and never found."

"So, not a robbery."

"Your usual robber doesn't slit his victims from gills to gullet."

"That's what killed them?"

"No. And this is where it gets even stranger. The doc who did the autopsy said both bodies had internal injuries consistent with being shot with an arrow. An arrow with a sharp broadhead. Not only that, some kind of animal had chewed Lacey's face off. And a big chunk of his arm."

"Were the arrows recovered?"

"No sir."

"Prints in the truck?"

"Everything had been wiped clean. The cab, the sides of the truck, the mirrors, even the bumper and the tailgate. The last line in the report said the cab smelled like vinegar.

"The House of Three Murders is the book that began the Smoke Tree Series. It was followed by "Horse Hunts," "Mojave Desert Sanctuary," and "Death on a Desert Hillside." If you enjoyed "Deep Desert Deception" and have not read the first four books in the series, I hope you will take the time to experience them. Although they are part of a series, each reads well as a stand-alone novel.

Also, if you like the book you just read, the author would be greatly appreciative if you would post a review on *Amazon* and/or *Goodreads*. We independent authors lack the resources of the big publishers; therefore, we rely on our readers to post reviews and tell others about our books.

Thank you for your consideration of this request.

Gary J. George